My Kind
of People

ALSO BY LISA DUFFY

This Is Home
The Salt House

My Kind of People

— A Novel —

Lisa Duffy

ATRIA PAPERBACK

New York   London   Toronto   Sydney   New Delhi

ATRIA
PAPERBACK

An Imprint of Simon & Schuster
1230 Avenue of the Americas
New York, NY 10020

First Atria Paperback edition May 2020

ATRIA PAPERBACK and colophon are trademarks of Simon & Schuster, Inc.

For information about special discounts for bulk purchases, please contact Simon & Schuster Special Sales at 1-866-506-1949 or business@simonandschuster.com.

The Simon & Schuster Speakers Bureau can bring authors to your live event. For more information or to book an event contact the Simon & Schuster Speakers Bureau at 1-866-248-3049 or visit our website at www.simonspeakers.com.

Interior design by Jill Putorti
Jacket design by Chelsea McGuckin

Manufactured in the United States of America

10 9 8 7 6 5 4 3 2 1

Library of Congress Cataloging-in-Publication Data has been applied for.

ISBN 978-1-9821-3715-1
ISBN 978-1-9821-3717-5 (ebook)

For my mother, Peg Hamilton,
with love and gratitude.

I shut my eyes in order to see.

—PAUL GAUGUIN

1

In the hours before dawn, she slips out of the house and runs. She knows the way by heart, even though she's only ten, and the land swells around her like the mother's bosom she never knew.

She follows the path that winds near the cliff, the edge nipping at her feet, threatening to swallow her whole. Spit her out on the rocky shore below.

She left the men sleeping.

Xavier passed out on the couch, but Leo roamed the house all night, as though he knew she might leave. Even stood over her bed once while she pretended to sleep, her back to him, his shadow on the wall looming through her half-lidded eyes.

When she finally heard his breathing, slow and deep from the other room, she left. Silently and swiftly, even though the night was soundless and black. She was good at that. Disappearing in the cracks between light and sound.

The wind licks her ankles. Spray from the water below clings to her hair, coats her legs and arms in the icy Atlantic.

She pauses on the cliff above the ocean. Her foot tingles, ready to step. But the night grips her body, presses against her until she's flattened, as though she's a leaf pressed between pages, the darkness sandwiching her in place.

She thought it would be easy.

Simple even. To step into nothing. To sail off the earth just like her parents had done, the wind taking her breath, filling the emptiness inside her body.

But Ichabod Island won't let her.

When her toes touch the edge of the granite rock, the island stirs. The trees bend. The wind howls and the ocean roars and the lighthouse glares until she turns and runs, her feet pounding the dirt path through the woods.

When the sun finds her later in a wooden house high in the trees, safely away from the cliff, sound asleep on a bed of feathers, she doesn't stir. She doesn't feel the day rise above her. The cloudless sky peering down with its bright yellow eye.

She sleeps soundly. On her own. Just like she should be. Just like she came into the world.

Nobody knows she's gone. The men don't know she ran away. When they find out, they'll ask why. Over and over, they'll ask why.

She won't have an answer. She never does.

She's not even sure there is one.

2

Across the street, Maggie Thompson is in bed alone, wondering when it was exactly that her husband fell out of love with her.

The day had started promising.

They'd gone to their first visit with a new marriage counselor; a thin, well-groomed man who ended the session by encouraging them to be more spontaneous.

Mix it up, he'd said, *and be nice to each other.*

On the ride home, Pete mimicked the counselor: the way he twiddled his fingers when he told them to mix it up, as though he were casting a spell. Maggie had giggled, a bubbling, young sound that made Pete laugh.

He reached over with his right hand and laced his fingers between hers.

Maggie didn't know the last time they'd done something like that—touched for touching's sake. Not the perfunctory, almost scripted caresses before they made love or the quick, tight-lipped kisses that followed each hello or goodbye, but a touch that carved a small spot in her memory.

The sort of touch that could nearly be felt again.

When Pete had come up behind her in the bedroom and whispered that they should follow the doctor's orders and be spontaneous, she agreed, because the warmth of his fingers still lingered on her own.

They undressed quickly, without pulling the shades, and climbed into bed, even though it was late morning. Since Maggie couldn't remember the last time they'd done that either, she considered this to be the spontaneous part.

After the usual foreplay and well into their missionary love-making, Pete whispered in her ear in a throaty voice, "Do you like that, you dirty slut?"

Maggie couldn't help the snort that shot out of her.

"Jesus," Pete said, pushing his weight up on his hands and frowning at her. "That was sexy."

She took her hand off his back and pressed it to her nose.

"Sorry," she said through her fingers.

She put her hand on Pete's back again and gave him a little tap to indicate that it was fine—that he should keep going—even though she could feel inside of her that it was not fine, and he was not going to keep going.

Pete rolled off her and lay on his back, his eyes on the ceiling.

Maggie sat up and leaned on her arm, turned her head to look down at him, trying not to wonder how her naked fifty-year-old body looked in the bright daylight.

"It surprised me." She rested her hand on the slight paunch of his belly. "Let's start again."

"Explain that to him." He pointed to his penis, which lay flaccid and forlorn on his thigh.

Maggie leaned down and wrapped her hand around the length of him, holding it like a microphone.

"Will the master of ceremonies please rise for the occasion and accept the apologies of the attendee? No offense was intended," she said in a formal voice.

She looked at Pete, waited for him to laugh, but he brushed her hand away and flipped the edge of the comforter over his midsection.

Maggie felt the heat rise up her neck. She had done it to be playful—to make up for her reaction—but in twenty-seven years of marriage, Pete had never talked dirty to her in bed.

Not like that, at least.

That feels good was his go-to line. Occasionally, if he drank too much, he'd whisper in her ear that she had a great ass, but in Maggie's mind that didn't exactly qualify as dirty talk.

"I didn't mean to laugh. Come on. Let's start again—"

"Can we not talk about it?" he said.

He stood up suddenly, pulled on his boxers, then his pants. Maggie tugged on both sides of the comforter, wrapping it around her body and tucking it under her arms like a towel.

"I didn't realize we started talking about it."

"Dr. Quack said to mix it up, so that's what I did. You want more sex and spice. Right? That's what you said. Just like that." He crisscrossed the room, looking for his shoe.

"I said passion, Pete. That I miss having *passion* in my life."

He found the shoe under Maggie's shirt on the floor and sat on the edge of the bed to put it on.

"Ah, yes, *passion*," he mumbled in a voice she was sure he meant her to hear.

"We agreed to see him to help us communicate better."

"Well, that was my impression. But come to find out—it's not just communicating that's the problem. It's my lack of passion in bed."

"I never said anything about us in bed. Why did you agree to go if you were going to use it against me later?"

Pete looked at her, shook his head, and disappeared into the closet. She sat in the middle of the bed, remembering that he hadn't really *agreed* to go at all.

More gave in to her nagging, it seemed.

They'd already gone to a different counselor last year. Right after Maggie had found the texts on Pete's phone. Text after text from his secretary.

None of them about work.

They made it two months in couples therapy before Pete refused to go back. He was tired of talking about it. Tired of explaining that it just *happened*—he never meant for it to go that far. Of course he hadn't slept with her—he hadn't even *kissed* her!

He apologized. Over and over, he apologized. Finally, she said she forgave him. They stopped going to therapy.

Everything went back to normal.

Except Maggie woke up every day with a weight on her chest. She went to the doctor. Tried antidepressants. Added in another day of yoga. She took baths and went for long walks. Still—she was joyless.

Passionless.

That's how they ended up with this new therapist. She'd begged Pete to come with her, said it wasn't about their marriage—she just wanted to see if they could communicate better.

She'd seen the look on Pete's face in the therapist's office after she said she wanted more passion in their life. It reminded her of the look the boys used to give her as teenagers whenever Maggie tried to show them affection in public—a mixture of shame and embarrassment. Maybe even a touch of anger.

She heard his voice again. *Do you like that, you dirty slut?*

Replaying it in her head now, she caught the edge in his voice. The blame.

Pete emerged from the closet. She watched him button his shirt, eyeing the patch above the breast pocket. He never talked about his job, even though he knew all the town secrets, working his way up from a patrolman to, now, chief of police.

The job stays at the job was his favorite line. She stopped asking long ago after what seemed like the millionth go-around of Pete dodging her questions about what happened on his shift.

"Who am I going to tell?" Maggie asked while they sat at the dinner table when the boys were little and she was craving adult conversation.

"The Russians," Pete said, with a smirk.

"I'm your wife."

"That's how the Russians work. They go through the women."

"What if you talked in your sleep? What then?"

"I'd have to kill you," he said, flicking his eyebrows.

It was funny at first, then it wasn't so funny, and finally, she stopped asking.

Pete leaned over and planted a kiss on the top of her head and said he had to go to the station. Maggie followed his eyes, watched the way they would not meet her own. She wanted to ask him if he'd heard the last part of the counselor's advice—the part about being nice to each other. But he was gone before she could gather her words, his footsteps echoing heavy and quick through the house and out the door.

Almost as if he were running from her.

Now, she's in bed. Naked. She's staring at the ceiling when the phone rings and the person on the other end tells her that Sky is missing.

That she left sometime after midnight, as far as anyone can tell.

"You mean gone," she says, knowing it's just a matter of time.

How many hours can a child linger in the forest, high in a tree house, before hunger strikes and her empty stomach sends her home?

She hangs up the phone and gets dressed, walks down to the kitchen just as the clock strikes noon.

When she turns to the back door, two blue eyes look back at her. And she has her answer.

Apparently, only twelve.

3

It's Xavier who discovers she's gone.

Leo is half awake, the sun peeking through the shade, when he appears in the doorway, leans against the frame. He doesn't need to say it. Disappointment is etched in his forehead.

"Not again," Leo sighs, sitting up.

"You had night duty——"

"I checked on her. She was sound asleep when I went to bed." Leo kicks off the covers and stands up, rummages through his suitcase for a clean pair of shorts.

This is how they've been living the past two months.

Out of suitcases Xavier replenishes when he returns from the city each weekend. Leo's existence in this house is one dress shirt, his favorite khakis, three pairs of shorts, four T-shirts, old sneakers, even older loafers, underwear, and his toiletry bag.

And his laptop, of course. According to Xavier, Leo's only connection to civilized life.

"So much for Saturday mornings in bed. Remember those days?" Xavier asks.

Leo picks up a T-shirt, gives it a sniff before he pulls it on. He ignores the comment.

Of course he remembers their Saturday routine. They've been married a year. Together two before that.

What his husband is really asking is: Do you remember I didn't agree to this?

Do you remember only your name is in the will?

"I called the police. Chief Brody's on it," Xavier tells him.

"Who?"

"Oh, come on. *Jaws*? The island police chief."

"*Jaws* was filmed on the Vineyard. Get your islands straight. Why did you call the police? She's probably where she always ends up."

"I called the police because this needs to stop. We're not getting through to her. As far as getting my islands straight—you've seen one, you've seen them all. I mean, we're out of coffee and not a Starbucks to be found."

Leo doesn't respond. He's heard it all by now—he's been hearing it for two months. Ever since Brian and Ann were killed in a car accident and Leo moved back over to the island to take care of Sky, their ten-year-old daughter.

Leo's ten-year-old daughter, according to the will that named him as her guardian.

"I'm going to the treehouse, then to Maggie's," he says. "Stay here in case she comes home." He walks past Xavier, kisses him on the cheek. "Good morning, by the way."

Xavier doesn't smile. Just looks at him with tired eyes. "How long are we going to do this?" he asks.

Leo knows his answer isn't the one Xavier wants to hear, so he just shrugs and walks away.

As long as it takes, he thinks to himself.

As long as it takes.

*   *   *

Ichabod Island is nothing more than a slice of land thirteen miles off the coast of New England, referred to by year-round residents as simply Ichabod.

Some say it sits in the shadow of the Vineyard like a disobedient child, wild and untamed, fog rolling over the land like a tantrum in wait.

Shaped like an enormous lightning bolt, the island is a jagged zigzag of land rising out of the Atlantic.

Which is why perhaps Leo always feels more alive when he's here. As though the red-clay cliffs and white-sand beaches and cobblestone streets are electric in some way, igniting the air in his lungs and the blood in his veins.

Now, he walks out of the house, blinks at the daylight. The dead-end street is narrow—they live where the land sharpens to a point high above the water.

Not far from the town dock, Winding Way is anything but winding—it's more of a slender, thumb-shaped cul-de-sac lined with a handful of small Cape Cod–style homes, one resembling the next.

Leo grew up here. Four houses down from Brian.

He still hasn't gotten used to parking in Brian and Ann's driveway, even though he's been living in their house for two months. When he first arrived, he sometimes drove straight past their house and pulled into the driveway of his childhood home. A reflex. Maybe to be expected.

But it was embarrassing—he'd reversed the car quickly, his face hot, hoping the tenant, Mrs. Pearse, hadn't seen him.

He's taught himself to avoid his old home—avert his eyes,

pretend it's just another house on the street. He feels as though he's abandoned it, turned his back on every single memory between those walls.

His parents had always assumed Leo would live in the house after they died. Use it as a weekend getaway from his place in Boston. A summer home when he could get the time off from work. His parents had paid off the mortgage. They knew how much he loved the island.

His mother got Alzheimer's and spent her last days in the nursing home, but his father took his last breath in his recliner in the living room, passing away quietly in his sleep at seventy-one after a series of strokes.

In the weeks before his father died, Leo had moved in to take care of him. His father had talked incessantly about how he wanted Leo to turn the small house into something spectacular. Knock it down and start fresh, his father kept repeating.

It was the last house on the street. The only house with a view of the water because of the way the trees sloped down the hill in the back of the property.

An architect's dream.

Then there was the awful night after his father's funeral. The night he got so drunk that he woke up next to a woman in his bed. The night that left him a stranger in his own home—no, a stranger in his own skin.

He left Ichabod the next day, went home to his condo in the city, and hired a property manager, putting him in charge of cleaning out and renting his childhood home. A month later, a tenant moved in.

Sweet, old Mrs. Pearse—spinster and the town historian. Even Agnes Coffin, who lived on the street, didn't complain. And she complained about every outsider on Winding Way.

Agnes Coffin acted as the island gatekeeper. Give her the opportunity and she'd raise a finger in the air to count her direct relation to the men who founded Ichabod Island. Proving to anyone within earshot that her right to this island was in her *blood*. She was only four wrinkled fingers away from the first settlers on Ichabod: *My father's* (pointer), *great-grandfather's* (middle), *uncle's* (fourth), *cousin* (pinky), she would say, all smug and content.

Like it was something she'd earned. As though she had more right to the island than a person who wasn't a *native*. Someone born on the island.

But Agnes Coffin couldn't complain about his tenant—Mrs. Pearse was a descendant of Captain Ichabod Pearse—the island's namesake.

Now, Leo walks down the street to Maggie's house, the smell of low tide at the base of the cliffs following him to the front door.

He knocks, and Maggie calls for him to come in.

He finds them at the kitchen table. Sky is halfway through a bowl of macaroni and cheese. She waves, looks down at her lunch.

"Sit," Maggie says. "Do you want some lunch?"

He shakes his head, resisting the urge to say, *No, thank you, Miss Maggie*. She was his fourth-grade teacher all those years ago, and old habits die hard.

He'd called her Miss Maggie once when they'd passed each other in the bank, and she'd rolled her eyes.

"You're not a kid anymore, Leo," she'd said. "That's my name during school hours to people who are only as high as my waist. Call me Maggie, please!"

Maggie walks to the counter, returns with a napkin and puts it on the table next to Sky.

"I just got off the phone with Xavier. He said you were walking over. My friend here and I were just talking about these nightly adventures. How they need to stop. We agreed to it. Didn't we, Miss Pope?"

Sky looks up and nods, returns to her bowl. Maggie glances at Leo and sighs, gives a slight shake of her head, as though she knows no such agreeing has taken place.

Leo clears this throat. "I was worried, Sky. It scares me when you leave."

His voice is gentle, soft. He wishes he were more like Xavier. He's never been able to sound firm. Like someone in charge.

"Don't be scared." Sky wipes her mouth with the napkin and sits back in the chair. "It's not like I'm lost or anything. I'm just in the tree house."

"I don't want you sneaking out in the middle of the night. Do you understand that?"

"I didn't sneak. I walked out the back door," she says innocently.

Maggie turns in his direction, shielding a smile from the girl, and brings Sky's bowl to the sink.

He pauses, decides to stay quiet.

They've had this conversation before. Three times to be exact. She's never apologetic. And she never lies—she hasn't once promised to stop leaving in the middle of the night. She just listens to him, tells him not to worry.

That she's perfectly safe. It's her tree house. On her island.

And somehow, he can't summon the will to argue with her. No—he doesn't want to argue with her. He doesn't want to make her afraid. He doesn't want to tell her all the horrible things that *could* happen. That *might* happen.

He's willing to be the one who's afraid. He doesn't want to change who she is.

A fearless girl who doesn't just *think* she's safe alone in the dark on an island in the Atlantic.

She *knows* it.

They don't speak on the way home. It's maybe thirty yards, door to door. No need to fill the silence on the short walk.

But Leo wishes they were talking. Mundane conversation. Stuff they used to talk about before her parents died.

He'd visit Brian and Ann, and Sky would sit at the table and tell him about scoring a goal in her last soccer game. Or what her favorite school subject was (gym!).

The only thing he can think to ask her now is: *How can I help?*

But he's asked several times, and the blank look in her eyes tells him everything he needs to know.

He remembers feeling the way she does. Or something similar to it. He remembers feeling lost. Untethered. Broken.

He was about her age when it happened.

Ten or eleven—he doesn't remember exactly. Only that he was in sixth grade when he fell in love for the first time. Or lust. It didn't matter—the feeling inside of him was the thing that took his breath away. Split him open.

The way the substitute teacher introduced himself wove itself into the seams of Leo's existence.

Mr. Baxter is what they want you to call me, the teacher had said. *But that's my father. So Mr. Ethan will have to do.*

Mr. Ethan Baxter, with his canvas backpack and worn jeans and unshaven face and no clue that four seats back, in the center row, young Leo Irving had just discovered something about himself that would change his life.

Leo had gone home after school, locked himself in his room,

and refused to come out for dinner. Told his mother through the door that he was sick.

Because wasn't he, for Christ's sake?

All his buddies were obsessed with girls. The entire cheerleading team, it seemed. Brian never stopped talking about Charlotte's breasts and Karen's ass and Meg's everything, and all Leo could think about was the substitute teacher in English class.

The *male* substitute teacher.

Leo had stayed in his bedroom all night, staring at the wall. His father had come in the next morning, sat on the edge of the mattress, asked if everything was all right. A sob had slipped out of Leo before he could choke it back. He'd felt his father's hand on his shoulder, but he hadn't turned. He couldn't face him.

How can I help? his father had asked.

And Leo had only shrugged, stayed silent.

What was there to say?

Even now, all these years later, Leo considered that question. If he could go back to that morning and answer his father—what would he say?

The closest Leo can come to an answer is this:

Just love me.

So that's what he does now with Sky. He just loves her.

Later that afternoon, while Xavier is packing for his early-morning return to the city, and Sky is in her room, Leo sits on the patio.

He looks at the backyard, the tree house barely visible in the distance. It still seems strange to sit here without his friends.

How many times had Brian and Ann fed him dinner right

in this very spot? He'd nearly grown up in this yard—it was Brian's childhood home. They'd played a million games of tag football on the grass. They'd camped in tents as boys, and later, had prom pictures over by the stone wall.

He remembers not wanting to leave Ichabod. It was the only place he'd ever lived for the first eighteen years of his life.

When he got accepted to his first choice of colleges, he knew it would break his father's heart if he didn't go. Never mind all the money his parents had put away over the years for his college tuition. A remarkable feat on his father's harbormaster salary. His mom contributing with her job as a nurse's aide at the hospital.

Leo was the first in his family to go to college—but his mother wanted degrees. *More than a thermometer*, she always told him.

After college, he was offered a job at one of the top architectural firms, and he took it, even though it was across the country, and he missed the island so much it hurt his bones. A constant ache no amount of promotions or raises eased.

Eventually, he moved east again, joined a firm in Boston, and after his parents passed away, he'd take the ferry over to the island to visit Brian, his best friend from childhood.

Brian had married Ann by then, and Leo would sometimes tease them when Ann would snap a picture on her phone of the three of them: Brian and Ann, blond and pale, and Leo, so dark, standing between them.

"You're *so* white," he'd joke, eyeing their matching Vineyard Vines pullovers. Ann would laugh and roll her eyes.

"Oh, please," she'd say. "You're the whitest black person I know."

"I'm the *only* black person you know."

Ann would laugh, but not Brian. He'd stay silent, his face clouded, and Leo would have to tell him to lighten up.

To not be so damn *serious*.

But he'd grown up with Brian. They'd been best friends since preschool, went to Ichabod High School together, and when Leo left for college, Brian stayed on the island, joined the fire department, and tried to start a family with Ann.

Brian didn't say out loud what they both knew—the color of Leo's skin wasn't invisible on an island that was mostly white.

Of course, Brian didn't know what was coming his way. He couldn't have known that one day, he and Ann would be parents to a girl who dropped from the clouds. A girl with dark skin and eyes so light looking at her was like tumbling into the crystal-blue sea.

And now Leo is her guardian.

It took him by surprise, even though Ann had told him years ago she was putting it in their will—that if anything happened to Brian and Ann, Leo would get Sky.

Leo had shrugged it off. Brian didn't drink. Neither did Ann. Most nights they were in bed before Leo was home from work. He'd been convinced that life wouldn't take away people like Brian and Ann, erase them from the world so brutally, so easily, when they were so good.

So loved.

My kind of people is what his father always said of Brian and Ann.

And then two months ago, they went out on a date.

They left Sky with a babysitter to celebrate their anniversary. Someone at the bar sent over two glasses of champagne while they ate dinner, but the bubbly sat untouched—Ann wasn't a drinker, and Brian gave up alcohol years ago.

No one will ever know why their car missed the turn by the

cliffs and plunged to the rocks below. Ann was driving, and the detective said the car left the road at a high rate of speed. Nobody saw anything. The night had been clear. The full moon the only witness to the accident.

They don't know if they died instantly or if they suffered— the fire erased all the answers. Left only dust and ash and charred wreckage.

And a girl waiting all alone in her bed across the island.

Waiting for parents who would never return.

4

When they ask her why she runs away, Sky doesn't answer. She can't find the words to describe her house now that her parents are gone.

How the silence is what hurts the most.

She can't hear her mother humming in the kitchen. Or the low rumble of her father's voice at the table, the *snap* when he'd straighten the newspaper in front of him.

After they died, the thought of never seeing them again left an empty space in the middle of her body.

She keeps her mother's perfume on the table next to her bed; her father's sweatshirt under her pillow. She can hold on to their scent. Imagine their touch. Feel the stubble on her father's cheek, her mother's hands braiding her hair.

But the quiet is something different.

She stares at the wall when she's supposed to be sleeping. She listens for the clomp of her father's boots on the wood floor. The whistle of the teakettle at night.

But there's only quiet. A silence threatening to swallow her.

It's worse on the weekends, when Xavier is there, because the house feels different. Like it's not hers anymore. She knows he doesn't want to be in her house—he doesn't even want to be on her island.

She's an outsider when he's there.

That's when she runs.

Outside, the night surrounds her, fills her ears and lungs. She runs to where the sound of the waves is deafening. High above the water on the cliffs, the surf pounding the rocks below, the noise of the island around her.

She sleeps in the tree house that her neighbor Joe built for her last year—a birthday present from her parents—although mostly from her mother. They'd all walked out to the woods behind the house, a blindfold over her eyes until her mother took it off and shouted, "Look up, birthday girl!"

Sky had blinked. It took a minute to see the square box through the thick leaves, a small house built into a big oak tree, tucked in the space where four large limbs reached out like fingers touching the sky.

"How did——?" her father had asked.

"Joe did it," her mother interrupted, then laughed. "Don't you love it?"

Sky nodded and hugged her mother, who couldn't stand still, her excitement spilling over to Sky.

Not to Sky's father, though.

"It's not good for the tree," he muttered, frowning. "And how's she supposed to get up there?"

"The tree's fine. And there's a ladder——" her mother began, but Sky already had her foot on the first rung. She could have reached the house without the ladder. As high as it was in the tree, the branches from the ground up were good for climbing. But she'd wanted them to stop fighting.

She'd thought then that her parents had just disagreed on her birthday gift. A minor fight. Looking back, it was the beginning of everything. The start of her family breaking apart.

When she sleeps in the tree house now, a small lantern lights the room, making a ring of yellow on the ceiling. Otherwise, the darkness would be so black, she wouldn't be able to see her hand in front of her face.

She lets the hum of the forest sing her to sleep. Safe inside the walls, she listens to the hoot owls calling back and forth, singing a song she likes to imagine is her very own lullaby.

Here, her heart stops racing. She's a hamster on a wheel, running and running, until she's curled tight in the feather bed on the wood floor.

The guilt weighs heavy each time she runs away.

She likes Leo—she's old enough to know she's making a bad situation even worse. And Leo is struggling too; she knows he misses her father.

The other day she walked into the living room to see him holding a picture up to his face. The one of her father on the town dock with a large fish in his hands, his smile big. She remembers that day. He'd won the fishing competition, and they'd brought the fish home and cooked it on the grill for dinner, the whole fire department in her backyard, eating off paper plates.

Leo had looked up, caught her watching him. He'd put the picture back on the table and smiled at her, but his lips were crooked, and she turned and left the room before the tears spilled down his face.

She's known Leo her whole life, but now that he's living in her house, things have changed between them.

He walks around her carefully. She catches him watching her out of the corner of her eye while she eats breakfast. She feels his eyes on her while she does her homework at the table, the night closing in on them, the quiet so loud she can't think.

She doesn't know anything about the will everyone keeps talking about. The one that says Leo is her guardian.

Her parents never asked her about that. Not that she would have had anything to say. In her worst nightmare, she couldn't have imagined losing them both.

Most days it doesn't seem real. Two months have passed since the accident, and she's still waiting for the front door to open. For the jingle of her father's keys dropping on the table. Her mother's voice calling her name.

She thinks about it all the time. Wonders if her parents are gone because they never belonged to her in the first place.

She said this out loud to Frankie the other day. She wouldn't have admitted this to anyone but Frankie Murphy—her best friend since the beginning of time.

They were walking home from school, and Frankie was telling Sky that she'd lost her favorite necklace at the beach. It just disappeared from the towel where she'd put it.

Frankie was sad until she remembered that she found the necklace in the first place. Right on that same beach the previous summer. That made it better.

"Maybe certain things are only meant to be ours for a little while," Frankie said.

Sky nodded. "Sort of like my parents, I guess," she said, kicking a pebble from the sidewalk to the hedge next to her.

Frankie screwed up her face and stopped in the middle of the sidewalk. "How are your parents like my necklace?"

Sky shrugged. "I don't know. They adopted me. So we never really belonged to each other." She shrugged again. "Just like you said. Some things are only supposed be ours for a little while."

Frankie eyed her. "That's the stupidest thing I've ever heard," she said finally.

"Why? You just said the same thing about your necklace."

"My necklace was a cheap piece of metal. Yours is . . . people!"

"Come on. I have to pee." She pulled Frankie's arm, and they started walking again, but Frankie kept stealing glances at her, as though she wasn't sure at all if Sky knew the difference between jewelry and human beings.

"Plus," Frankie said, out of the blue, "you had the best parents in the world. Doesn't matter if they adopted you. If anyone gets to say they don't belong in their family, it's me, not you."

Sky didn't answer, because she couldn't argue with that.

Sky always thought the Murphy family Christmas card could have been ripped from the pages of the L.L.Bean catalog her mother used to keep on the coffee table.

Frankie's mom and dad, her two brothers, and Frankie all sitting on the steps in front of their huge house. All of them pale and blond, dressed in plaid, even their dog, with his yellow fur and matching outfit.

But Sky knew what went on in that house. Frankie's mother had wanted Frankie to be just like her star-athlete brothers, twins and seniors at Ichabod High School, cocaptains of every team they played on.

Sky only knew them as Big Murph and Little Murph, just like everyone else on the island. Their faces looked identical, except Big Murph was over six feet and thick and Little Murph was shorter and wiry.

Sky would sit in the bleachers with Frankie at one of their games and she'd hear someone ask, "Who scored that goal?" *Big Murph.* Or "Who hit the home run?" *Little Murph.*

Mrs. Murphy never missed a game. She dressed in the school colors and cheered the loudest. She insisted she wasn't competitive—just happy that her children were *involved*.

By the time Frankie was five, she was on six teams. Soccer in the fall. Basketball in the winter. Softball in the spring. Gymnastics throughout the year. Summer was swim club. Tennis every Sunday.

It's how Frankie and Sky met.

Frankie was the only other girl who could keep up with Sky. Forwards on the soccer team, they traded goals like playing cards. Sky loved playing on a team with Frankie.

Except Frankie hated it. Even at five years old, all Frankie wanted to do was draw. And sketch. And paint.

Frankie's mom thought it was *cute*—but hobbies like art didn't get you into an Ivy League school. By the time they were seven, both Frankie and Sky would mimic Frankie's mother when she said this. They'd mouth the words behind her back, giggle when Mrs. Murphy caught them and frowned.

When Frankie was eight, she tried to quit every sport, but her mother wouldn't let her.

A year later, Frankie chopped off all her hair with a pair of dull scissors to prove to her mother that she couldn't control *everything* Frankie did.

Then this past winter, something snapped inside of Frankie. She traded her UGGs for black combat boots. She wore them with black leggings and her brother's hand-me-down plaid shirts.

She tucked her white-blond hair into a black knit cap.

She told everyone she would no longer answer to Francesca. Now, she was Frankie.

That was the last straw for Mrs. Murphy.

She threatened private school. Frankie, the little sister of two of the toughest boys on the island and no stranger to threats, simply ran away. Disappeared in a blizzard in the middle of February.

The search lasted three days. The whole island went looking for Frankie, the Coast Guard too.

They located her when a guy on a fishing trip returned to his houseboat to find a young girl in his bed, a sketchbook on her lap, the electric heater blazing so hot he could have stripped to his underwear and still have been warm.

Frankie had a cup of hot soup on the table next to her. She'd showed him the sketch of the inside of his boat while he called her parents.

After that, Mr. Murphy, Frankie's father, a large man in expensive suits who spent most of his time on the mainland, told Mrs. Murphy that enough was enough—to let the girl be, for everyone's sake.

From then on, Frankie got to spend her time drawing and sketching and painting. Mrs. Murphy got to pretend the whole mess was just a silly misunderstanding. The island got a Frankie Murphy original piece of art—the sketch is still framed on the wall of the town pub. Not because anyone really wants to remember the three days Frankie went missing.

More because the owner of the houseboat also owned the pub, and the sketch was just that *good*.

Everyone moved on.

Except Sky knew that Frankie never felt at home in her house. And Sky, without parents now twice in her life, knew what it was to be alone in the world.

That's why Sky and Frankie are best friends. Why Sky would do anything for Frankie. And Frankie would do anything for Sky.

They both know sometimes the strongest friendships come from the loneliest despair.

5

She comes to the island with next to nothing. A duffel bag the size of a large watermelon. A purse small enough to fit in the palm of her hand.

At the inn, the front-desk clerk takes her credit card, runs it through the machine.

"You here for work?" he asks, letting his fingertips brush her hand when he passes her the key to the room.

She doesn't answer, just opens her purse, slips the key inside.

"I was asking because you look like one of those models who stayed here last week," the clerk says, his thick New England accent spilling on the counter between them like a stain he can't wipe away.

"Whole bunch of them did a beach shoot here last week," he continues. "No joke—you could definitely be one of them."

She thanks him. He asks if it's for the compliment or for checking her into the inn.

She's not sure, so she smiles and walks away. She feels his eyes on her ass. This makes her feel sorry for him.

He's young, full of life.

She's rotting from the inside out.

*   *   *

She's come to Ichabod to die. The thought doesn't even make her sad anymore. The disease has been part of her for so long now—it's a relief to just be. To let it have her, fully.

Absurd, given that she's only in her third decade.

Even more absurd that there's not a single person on this earth who will miss her. Her mother will cry—of course she will. Because mothers are supposed to cry. It's the appearance that matters to her mother. She learned that years ago. Learned that not every girl had an empty space inside where a mother's love could have been—should have been.

Her whole life she's been filling up that empty space inside of her with poison. Alcohol and amphetamines. Then heroin, her drug of choice. The one that ruined her modeling career. But it was the chemo that made her want to die. When they found the cancer the second time, she was almost glad it was everywhere. Untreatable.

She's done a lot of bad things in her life. Lied, stole. Cheated on every man she ever loved.

But here, on Ichabod, is the best thing she ever did.

The best part of her sorry, wasted life.

Now, she stands at the slider, looks out at the harbor. The sea flat and calm on the other side of the glass door.

And for the first time in as long as she can remember, her future seems bright.

6

Summer descends upon Ichabod the same way the tide rolls in, little by little, and then seemingly, all at once.

The population swells. Tourists arrive on the ferry. Some for the summer. Others, a week or two.

More than a few simply never leave. Perhaps the beauty of Ichabod is what grabs them. Maybe a chance at a fresh start.

For Maggie, it was both.

Which is why she's nostalgic at the beginning of every summer. Yesterday, she took the long way to work, through the center of town and by the water. The ferry was docking, and she pulled into an open space, put the car in park, and just sat.

She still remembers seeing Ichabod for the first time. Standing on the bow of the ferry as the fog lifted and the island materialized before her eyes. The red cliffs blazing and the trees glistening with dew. The land appearing as though it had suddenly risen straight out of the sea.

Almost three decades have passed since she was that twenty-two-year-old girl arriving alone, accepting a last-minute invitation from Agnes, her college roommate, to a Fourth of July party at her family home on the island.

Maggie had planned to stay only the weekend.

But two days turned into a week, and she found herself falling in love with Ichabod, inch by inch, so much that when she saw the Help Wanted sign in the window of the quaint inn on Main Street, nestled in the center of the island, she knew even before she got the job as the front-desk receptionist that she was going to stay.

That Ichabod Island would become her home.

All these years later, she doesn't regret staying.

Even when it's the dead of winter, and there's only two restaurants open, and it seems like every other day the heat in her classroom breaks, and she has to wrangle all of her fourth graders into the gym where it's warm, just so they can do their worksheets without their fingers and toes going numb from the cold.

But it's this time of year she loves the most.

Early summer, before the season really kicks off. When stores and restaurants reopen, and the days are longer, and the air warmer, yet the island is still quiet.

Still *hers*.

Although she woke up in a foul mood today—gloomy and anxious—even though there's no reason why she should be gloomy and anxious today, the last day of school and, therefore, the last day she needs to get up and go to work for the next twelve weeks.

She's aware she's likely the only teacher on the island (maybe the planet), who isn't happy it's the last day of school.

Hell, she remembers a younger version of herself counting the minutes until the year ended. Especially when the boys were little. When she had beach days and s'mores over campfires and lazy afternoons at the park to look forward to. When she had people to take care of—to talk to!

Back when her marriage was a living, breathing thing.

Now the boys aren't little anymore.

Michael, her baby, just turned twenty-four and PJ is two years his senior. Both living on the West Coast, busy with their own lives. She's lucky if she sees them a handful of times each year.

Summer stretches out lonely in front of her.

She knows today is supposed to be a fun day—a celebration, really. Games and hot dogs and burgers and ice cream. The entire elementary school on the large grassy field for a field day and a cookout—an Ichabod Island tradition.

Still, she drags herself out of bed and into the shower. When she's dressed and downstairs, she thinks about calling Pete. See if he wants to meet her for a drink on the harbor later.

But they've barely spoken since that awkward mess in bed, and honestly, she doesn't have the energy to cajole him out of the seemingly never-ending bad mood he's been in for a year.

Downstairs, she grabs her keys and walks out the door.

Joe is across the street, standing in his garden, his usual spot. He has a mug in one hand and a watering can in the other.

Joe's garden is a work of art. And he's usually outside tending to it, especially now that he's out of work.

Maggie calls out a hello, and Joe looks up, stops the stream of water on his vegetables, and puts down the can. He waves to her, and she crosses the street, kicks off her flip-flops and walks up the front lawn to the side of his house. His lawn is plush—so green and thick under her bare feet, she wishes she could just sit. Maybe lie down in the sun.

"Hey, stranger," he says when she reaches him. "I was starting to think you were avoiding me."

"I've been meaning to stop by and see how you're doing. Huge neighbor guilt here. I've felt awful about it all week," she says, eyeing the angry scar on his leg.

Joe Armstrong was the busiest builder in town until six

months ago, when he fell off a second-floor scaffolding at Brian and Ann's house. Maggie doesn't know the extent of his injuries, but it's bad enough that he might never climb a ladder again.

"Don't say that," Joe says. "Nothing worse than making a woman feel awful and not knowing a thing about it. Besides, your husband stopped by for a beer the other night. I told him to say hello for me. I take it he didn't?"

Maggie shakes her head.

"Well he did a hell of a job cheering me up. Can't be down with that guy around."

"No, I guess you can't," Maggie says dryly, and Joe looks at her, his eyebrows up, but she's saved from explaining by Xavier, who's just come out of the house next door and called loudly to both of them to hang on a minute—he's coming right over.

"Lucky us," Joe mutters.

"What's wrong?" Maggie whispers out the corner of her mouth, watching Xavier squeeze through the hedge between the driveways. "He seems nice."

"Really? I think he seems like a first-class asshole. Showing up in his Range Rover every Friday night even though it sits there all weekend. I guess the ferry fee to get it here is just chump change. Plus, he never gets my name right. Watch." Joe lifts his chin in Xavier's direction, as though Maggie should pay attention to the show that's about to go on.

"Hey, neighbors," Xavier says when he reaches them.

He's dressed in pressed jeans and loafers. A skintight T-shirt tucked in and stretched over abs so pronounced that Maggie has an urge to reach out and touch them just to make sure they're real.

Maggie says hello, but Xavier is already turned away from her, looking at Joe.

"It's Jay, right? Look—we're going to need your help with the girl. The path to the tree house is almost in your backyard. Be great if you can keep an eye out. Let us know if you see her when she takes off at night." He gestures to Joe's lawn, frowns at it as though it's let him down in some way.

"It's Joe."

"What?"

Joe holds up his mug. "Like the coffee. Not Jay. Not Jeff. Not Jim. Just Joe."

Xavier takes off his sunglasses, squints at Joe. "Sorry. Lots of new names in my life lately. Guess I'm playing catch-up. Anyway, the girl took off again—"

"Sky," Joe interrupts, pointing to the clouds above. "I can make name tags if you need. Go around the neighborhood and stick them on folks until you learn them." He leans over and dumps his coffee in the bushes.

Xavier jumps back, straightening each leg in front of him to see if the brown liquid has splashed on his pants. When he's finished, he looks at Joe, clears his throat forcefully, as though he's commanding the attention of a roomful of people.

"Look—I'm just asking you to keep an eye out. I'm leaving for the week, and Leo will be alone. I know he's her guardian, but this can't be just his problem. I mean, there's a whole island full of people who seem to be very—" He glances at Joe, then Maggie, and stops.

"Very what?" Joe asks, but it's more of a bark, and Maggie's pulse quickens.

She doesn't like confrontation. Never has.

"Concerned?" Joe continues.

Xavier shifts his weight and nods, even though it's clearly not the word he was looking for.

"We'll all keep an eye out," Maggie offers, trying to smooth Joe's rough edges.

She doesn't know Xavier at all, but she does know Leo. And she loves Leo.

So even though she can't disagree with Joe—Xavier does come off as sort of . . . abrasive (*first-class asshole* seems extreme), he's also Leo's husband. Maggie wants to be on good terms with Xavier for this fact alone.

"Not used to island life, huh?" Joe taunts.

Maggie winces.

"All the closeness?" Joe says.

"I'm a city guy," Xavier replies, nonplussed. "Where I come from it's called meddling."

"She stayed put all week, right? When it was just her and Leo?"

Xavier shrugs. "Far as I know."

"Maybe there's your answer."

"What's that?"

"You leave, and she stays put. You come back, and she takes off. Could be as simple as that. Maybe it's you she's running from."

"Thanks for your help," Xavier mutters and stomps away, trampling through the hedge.

"No problem," Joe calls after him. "Where I come from it's called neighborly advice."

Maggie winces again. "Have a good day!" she shouts weakly to Xavier, who either doesn't hear her or doesn't care to respond, the car door slamming after he disappears inside the Range Rover.

Maggie frowns at Joe after Xavier drives away. He looks at her, lifts his shoulders, and drops them.

"Look—I don't care if he doesn't know my name. But he sure as shit better get hers right." His voice cracks, and he straightens, clears his throat.

He's talking about Sky—Sport, he calls her. She's in Joe's yard often. Picking flowers or vegetables or petting Joe's cat. He even made Sky her own garden, a small one that Maggie has helped Sky weed on cooler afternoons.

She puts her hand on Joe's arm. "It's going to be okay," she says.

She's known Joe Armstrong for a lot of years. He lost a wife to cancer. A son to drugs. Now, perhaps, his livelihood is gone.

Her own life is not what she thought it would be. Her days so void of . . . *joy* . . . that lately she wonders if she's depressed.

Her friend Ann is dead. Along with her husband. And now, Sky, the sweetest child Maggie's ever met, is an orphan for the second time in her short life.

And all Maggie can think to say is: *It's going to be okay*.

She takes her hand off Joe's arm. She can see her words fell flat, but she simply turns and walks away, crosses the street and gets in her car. She shuts the door before her big mouth betrays her. Before she can open her mouth and tell another absurd lie.

It's going to be okay, she mimics out loud, sings it really, her shaky, high-pitched voice filling the car. She laughs at her own ridiculous words, doesn't bother to wipe away the tear sliding down her face.

All morning Maggie tries to get out of her miserable mood. A *funk* is what her mother would have called it.

By lunch, she's given over to it.

She should be sitting under the tent with the other teachers.

Instead, she's on the bleachers with a hamburger balanced on a paper plate in her lap.

There's a frenzied excitement in the air. She can hear the high schoolers on the football field even though they're a half mile down the road. Music drifting over on the breeze.

She watches a group of boys play kickball. She'll miss seeing her students and having a schedule to fill the hours.

She's contemplating this when she hears her name and looks up to see Agnes walking toward her. As the school nurse, health teacher, and coach of the varsity crew team, Agnes Coffin wears a lot of hats.

But to Maggie, she's her old friend. Her roommate all four years of college.

The one who knows that when Maggie Thompson sits by herself on the bleachers, far away from the fun, something is wrong.

Agnes plops down next to Maggie, waves a fly away from the ice-cream sandwich in her hand.

"You're missing all the good dirt," Agnes says. "Apparently, the entire guidance department is sleeping with each other."

Maggie smiles. "Which would be interesting if there were more than two people in the entire guidance department. And they weren't married. To each other."

Agnes shrugs. "I was going to say something more off-color, but we're still on the clock. At least I got a smile. That's the first one I've seen from you all week."

Agnes leans forward, eyeing Maggie, her broad-shouldered, six-foot frame casting a shadow over Maggie even though they're both sitting. Agnes is the reason Maggie's on this island. Living this life.

Agnes's hair has grown back after the chemo, but thinner,

her blond curls replaced with a short wispy cut that's now lit by the bright sun behind her, making her look as if she's wearing a halo.

Maggie tells her this, and Agnes grimaces.

"You know me," she says. "Goddamn angel in disguise."

"Well, you are. Some days, at least," Maggie jokes.

"Tell that to William. I almost threw a spoon at his head last night. Over laundry. Laundry!"

"At least it wasn't a knife," Maggie offers, and Agnes nods, like she has a point.

"I heard Sky showed up at your house again this weekend."

Maggie nods. "Poor Leo looks like he's dropped twenty pounds since he got here, and he didn't have it to lose in the first place. Wait—how was your checkup in the city? I thought you and William were going to stay an extra day? Stay in a fancy hotel. Make a little vacation out of it."

"I changed my mind. We came home right after the appointment. He wanted me to be cheery, and I didn't want to be cheery after I was poked and prodded."

"Was that the argument behind the laundry?"

Agnes waves away the question. "It's about his work, as usual. How he's never home. It's not worth talking about. I'll only get mad again. By the way, I saw Lillian on the ferry. I went over and told her I was very happy to see her and that I hoped she was staying for a while."

Maggie looks at Agnes blankly. "Lillian?"

"Lillian, Maggie. Ann's mother. Sky's grandmother!"

"Why are you saying it like I should know who you're talking about? I haven't met her."

"Well, you've heard me talk about her. I was the one who had to call about the accident."

"I seem to remember you volunteered to call Lillian."

"It came down to either me or Leo, so I was the obvious choice. I mean, Lillian and I are friends."

Maggie frowns. "Friends? I never heard you talk about this person until two months ago!"

"We *were* friends until she left Ichabod. She's a native, you know. Her mother and my mother went to church every Sunday. She moved away when we were ten. Eleven, maybe. I remember she was very nice."

"Nice? Agnes. She didn't come to her own daughter's funeral. Maybe she's changed in the forty years since you were *friends*."

"That's not fair. Lillian explained that she wanted to hold her own services on the mainland. And the only reason she didn't come to the funeral was because of Sky. They haven't seen each other for quite some time, and she didn't want to make things even harder for the girl. Frankly, I think she was still in shock. Losing her daughter *and* finding out that her own granddaughter is now being raised by a man. A man she hasn't even met!"

"Leo isn't just some random stranger. He was Brian's best friend. And Ann loved Leo. Did you bother to ask her why she hasn't seen her daughter or granddaughter in 'quite some time,' as you put it?"

Agnes rolls her eyes. "Yes, because that would have been an appropriate thing to ask at that particular moment. *Hello, Lillian—I'm calling to tell you there's been a tragic accident and your daughter was killed. And by the way, what exactly was the issue between the two of you?*"

Maggie tilts her head at Agnes and sighs. She's fairly certain Agnes getting involved in this is really about Grace, Agnes's only child.

Grace lives in Vermont with Julie, who Agnes refers to as Grace's *roommate*, even though Grace is a twenty-six-year-old woman who has lived with Julie in the same one-bedroom condo for four years.

Grace doesn't come to Ichabod often. Never with Julie.

Agnes has never said out loud that she has a problem with Grace's sexuality. Maggie learned early on that Agnes's faith came first in her life.

If the church didn't support something, there was a good chance neither did Agnes.

Maggie wasn't religious. But she couldn't deny that Agnes's faith was a source of support for her friend, even if it was hard sometimes to understand *why*. Especially when Agnes kept going to church regularly, straight through the sexual-abuse scandal. When every headline in the news seemed to name another parish. Another priest.

Maggie had long ago settled with the decision that she would love Agnes for her quick wit. Her huge heart. Her *capableness*.

They didn't talk about religion or politics. That's how they stayed best friends.

"Don't get in the middle of something you don't know anything about," she says.

"All I'm saying is Lillian has a right to be in that child's life. And I wanted her to know that I support that—she should be in Sky's life. Don't tell me you disagree—what if PJ or Michael had a child and, God forbid, something happened? Wouldn't you want a chance to raise your own grandchild?" Agnes clears her throat. "I'm not the type to meddle. But this is important."

Maggie snorts. "You were born to meddle. Despite this, I still love you. Let's just change the subject. Pete was on the ferry yesterday. Did you see him?"

"See him? The whole boat was watching him. You know your husband, always the center of attention."

Maggie wants to kick herself for bringing Pete into the conversation. Agnes has never liked him. Hasn't from the first day he showed up on *Agnes's* island all those years ago with his beat-up Jeep loaded down with surfboards.

Maggie and Agnes had been kids just out of college. They were shopping in town when Pete pulled over in his Jeep, asked them for directions to Crane Beach.

"It's Crane's," Agnes told him. "*Crane's* Point."

He smiled. Two rows of perfect teeth in his perfectly tanned face. "Right on. Big swells there, right?" He held out his arms, surfing an imaginary wave.

Agnes scowled at him, but Maggie nodded, mesmerized. Agnes had told her later that she looked like one of those bobbleheads people stick to their dashboards. But Maggie couldn't take her eyes off Pete. He was the most handsome man she'd ever come even close to standing next to.

"The best," Maggie said. "Is this your first time on the island?"

He nodded. "You guys locals?"

"Agnes was born here. I moved here a month ago. You're going to love it. It's the best," Maggie gushed.

"I think I already love it," he said, winking at her.

Maggie giggled. "Where are you staying?"

"Wherever I land." He winked again and drove away. Agnes muttered that she hoped he landed somewhere *off* her island.

But a week later, Maggie showed up with him to dinner. And then *Bam!* they were married, and *Pow!* two kids came along, and *Splat!* just last year, twenty-six years in, Pete cheated on Maggie. With his secretary no less.

The secretary. How predictable, Agnes liked to say.

It was a sin Agnes couldn't forgive.

She didn't care that Maggie had forgiven him. That they'd spent months in therapy trying to save their marriage. Agnes never cared for Pete. And she wasn't about to let him off the hook for shattering her best friend's heart.

She knows she shouldn't ask Agnes what happened with Pete on the ferry. But she can't stop herself.

"He does like a crowd," she agrees. "What happened?"

"One of the pretty young galley girls cut her finger. Pete came to the rescue." Agnes rolls her eyes. "Mr. First Aid himself."

Maggie doesn't mention that Pete is a trained EMT. Or that some of the ferry crew are hired through the town, which is technically under Pete's jurisdiction.

"I'm sure he was just helping one of his employees," she offers instead.

As soon as it passes her lips, her cheeks color. His secretary had been his employee. The one who texted him heart emojis and called him *Babe*.

"Well, I took a picture. You can judge for yourself." Agnes digs in her pocketbook for her phone.

"You took a picture of Pete with the galley girl? What—as some sort of proof?"

"Calm down. Of course not. I was trying to take a picture of the rainbow in the doorway behind them. But I didn't have my cheaters on. And by the time I snapped the picture, the rainbow was almost gone and all I got was Pete leaning over the counter with the girl's hand in his arm and his lips nearly touching her swanlike neck." Agnes holds up her phone. "See? Look."

Maggie shakes her head and pushes the phone away. "I know you're just trying to protect me, but I have better things to do than worry about Pete bandaging some teenager's finger."

"Suit yourself." Agnes drops the phone in her pocketbook.

They don't speak. She feels Agnes's eyes on her, but she tilts her face, pretends she's just relaxing in the sun instead of wishing Agnes would go back to the tent with the other teachers.

Agnes clears her throat loudly, as though she can sense Maggie's desire for her to leave.

"So, what's wrong with you anyway? That's what I came over to ask. Why are you over here all alone?"

"Nothing's wrong," Maggie lies. "I just wanted a little sun. When do you get your results from the MRI?"

"I don't know. Let's not talk about it."

They sit in silence while Maggie takes a bite of her burger and Agnes eats her ice cream.

After thirty years of friendship, they both know when to leave well enough alone.

7

Across the field, Leo flips the last hamburger on the grill, presses the spatula against it until the juices run clear.

Then he puts it on the platter where it's whisked away to the food table. He places six more burgers on the grill, even though they're probably not needed. Most of the kids have gone back to playing, and there's still a stack of burgers left on the table. But he's happy to be doing something useful.

Grilling, he can do. Parenting is another story.

He's here as a volunteer. Sky's parent. Which, at this moment, seems laughingly absurd because he's just learned that he forgot to send the paperwork and the payment to the day camp where Sky is supposed to start tomorrow at eight in the morning.

And now, she can't go. Because of him.

An epic fail, Xavier would say.

Leo learned this bad news the way all bad news seems to find him these days. Suddenly and without warning. Not even a whiff of premonition.

He was having a perfectly nice conversation with a young woman named Lori while they stood at the grill.

He cooked. She set the buns on the plate.

In the interest of small talk, he asked Lori if she had any special plans this summer. She looked at him with a puzzled expression and told him she ran a day camp on the island.

"You run it? By yourself?"

"Well, no. I'm the director. It's a pretty big camp."

"Oh, yeah? Which one? Sky is going to camp too. I forget the name of it. Camp Tekawho or something like that."

Lori paused. "Tekawitha."

"That's it. I forgot to get the paperwork in and thank God they called me. The principal even sent home a letter in Sky's backpack."

She paused again. "That was actually me. I'm Lori Ward. The assistant principal . . . Ms. Ward."

He looked up, startled. The hamburger he was flipping slid off the spatula and landed on top of a cheeseburger. He sorted the mess while studying her out of the corner of his eye. How was it possible that she was the assistant principal? Fresh-faced and sporty with her long dark hair pulled back under a coral Lululemon headband, she could've blended in with the senior girls at the high school.

When did he get so old?

He groaned, gave her an apologetic look. "I'm sorry—you just look so young. I didn't put two and two together. Thank you, of course. For following up. I have some big shoes to fill, and I seem to be stumbling here."

Her face colored. "I, um, well—I never heard back from you. I sent the stuff home with Sky and then I called too. When I didn't hear back, I figured she wasn't coming this year."

The minute she said it, Leo saw the letter on the table. He'd read it. Put it aside until he had more time in the day. And somehow, in his mind, he wrote the check and sent the paperwork. But he hadn't.

The day with more time in it had never come.

He felt her hand on his arm.

"Look—I can't do anything this session, but I'll put her on the wait list for the other sessions. Sometimes kids drop out. I'm sorry. I would make an exception—it's understandable how this happened—but we're at capacity, and once I bend the rules for one person, it's a nightmare. A lesson I learned the hard way."

She left him standing at the grill, wondering how to tell a ten-year-old girl, whose whole world had recently collapsed, that her summer was off to a similar start.

By the time the school bell rings at the end of the day, Leo has forgotten about Camp Tekawitha and his epic fail.

He has bigger problems.

He's missed three calls from Xavier. Three voice mails that Leo listens to, each making him feel a little bit worse.

The first is Xavier telling him that he's leaving for the city a day early, but he went downstairs to get his laundry and there's a foot of water on the basement floor.

The second voice mail relays that by the time Xavier made it back upstairs, after wading through ankle-deep *muck*, there was a message on the answering machine from Sky's grandmother.

The third one is an apology—or so Xavier says, but Leo's never heard an apology sound so unapologetic.

Xavier feels bad for dumping things on Leo. But he has no idea what to do about the water. Ditto for the grandmother. And Xavier would have come up to the school to say goodbye, but he's late for the ferry, and since everything takes *ten times* longer here, he has to go right now if there's any chance of getting a goddamn latte before the ferry takes off.

The seasonal coffee shack on the dock opened last week. Overpriced and overrated to the locals, but Xavier can finally get his preferred caffeine fix. Now that the summer shops are beginning to open, Leo has heard less grumbling from his city-loving husband.

Lola's sushi bar, set to open on Saturday, seems to be the only reason Xavier is excited to come back to Ichabod next weekend.

When Xavier had gone on and on about it, Leo briefly wallowed in the thought that his husband had more interest in a selection of raw fish than in him. Then he felt melodramatic and selfish for thinking it—Xavier had made it clear that he missed *everything* about their life in the city—even the noise!

It's so goddamn quiet. I can't sleep! Xavier said every night of his first weekend on the island.

Most weekend nights now, Xavier falls asleep in front of the television. The volume droning out the chirping of the crickets, the tinkle of the wind chime, the call of the owls—sounds that Leo listens for in the quiet of the bedroom, where a peacefulness settles inside of him that he has no right to feel given that his husband is miserable.

Xavier is tired of commuting to and from the city, tired of living inside this cramped house that once belonged to people Xavier barely knew—he'd met them only once, at their wedding ceremony last year.

Leo never could get him over to the island to visit his childhood friends. Xavier didn't like boats. Or water, for that matter. He'd had a near-drowning experience at the town pool as a kid, but Leo didn't know how much of that was true. Xavier's sisters always rolled their eyes when he told the story and spent the next ten minutes laughing about how much Xavier loved to exaggerate.

Leo can't fix how Xavier feels about the island. He hopes Xavier will just give Ichabod a chance.

Because Leo's not going to leave Sky. And he would never ask her to move.

Leo didn't ask for this life, but now that he's here, back on the land where he grew up, somehow, *someway*, he's calmer.

And, so, Ichabod has become a thing between Leo and Xavier. This single island alone in the water.

A glacial deposit formed into cliffs and beaches, forests and inlets that has risen up between them like an enormous summit, wind-whipped and avalanche prone, with their new marriage, just one year old, sitting in the path of destruction.

Each time Xavier tells Leo he hates the island, Leo feels the earth shift, the land beneath his feet shudder.

For this reason, and others he can't put words to, when he replays each voice mail for the second time, he doesn't call Xavier back.

He just puts the phone in his pocket and walks off the field, in search of the child he's been entrusted to care for, his mind on how best to deliver the bad news about camp.

When Leo finally finds Sky in the crowded parking lot, she is surrounded by women. And nobody is speaking.

Ms. Ward is studying Sky. Maggie has her arm around Sky's shoulders. Agnes has her hand on Sky's forehead.

"She's not warm," Agnes announces just as Leo reaches them. "But sometimes that doesn't mean anything."

"I feel fine," Sky says. "I just don't want to go."

The three women frown in unison. Leo clears his throat.

"Go where?" he asks, and they all turn.

"I just found out we have an opening in Sky's age group for the first session," Ms. Ward says. "Molly Bench broke her ankle this morning. I was telling Sky that she's welcome to come to camp tomorrow, but she said she doesn't want to."

"Could be Lyme too. Makes everyone lethargic. Have you found any ticks on you lately?" Agnes asks Sky, who shakes her head.

"I feel *fine*. I'm not sick. I just don't want to go."

"But you love camp," Maggie offers. "You go every year."

"Well this one's different," Sky says, in such a way that the women simply nod.

Leo clears his throat again, feeling as though maybe he's to blame for the whole mess. "Sky—this is my fault. Not yours. I forgot to sign you up. But everyone wants you to go."

"You didn't forget. You left the stuff on the table, and I threw it out," Sky tells him.

Agnes clucks, and Ms. Ward holds up her hands in resignation.

"Oh, Sky," Maggie sighs.

"I'll keep the spot open until the end of the day, Leo," Ms. Ward says. "I have a wait list and frankly, I'm bypassing that right now. I hope you change your mind, Sky. You know we'd love to have you." She pats her lightly on the back and walks away.

Sky turns to Leo.

"Can I go?" she asks. "Frankie's waiting for me to walk home with her."

"I can drive you both," Leo says, but he knows the answer is no. Sky has two favorite places in the world: one is next to Frankie, and the other is roaming Ichabod.

Which worries him more than ever right now.

He's had to keep track of her only after school hours. They'd agreed she would come home no later than four thirty in the afternoon. She's never been late.

Now the summer days stretch out. And he's supposed to be on the ferry off the island tomorrow for a meeting in the office.

Sky waves goodbye and turns. They watch her walk away in silence.

Leo should be rushing home to deal with the water in the basement. And the phone call from Ann's mother, the one she hadn't spoken to in years. But he stands in the parking lot with Maggie and Agnes, too tired suddenly to move.

"I'm screwed if she doesn't change her mind. I have to work all week," Leo admits. "Can you force a child to go to camp?"

"Of course," Agnes scoffs. "Mothers have been forcing children to do things they don't want to do since the beginning of time. Welcome to the club."

Maggie frowns at Agnes, but Leo ignores her. Her comment is just one in a handful of things she's said to him since he returned to the island two months ago.

He's used to Agnes's gruff nature—she was the school nurse way back when he was a student. And he grew up two doors down from her on the same street.

Honestly, until recently, Agnes Coffin was just an adult in his life. The school nurse who kept a jar of animal crackers on her desk.

Now, as an adult, he finds her rude. Small-minded, even.

She calls him *city boy* and *hot shot*. One Friday afternoon, he passed her on the street on his way to meet Xavier at the ferry, and she pointed to the clouds, the rain starting to come down.

"Just saw your boyfriend getting off the ferry. Looks like he brought the bad weather with him from the mainland," she said.

"Husband," he corrected, and she waved him away and kept walking, as though he were a bigger inconvenience than the tiny drops falling on her head.

She had a habit of fingering the cross around her neck when she made these comments, as though she knew she should be seeking forgiveness even as the words crossed her lips.

Now Maggie puts her hand on Leo's arm.

"I'm no expert, but I think forcing Sky to do anything she doesn't want to do right now seems unnecessary. She's dealing with enough change, don't you think?" Maggie asks, and Leo nods.

"Well what do you suggest, Mother Teresa?" Agnes asks. "Perhaps a flock of sheep can tend to the child each day." She smiles innocently at Maggie, who ignores her.

"What if we watch her a couple of days a week? I think she'd agree to it," Maggie says.

"We who?" Agnes asks.

"I can't ask you to do that," Leo says. "It's your summer."

"Damn right," Agnes mutters.

"Oh, stop it, Agnes. You know you'll be calling me next week, bored out of your mind and asking me to do *something*. Besides, I *want* to do it. These kids keep me young. And she'll be good company."

"That's exactly my point," Agnes tells Maggie. "I want to call you and do *something*. Not watch a child—which is what we do all year!"

"There's plenty of time for both. I'm happy to do it."

"Are you sure?" Leo asks. "I mean, she loves you. She ends up at your house all the time anyway."

He doesn't mean for this to come out like it does. Sad and pathetic and whiny. But there it is. Out in the air just like that. Maggie's quick to respond, patting his arm.

"Don't let that bother you. I used to watch Sky when she was little and Ann was working part-time. She'd drop her off if Brian was at the station. Never mind that I'm her teacher. It's just familiarity she wants right now. She'll stay put when she's ready. Just give her time."

"Xavier wants me to put a lock on her bedroom door. He takes a harder line than I do, I guess," Leo admits.

"Well, you're a parent now. Nobody said it was easy. If you don't know where she is at night, a lock isn't the worst idea. Remember, it's your job to keep her safe," Agnes lectures, as though this has somehow slipped his mind.

Maggie frowns. "It's not a mystery where she's going, Agnes. She's in the tree house, which is technically on their property—"

"In the middle of the woods!" Agnes says.

"In *her* wooded backyard," Maggie corrects.

"It's not just the running away," Leo cuts in. "I've known Sky since she was, I don't know, a week old. I mean, coming into the world like that—being abandoned and then fate somehow giving you two of the best people as parents. That's just . . . luck. Amazing luck. And Sky knew it. The three of them were inseparable. And now she's just sad. I mean, it's all over her face—I can feel it. I guess I just worry about her . . . you know. *Doing* something."

"Don't say such things," Agnes chides. "God won't allow that to happen."

"Maybe you could talk to her?" he asks Maggie. "It can't hurt—"

"I gave her a wellness evaluation just two weeks ago," Agnes interrupts. "And as a *professional* in the medical field, I can assure you she is not going to hurt herself. That's something I'm trained to be aware of."

"Are you aware that she's been writing letters to her parents? Each one is signed: *See you soon*. I'm not a trained professional, but that seems pretty serious, doesn't it?" Leo snaps.

"Oh, good Lord," Maggie says.

Agnes rolls her eyes. "Children are fickle. Who knows what nonsense they get in their heads? Let's just keep an eye on her and say our prayers, and this will all pass. Calling attention to it is just going to reinforce the behavior."

"Right. Ignore it and pray. Problem solved," Leo says, his temper running away from him.

"I didn't say *ignore* it. I said don't call attention to it. And damn right I pray. Perhaps *you* should, too!"

"What's that supposed to mean—"

"Let's just calm down," Maggie says quietly. "We're all on the same side here. Right, Agnes?"

"I'm not the one who was sarcastic, was I?" Agnes crosses her arms, and Leo sighs.

"Agnes, I apologize. Look—I know you both love Sky. I'm just trying to do my best here. Maggie, it would be a huge help if you could watch her. I'm sure she'll be excited."

He says goodbye to them, notices how Agnes won't even look at him.

He's walking away when he hears Agnes say to Maggie, "Are you planning on saving all the children on the island? One at a time?"

He doesn't hear Maggie's response. But he doesn't care. He's not interested in all the children on the island.

Just one.

8

There's a story everyone on Ichabod likes to tell about Sky's father. Sometimes she tries to remember when she first heard it, but she can't. Her memory doesn't go back that far.

It goes like this:

Brian Pope was born dead. All seven pounds of him appearing suddenly in the sixth inning of a Red Sox game at Fenway Park.

Three weeks early, he came into the world as though he were sliding headfirst into home plate. A heaping pile of baby nearly landing on the peanut-shell-covered floor in the bleacher seats.

His parents were surprisingly calm.

Brian's father was halfway through his fifth beer, and the Yankees were at bat, and he hated the Yankees, every one of them. As did everyone around him. Between the booing and hissing and name-calling, he didn't hear his wife call out.

He didn't notice her get up from her seat and double over on the wide cement steps in the aisle. His eyes were on the batter and, sure, he felt someone tap him on the back, maybe even a tug on his sleeve, but that was because he was screaming, telling the batter what a *lousy bum* he was, and everyone was cheering, agreeing with him.

Then he heard the crack of the ball against the bat. His eyes went skyward, searching. But there was no ball. From his seat way out in center field, he watched the *lousy bum* of a batter at the plate walk to the dugout.

Three strikes on the board.

Only then did he notice the commotion beside him. His wife on her back, her sundress tented over her spread legs, and a policeman kneeling between them, holding a blue-faced, lifeless, newborn baby.

The crack of the ball against the bat was the policeman's open palm bouncing off the baby's round bottom, desperate to get him to breathe. The rookie policeman wasn't trained for this—he'd only just graduated from the academy last year. He'd cleared the baby's mouth with his finger already. He couldn't feel a pulse.

And the mother was up on her elbows, staring at him, so stunned that her expression looked almost serene. She hadn't even pushed. The baby just slid out.

The rookie policeman did the only thing that seemed reasonable. He slapped the baby on the behind. Not too hard—just enough to say: *Wake up!*

He thought he saw the infant's eyelids flicker. He did it again.

A second slap, just as the small crowd that had gathered went quiet with horror at the silent infant cradled facedown in his hand.

The baby jolted, arms jerking, his mouth opening. Seconds later, a shaky wail filled the air.

The crowd cheered while the baby took his first breaths, the Green Monster peering down on him as though it were his very own guardian angel.

The story made the newspapers. *Miracle Baby*, they called him.

The story followed the new parents back to their home on Ichabod, and the infant, Brian Pope, earned a reputation before he even shed the remnants of his umbilical cord.

Tough, they called him. A *survivor*.

Not a weak bone in his body—a fighter, that kid.

Sky heard that story over and over. The priest even slipped it into her father's funeral: No one knew what happened in that car. What tragedy led to the accident that took both Brian and Ann.

But the priest *knew*. *God* knew that Brian Pope did everything in his power to save himself and his beloved wife.

Because that's the kind of person Brian was. A *fighter*.

Her mother hated the story about Sky's father's birth. She'd wince when anybody told it.

"Isn't that a burden to carry through life?" she'd muttered once to Sky. "So small and you're already *tough*. Already a *fighter*. Quite a thing to live up to."

Sky hadn't understood what her mother was talking about. But this last year, she didn't understand a lot of things that were happening in her house.

Things she didn't tell anyone.

Not even Frankie.

She didn't have the words to explain the growing pile of empty bottles under the stairs in the basement. Her father disappeared down there most nights.

She also couldn't figure out her mother's moods. How she was happy one minute. Crying the next.

In the months before her parents died, Sky didn't know which mother she'd wake up to in the morning. The mom she'd always known, or the other woman—the one who dressed in heels and wore red lipstick and said things that made Sky look at her sideways.

The one who decided they needed all new plates and glasses one random day. Her mother had gone to the store and returned with boxes filling her trunk. She stayed up all night unpacking them, putting the expensive-looking china in the cabinets. Sky could hear her from her bedroom, muttering something under her breath.

But when Sky came home from school the next day, the old plates and glasses were back in the cabinet. Her mother had taken the new china back to the store. And she was herself again. Calm and smiling, apologizing to Sky for being *so caught up* in that silly project.

"You know how I get sometimes," her mother had said. "Silly and impulsive. Crazy ideas in my head."

No, Sky had thought to herself. *I don't*.

Sky had never known her mother to be impulsive. And *silly* was about the last word she would've used to describe her. *Dependable. Reliable.* Maybe even *boring.* These were the words she would have used to describe the only mother she'd known since birth.

But something inside of her mother's mind had changed.

Her father knew it too.

Sky saw it in the way he watched her mother. Sometimes, if her mother was acting that way, he'd come into Sky's room at bedtime, sit next to her, his back against the headboard, ask her about her day. He'd stay in her bed and pretend he'd fallen asleep.

But she'd catch his eyes open when there was a noise in the house. He'd look at the door, and she'd hold her breath even though she had no idea what they were waiting for. She got the impression he was protecting her. Standing watch.

She'd never even heard her parents argue until this past year. But once they started, they never stopped.

Her mother yelled at her father about the bottles in the base-ment. How he needed *help*.

Most times, her father walked into the bathroom, opened the medicine cabinet, and returned with a bottle of pills in his hand.

He'd shake it, a thick rattle going through the house. "Did you even take one? A single one?"

"They make me feel sick," her mother would explain.

Her father's answer was always the same. "You are sick," he'd say. "You have a disease."

"So do you!" her mother would shout, ready to fight.

And Sky would close her bedroom door. Or slip outside, run to the tree house. Or sometimes she'd go next door to Joe's.

Joe never came over anymore. He used to be at her house all the time when he was putting the dormers on the front of their house. Then, one day after school, Sky came home to an ambulance in the driveway and Joe, unconscious on a stretcher, and that was the last time he was over at her house.

He'd fallen off the scaffolding, her mother had said.

Sky still remembers her mother standing in the driveway. Shiny red lipstick on her mouth, so heavy and bright she looked like a clown.

Sky should've been watching the men load Joe into the back of the ambulance, checking to see if he was okay. But she hadn't taken her eyes off her mother. But it wasn't really her mother. It was the other woman.

The one with the blank eyes and the red lipstick. And the crazy ideas.

Now that her parents are gone, everyone talks about what a perfect couple they were. But she knows they weren't. They were just people, with problems and secrets, just like everyone else.

She writes them letters sometimes. Tells them about her day. Or what the weather is like. Nothing important, because the thing she misses the most is talking with them about nothing important.

It's silly. A waste of time. But it always makes her feel better. It reminds her of when she went to overnight camp and she'd send home letters almost every day.

She throws each one in the trash though. There is nowhere to send them. No return letters coming her way or care packages in the mail.

Still.

A letter each night makes her feel as if they're still here. As though they're somewhere out there. Still listening. Maybe reading the words over her shoulder.

See you soon.

9

The sun is already blazing in the morning sky when Leo walks out of the house. He's wearing a collared shirt tucked into khakis. A belt even.

Dressed up from his typical shorts and T-shirt, he's already uncomfortable in the heat, but he wants to make a good impression today.

He hears a whistle and looks over to see Joe sitting in a lawn chair in the shade, a hose pointed at his garden.

He's smiling at Leo, as though he's a construction worker catcalling a pretty girl instead of an out-of-work sixty-year-old man teasing his gay neighbor.

Leo laughs and walks over.

"You approve?" he says, and holds his arms out, spins in a slow circle. "Work on your whistle, man. My mother had better pipes."

Joe grins. "Your mother probably could've kicked my ass right now too. Watering these plants has me out of breath."

Leo waves him off. "It's only been a couple months since you got hurt. You'll be good in no time."

"Couple, my ass. Six months as of yesterday. Doc says I'm healed, but my back seems to think otherwise. Starting to wonder if it's all in my head. I should probably take my sister's advice. Hang up my hammer. She keeps telling me to get a job on the mainland. A regular gig at Home Depot or Lowe's. Some place so big even the damn birds in the rafters can't get out."

"Come on now—the one and only Joe Armstrong! Best builder on the island. Guys like you don't go silently into the night. Where's the fight in the old dog, huh?" Leo puts his hands up, punches the air.

Joe watches him for a minute, raises his eyebrows. "Sky could take you in a brawl. You ever get in a fight, let Xavier handle it."

Leo drops his arms. "He's not any better. We have a couple of lesbian friends we bring in for the real muscle. Nobody messes with them."

Joe smiles. "Speaking of messing with people—don't answer your door if somebody knocks. The warden's trying to set up a neighborhood meeting."

Leo rolls his eyes. "Thanks for the warning. You two any friendlier?"

There was no love lost between Joe and Agnes. The whole neighborhood knew they didn't like each other. Maybe the whole island.

"I laid off her when she was sick. But she's back to acting like she owns the street."

"Well, she might. She's been here long enough. Isn't just the street either. Agnes thinks she owns the island."

"Speaking of—I didn't know she owned that house too." Joe nods to the vacant house down the street. "I thought it belonged to the town or something. They always have meetings or whatever there. Church fund-raisers."

Leo nods. "She grew up in that house." He pointed to the one Joe was referring to. "Then she got married and moved across the street. When her parents died, she inherited the one she grew up in. She didn't change one thing in there. Place is like a shrine. She won't sell it. Won't rent it. Says she doesn't want strangers moving in."

"Well, apparently it's the site of our weekly neighborhood meeting. Twice this week, she's knocked on my door. First to tell me it's my duty to show up at the neighborhood meeting—'course, I didn't even know about any of that. Two days later, she's back. Says there's an unknown car parked on the street and do I know who it belongs to? Middle of the day and she's worried about a goddamn sedan parked outside my house."

"What'd you say?"

"I said 'Unknown to who'? Cars don't drive themselves. It sure as hell wasn't unknown to whoever parked it there."

"Bet that went over well."

"'Course it didn't." Joe smirks. "But I wasn't going to tell her it belonged to the massage therapist waiting for me to get naked in the den. None of her damn business. It's not a goddamn gated community. It's a public street."

Leo raises his eyebrows. "Massage therapist, huh? You don't seem like the type."

"I'm not. And he's a guy too. Big Tarzan-type dude. My sister talked me into it. It took some convincing to get me in a towel on a bed in front of this guy. But then he started on my shoulders. He worked out knots I didn't even know I had. I never understood the guy-on-guy thing, but every time Tarzan works his magic, I think if I was smart, I'd switch teams."

Leo laughs. "Never too late, Joe."

A screen door slams behind them, and they both turn to see Sky, walking up the driveway toward them. She's still in her pajamas, walking on the crushed seashell driveway with bare feet as though it were soft grass.

She'll be a beautiful woman someday, Leo thinks, *with her light eyes and dark skin, features sharpening as she matures.*

But right now, she's just a kid.

Tall and skinny, all elbows and kneecaps, limbs that need growing into. Of course, it wasn't like they could look at pictures of Sky's parents to see what she might look like when she was grown.

Nobody had any idea who her parents were. Sky was the island mystery.

The newborn left in the fire station a decade ago during Hurricane Skylar, the worst storm in Ichabod history.

It was Ann who found her. She was dropping off dinner for Brian when she heard a noise in the empty firehouse. She knew all the men were battling a blaze on the waterfront, and she wanted them to return to a warm meal. Swaddled in a basket on the table was a baby.

A newborn.

Most longtime islanders know the story by heart.

How not a soul came forward to claim the healthy eight-pound baby girl with a shock of dark hair and skin to match.

The story made regional headlines. State police and DCF were contacted, and they insisted the newborn be brought to the city. The Ichabod fire station was a safe haven—but there were still rules.

Laws to abide.

But the hurricane raged on, taking out power lines and canceling ferries, and, all the while, the abandoned newborn thrived in the island hospital nursery. Nurses fell in love with her. Tiny homemade knit hats were dropped off at the hospital. Blankets and quilts. The baby was the most exciting thing ever to happen to Ichabod Island.

A week passed, then two. The story died down, and city officials finally made it over to the island, prepared to take the baby and place her in foster care. They had a long list of waiting applicants.

But there she was, the newborn. Already sleeping peacefully in a crib in her very own nursery. Ann and Brian told the officials they wanted to adopt her—she'd already slept over two nights!

Leo's best friends had wanted kids. But Ann couldn't have them. Over the last year before the storm, they took all the foster-care classes. They had their names on a list to adopt. And then this child appeared, belonging to no one.

It made sense to the residents of Ichabod. Ann was a midwife—a baby whisperer, everyone said.

Brian was a firefighter, no doubt the future chief with the way the men regarded him.

Churchgoers and charity-event organizers, Brian and Ann were the golden couple of Ichabod.

Ann found the baby, everyone said.

It was meant to be, everyone agreed.

Even the Department of Children and Families couldn't argue. Or maybe they did. But now that they were on Ichabod Island, the residents had spoken.

Like pieces of a puzzle sliding into place, the abandoned newborn's future suddenly took shape. Brian and Ann named her Skylar, after the hurricane. Her last name, Pope, was theirs. And just like that, they became Ichabod Island's cherished family.

This was the story the island knew. But Leo knew more than that.

He knew his friends had struggled for years. Ann couldn't have children. Brian never said why—just that it wasn't "in the cards." Adoption was expensive. Especially for a baby. Ann suggested an older child. Brian refused. A family member out west had gone that route and according to Brian, it was a *shit show*.

Leo knew from the very first day his friends brought Sky home, they fell in love. How they said she saved them—not the other way around.

And now it was just the two of them. Leo and Sky. And Xavier, of course. His husband who wanted to be anywhere but on this island.

How do you build a new life? Leo wonders. How do you fill shoes so goddamn big?

"Earth to Leo," he hears Joe say. When he blinks, Sky and Joe appear before him.

"Where did you go?" Joe asks, but Sky just looks at him, as though she knows what it's like to be standing in front of someone and disappear in your own mind.

When Leo doesn't answer, Joe winks at Sky. "Hey, Sport. Why are you up so early?"

"We're going to the beach," says a voice from behind him. Leo turns to see Maggie standing next to him. She's in a sundress, bathing suit straps tied around her neck, a cup of coffee in her hand.

"I was just coming to make sure you were awake, Sky. It's going to be in the nineties today, so we'll want to get there early to get a good spot." She looks over at Leo. "You sure you can't come? Blow off work for the day?"

"I wish," he says.

She turns to Joe. "How about you? Feel like joining us?"

"You should come!" Sky says to Joe.

"To the beach? Oh, no. They'll think I'm a whale and harpoon me."

"Oh, you should come!" Maggie adds.

"I don't own a bathing suit."

"All the boys wear shorts just like that." Maggie points to Joe's gym shorts. "Plus, Sky never gets out of the water. I can only stay in so long before my toes are numb. You can sit in a chair at the edge and keep me company."

Joe looks at Leo for help, but Leo only shrugs.

"I have towels, sunscreen, drinks, sandwiches, fruit. Plenty of beach chairs already in the back of my car," Maggie says. "Don't rush today, Leo. We'll be just fine. See you in fifteen minutes, Joe."

She turns and walks away before Joe has a chance to argue. Sky skips off, and Leo looks at Joe, who stares back at him blankly.

"What just happened?" Joe asks.

"Well, if I'm not mistaken, you have approximately fourteen minutes and thirty seconds to get your ass ready for the beach." He slaps Joe on the arm and walks away. "Don't get harpooned," he yells over his shoulder and laughs at the insults Joe hurls back at him.

Now that it's nearly July, they have the schedule worked out.

Leo works from home three days a week, and Maggie watches Sky the other two. For the most part, things run smoothly.

Except when Frankie comes over for the day and, by mid-morning, they've talked Leo into some adventure. Sailing on Leta Pond or surfing at the Point or jumping off Shoal Bridge into the bay.

Today though, Leo has to do something he's been avoiding for weeks.

Sky's grandmother has been asking to meet with him. Lillian is her name.

He doesn't know what she looks like. Not even a picture or a description.

He knows only her voice from conversations over the phone. Twice Lillian has asked him to meet with her in person. Twice he canceled.

The last time they spoke, Lillian said she wanted to meet to discuss the *future*. The way she said it sounded ominous to Leo.

She had a slow, precise way of speaking, as though she were cherry-picking every word before it passed her lips. She had paused before *future*. A long enough pause that Leo had looked at the screen to confirm the call hadn't ended unexpectedly.

When the word *future* finally traveled through time and space and trickled through the cell phone pressed to his ear, he flinched.

It was then that he wondered if she would contest the will. If she would try to take Sky away from him.

Lillian was family, after all. Sky's grandmother.

Which is why he'd put off meeting her.

When she called the third time to reschedule, it seemed rude to put her off. He heard his father's voice in his head, telling him to *get it done*.

Tide waits for no man, his father liked to say about pressing matters. A navy man and the harbormaster of Ichabod, Leo's father had no use for procrastination. Even though his father died a decade ago, his voice still ran through Leo's head.

Some days, Leo welcomed it. Other days, like the one that made him agree to this meeting about the *future*, he wished he could just shut the old man up.

Now, he's sitting on a bench, waiting for the ferry to unload.

"How will I recognize you?" Lillian had asked on the phone.

He told her to look for the only black guy on the dock. A silence had met him on the other end of the line and Leo hadn't known if it was because she'd just learned he was black, or that he'd said out loud what everyone already knew.

Ichabod Island was, except for several Asian families and a crew of Jamaicans who were farmworkers at Bass Farm, all white.

Leo's scanning the dock when a woman steps through the crowd. She shields her eyes with her hand, then walks his way.

"Leo," she says when she reaches him, extending a hand. "Lillian."

She pushes her sunglasses up on her head while they shake. She's in her fifties or sixties—it's hard to tell from her hair and clothes.

Chin-length black hair cut in a sleek bob. White T-shirt. Black linen pants. Flip-flops. Silver rings. A small moonstone medallion around her neck.

Leo had expected an older version of Ann. Blond and preppy—the only jewelry he remembers Ann wearing was her wedding band and the simple gold cross around her neck. Both matching Brian's.

You're not what I expected, he almost blurts, but stops himself.

"I'm sorry for your loss," he says instead.

Ann had always described the relationship with her mother as dysfunctional. Apparently, at some point, Ann cut all contact with Lillian, so Sky hadn't seen or spoken to her grandmother in quite some time. This past year, when Ann spoke of her mother, she referred to them as estranged.

Still. She was Ann's mother. Estranged or not.

"Thank you. To you as well," Lillian says. "I understand Brian was a childhood friend. And for Ann—for both of them—to leave Skylar in your custody. You were obviously important to them."

This is delivered kindly. Leo searches her face for clues—a twitch of the lips, maybe. A glance down so he won't see her true feelings. But no, she's looking straight at him. Brown eyes, clear and honest.

The way she calls Sky by her full name—Skylar—shows an unfamiliarity with her own granddaughter. Sky has always been just Sky to everyone who knows her.

"Should we sit?" He points to the restaurants in town. "Have lunch?"

She follows where he's pointing as if surprised by the question.

"I'm sorry. I thought I mentioned I don't have much time. I really just wanted to meet and talk a bit. Say hello. Face-to-face."

"That's quite a trip to say hello."

She points to the bench. "Shall we?"

After they settle next to each other, he looks at her and waits. She clears her throat, faces him.

"I came here on the ferry a couple of weeks ago. Walked around a little bit. Just to reacquaint myself. The island's changed since my last visit." She smiles. "Sorry—that isn't really relevant. It's just—I was born here. My family moved away when I was ten. After Ann moved here, I'd visit. But I haven't been here for several years. It's strange to be back. Hard too. With everything that's happened. But I took an earlier ferry over this morning to see more of the island. So, I am here to say hello, but my visit is more than just that."

He swallows, keeps his expression from showing how his pulse has quickened. *How much more?* he wants to ask. The question lingers in his mouth.

"Look, Leo—I don't know what Ann told you about our relationship," Lillian says softly. "When I said I wanted to talk about the future, I meant that I would like to be part of Sky's future. I'm here because there is a grandchild whom I don't know very well. And I guess, perhaps—"

"Why don't you know her well?" Leo interrupts. No sense dancing around it.

The tide waits for no man.

Lillian breaks their eye contact for the first time. Looks out at the water.

"I wish I had a simple answer for you. But there isn't one."

"It doesn't have to be simple," he presses, but she shakes her head, pauses.

"I didn't come here to talk about the past. Just the future," she says finally. Resolutely. "I don't know what that means yet, in terms of my involvement in Sky's life. Certainly, I'd like to see her as soon as it's convenient."

He nods. Not in agreement. More in response to understanding her desire to see her own granddaughter. Fact is though, he's her guardian. And Lillian doesn't want to talk about why she wasn't in Ann's life. Or Sky's.

"I'll talk to Sky. See how she feels about it. But we can agree to move slowly here. Yes?"

"I think I have moved slowly. I've given her space since the acci—" She stops, clears her throat. "I'm ready to move forward. I wanted to tell you that in person. I know you probably have a lot of questions. But just know that I have Sky's best interest in mind."

She stands before he can respond. "I better go." She gestures to a line of people filing up the gangway onto the ferry deck. She holds out her hand and after they shake, she turns and calls out a goodbye.

He watches her find her way to the bow of the boat, where long benches sit in even rows.

Instead of walking to his car, he sits back down on the bench. Somehow, it's important that Lillian sees he's still here.

That he's not going anywhere.

He sits while the boat pulls away from the dock. Dark clouds have formed overhead. The air is suddenly wet, a cold mist rolling off the white-capped bay, sending a shiver through him.

An old back injury that flares up in bad weather makes him lean forward, elbows on his knees.

Still, he refuses to leave.

He sits motionless long after the wake vanishes and the fog swallows the ferry and all he's left with is a storm brewing around him and a cold, lonely ache settling in the length of his spine.

Later, when Sky comes back from her day with Maggie and Joe, Leo tells her to wash up and meet him outside. He has a job for her.

Friday nights have become a tightrope walk for Leo.

Over the last month, this is how the night has unraveled:

Leo works on Fridays, holed up in the den, hunched over his drafting table for hours. Xavier arrives at the house at five o'clock, give or take fifteen minutes depending on the ferry. Sky spends the day with Maggie, until around the time Xavier walks through the door.

All three of them together in the small house, at exactly the same time. Sky and Xavier both immediately vying for Leo's attention.

So far, it hasn't gone well.

Leo learned this by saying or doing something that made Sky

go to her room and shut the door or Xavier go for a walk to *regroup*, one of his favorite words these past weeks.

Which is why tonight Leo is prepared.

He sets the outside table for dinner. The sky has cleared since he was on the dock earlier. A perfect night for a cookout. He's keeping it simple: burgers on the grill. Potato salad. Corn on the cob.

When Sky skips out to the patio, he hands her a paper bag full of corn.

"Start husking," he says, and she smiles, takes the bag, and settles at the table.

He glances at her, busies himself with cleaning an ear of corn while he plays with the words he wants to say in his head, trying to make them come out of his mouth in a way that doesn't alarm her.

Finally, he gives up. Decides to just spit it out.

"Your grandmother got in touch with me," he announces, placing the corn on the table. "She said she'd like to see you."

He pauses, waits for her reaction. She meets his eyes, looks back at the corn in her hand, her expression unchanged.

"How do you feel about that?"

She shrugs. A noncommittal lift and drop of one shoulder. As though forcing the other shoulder to answer isn't necessary.

"I hadn't met her before today," he continues. "She seems nice." He waits. "Is she nice?" he asks finally.

"I don't know," she says plainly.

"She said you hadn't seen each other in a while."

She shrugs again.

"Do you know why you haven't seen her? Did something happen?"

"Mom said every time she came to the island, they fought.

My dad would get mad and tell her that if all they were going to do is fight, then she should stop inviting her. I don't know anything besides that."

Leo sighs. "Okay, well. Would you like to see her? I can set it up."

"Do I have to?" she asks, meeting his eyes.

The question takes him by surprise. So much so that he doesn't know what to say.

He thinks about his own grandmother. She never moved from the house his mother had grown up in just outside of Syracuse. A ferry ride and long drive from Ichabod, so they didn't visit more than a couple times a year. She died when he was eleven, but he remembers the smell of her kitchen. The way she threw her head back when she laughed. The sound of the grandfather clock in her living room.

"Do you not want to see her?"

"Can we talk about something else?"

He studies her. "Yes. But think about it, okay? I do have to give her an answer."

She nods, puts a knee under her and sits up taller. "Me and Frankie joined the surfing team today," she tells him nonchalantly, then giggles when she sees the surprise on his face. "I said *surfing team*. Not, like, something amazing that would make you look at me like that."

"I think it's amazing! How did I not know such a team existed?"

"It's not really an official team. Just a bunch of older kids who surf together. They're really good though. And nice—Maggie said to tell you that."

"How did you sign up to be on the team?"

She giggles again. "That's not how it works. They saw me and

Frankie surfing the last couple of weeks. One of them waved us over. Asked if we wanted to surf with them."

"I knew you were good. I didn't know you were *that* good."

She shrugs. "Frankie's better. She's not afraid of anything. Huge waves and she just goes for it."

"Well, I think you're pretty fearless. Hey—I was going to wait for Xavier, but I think this calls for a celebration. Hold on." He disappears into the kitchen, watches Sky through the window while he gets what he needs.

Minutes later, he emerges with two champagne flutes filled with a strawberry-colored liquid.

"Shirley Temple for the lady," he says, and hands one to Sky. She beams while they clink glasses. He takes a sip and hides his distaste for the sweet concoction.

He bought the ingredients earlier after racking his brain for a solution to Xavier's desire to have a drink together the minute he arrived.

Cocktail hour on the patio, Xavier called it.

Guaranteed to send Sky to her room. Or to the den to watch TV. Nothing more boring to a ten-year-old girl than two men drinking white wine and *reconnecting*, another one of Xavier's recent words.

Leo hasn't wanted to admit it to himself, but it's glaringly obvious that Xavier's presence in the house on the weekends throws Leo and Sky off-kilter.

During the week, when they are alone, their nights have had a certain flow to them. Sky talks nonstop through dinner. They watch a movie some nights. Other nights, they go to town for ice cream. Or go back to the beach.

Which is why, now, Leo holds his breath when he hears the Range Rover pull in the driveway.

Sky is telling him a story about Frankie's epic crash on a huge wave this morning, but she stops talking when Xavier opens the door and steps onto the patio, holding a bottle of wine and two glasses.

Oddly, he looks surprised to see Leo and Sky sitting at the table.

"Hello," he says formally.

Leo senses immediately that Xavier is in one of his moods, but he smiles at him, rises, and walks over to give him a kiss. Xavier waves him off.

"I smell like a dog after being crammed on that ferry for the last hour."

"I think I'll live." Leo laughs and leans in, but Xavier shifts, and the kiss lands on his cheek. The air has changed, thick with tension now. Sky is concentrating on the corn with a laser-type focus.

"Let's go in for a moment," Leo suggests. "Want a refill, Sky?"

She nods shyly, her eyes flitting to Leo, then Xavier, who has yet to acknowledge her.

"Sky made the surf team today," Leo says loudly. Too loudly. "We were celebrating with Shirley Temples."

Xavier gives them a forced smile. "Congratulations, Sky. Well, by all means, continue," Xavier says, and disappears inside the house. Leo follows and finds him in the kitchen, uncorking the wine.

"Let me get that while you clean up. I'll pour you a glass and meet you outside. I was just about to throw some burgers on the grill."

Xavier frowns, looks at the raw hamburger patties on the counter. "I was hoping we could go to Lola's tonight."

"The sushi bar? It just opened. It'll be a mob scene. I thought we'd wait a week or two." Leo pops the cork on the chardonnay and pours a glass. "Plus, it's not exactly kid-friendly."

"I was hoping you'd lined up a babysitter. We haven't been alone for weeks."

"We were alone this past Tuesday. Was it that forgettable?" Leo jokes.

He'd gone to the city for the day and managed to sneak out of work for lunch. Xavier was working from home, and they'd spent the lunch hour in bed.

"Don't do that," Xavier says. "Stopping by our home for a quickie and to repack your bag isn't exactly what I had in mind for quality time."

Xavier's anger is palpable. It takes Leo by surprise. They've never argued like this before.

Actually, they've rarely argued. In the three years they've been together, he can count on one hand the number of arguments they've had.

But what was there to argue about?

They met through a mutual friend who knew both Xavier and Leo were looking for a long-term relationship.

Leo hated dating. Xavier hated it more.

Their physical attraction was immediate. Leo loved Xavier's masculinity. His athleticism and muscled frame. Xavier loved that Leo hadn't stepped foot in a gym since high school, yet his body was lean and sinewy, and he made Xavier stay in bed on Saturday mornings instead of going for his daily workout.

They fell in love quickly and deeply. Leo cooked meals that made Xavier smile and tilt his head to the heavens. Xavier made Leo laugh out loud at least once a day.

They both made good money. Had similar taste in houses

and vacations and cars. They were both frugal. Neither of them wanted kids.

What was there to argue about?

Nothing. Until now.

"You're angry," Leo says. "Every time you come here now, you're angry."

"Well, maybe I just shouldn't come," Xavier replies, his voice loud.

Leo reaches to shut the window over the sink, the one that sits directly over the patio table, when he hears a chair leg scrape against the tile. He looks out the window at Sky, walking across the backyard, away from the house.

Away from them.

"Nice job," he says to Xavier, gesturing to Sky. But Xavier doesn't hear him. He's already walking to the bedroom, slamming the door behind him.

Leo leans against the counter. There's a picture of Brian and Ann on the refrigerator. He picks up the glass of wine, holds it up.

"Here's to fucking up raising your kid," he says quietly, and downs the clear liquid in one gulp.

10

She checks out of the inn and has a car waiting at the curb. The drive isn't long—the studio is just outside of town, high on a cliff. They turn down a long driveway and follow it past a farmhouse, then a barn, until the forest is in front of them, the studio to her left.

She pays the driver and gets out of the car. There's an envelope taped to the door, a key inside, and she lets herself in.

It was the location that mattered the last time she stayed here—if she walked to the very edge of the property and peeked through the trees, she could spot Mac's backyard in the distance.

There's a knock on the door, and she calls out that it's open. A woman's face appears.

"My husband said he left you the key," she says. "I can come back if it's a bad time."

"Now's fine."

"I don't want to disturb you. I'm Greer—I know we met, but it was so long ago. It's Henley, right?"

"Yes," she lies.

"Give a fake name," Mac had said, years ago. "Just in case."

And then they'd forgotten to agree on one and when Greer had asked her for her name years ago, her mind went blank. Absolutely blank.

"Henley!" Mac had said when she told her later. "Like the shirt?"

She'd nodded. "I panicked. And I was staring at her and saw her shirt and it just popped out."

Mac had snorted. "Good thing she wasn't wearing a button-down sweater. I'd have to call you cardigan for the next two months."

"Are you living on the island?" Greer asks now. "The only people who know about this place are the artists from the co-op in town."

She shakes her head. "I'm just visiting. I had your husband's phone number from when I stayed here before. I took a shot that you were still renting it out. Well, offering it up, I should say, with how inexpensive it is."

Greer laughs. "I wouldn't feel right charging more than we do for this place. That's still the only heat." She points to the woodstove. "I still think you were nuts staying here in the winter like you did. I know it's been a while, but things haven't changed. We're still busy as hell. Holler if you need anything. Otherwise, we're not likely to cross paths."

Greer waves and turns to leave, then sticks her head back through the door.

"I meant to ask—what did you end up having? We never heard anything after you went back to the city."

"A girl," she answers.

"I thought so—the way you were carrying. Gosh. Time flies, huh? I remember your husband was in the military. I hope he made it home for the birth."

"He did." She touches her thumb to her ring finger, finds it soft. She'd forgotten to put on the ring. "We're not together anymore," she says quickly.

Greer gives her a sympathetic look. "Well, it happens. Sometimes for the best. Is that where your daughter is? With her dad?"

"She's at camp," she says, sticking to her original lie. "But then with her dad, yes. They're taking a trip together."

Greer nods and waves again. "Well, enjoy the time alone. God knows, it's good for the soul."

The door shuts, and she's alone in the small room.

Her cheeks are warm.

She was never very good at lying—Mac was the one who could do it. Look straight at someone and, cool as anything, say things that were completely false.

She'd meant to slip a cheap ring on her finger. Explain her time here on this island away from her family as normal—a child at camp. A husband overseas.

She'd have a couple of weeks before Greer started asking questions. But this new lie has just bought her some time.

Now, she has a fake ex-husband to take care of her nonexistent daughter.

11

Maggie is on the phone with Agnes. The conversation isn't going well.

They've had lunch on the calendar for weeks. And now, just two hours before they're supposed to be sitting at the restaurant on the harbor, sipping a cocktail, Maggie's called to say she has to watch Sky—Xavier is in the emergency room, his ankle swollen after an accident at spin class. Leo's trying to catch the ferry back to the mainland.

Agnes tells Maggie that she just knew Maggie was going to let this *full-time nanny job* take over her summer.

"We haven't seen each other in weeks!" Agnes exclaims, her voice tight on the other end of the phone.

"We just saw each other yesterday," Maggie replies, as gently as she can muster.

"We bumped into each other getting the mail," Agnes says. "And I couldn't get a word in edgewise with Leo talking your ear off. I'm worried you're getting too involved. You're practically a full-time nanny."

"Yes, you mentioned that yesterday. Five times, actually."

She'd hoped Agnes might be nice about it. Tell Maggie that changing their plans last minute wasn't a problem.

And even though Maggie is at fault, she's irritated by Agnes's reaction.

No—she's irritated with Agnes in general, actually.

"Well, it's true. Every time I call you, you're watching Sky. And now, apparently, you're on call when there's an emergency."

"Oh, stop it. I offered. Frankie's over at Leo's and he was ready to take both of them with him to the city. He would have had to drag them to the hospital."

"The hospital? For a sprained ankle?"

"It could be broken, Agnes. We don't know."

Agnes makes a noise on the other end of the phone. "Well, I hope his *husband* appreciates you dropping everything at a moment's notice. And canceling our lunch. Our annual lunch. That we've had on the calendar. For weeks."

Maggie sighs. "I'm not canceling. I told you I'd make lunch here. We can do our annual lunch a different day."

"I was looking forward to sitting on the outdoor patio, catching up with you, and making fun of all the tourists getting off the ferry."

"I don't make fun of the tourists."

"It's not like they can hear me. Besides, I only make fun of the ones who deserve it. Remember the woman last year who got her stiletto stuck in the cobblestones? Don't tell me that wasn't funny."

"It was until she bled all over the street."

"Oh, she was fine by the time they got her up and put her ridiculous Cinderella slipper back on. Besides, I was looking forward to talking about something other than the party. To be honest, I'll be glad when it's over."

"Are you ready?" Maggie asks, happy to change the subject.

She knows the answer already—of course Agnes is ready.

She's been hosting her annual Fourth of July party for decades—her parents hosted it for decades before that—her grandparents before that.

The enormous tent is already set up in Agnes's backyard. The tables arranged. Flowers ordered. Vans rented, ready to shuttle people from the town lot to the party, then back again in time for the fireworks show on the harbor.

The caterer knows the menu by heart—it's been the same for years now.

Clam chowder and lobster rolls. Oysters and shrimp cocktail. Corn on the cob and potato salad. Vegetable and chicken kabobs. Ribs and pulled pork. Something for everyone.

And that's about who shows up. Anyone who's anyone on Ichabod.

"It's like a goddamn wedding," Pete complained, just this morning. "Whatever happened to sparklers in the backyard and a hot dog off the grill?"

Maggie would be going alone. Pete hadn't been to the party since he took the job with the police force decades ago. He said it was because he had to work. But it wasn't Pete's crowd anyway.

"Ready as any other year," Agnes replies. "Of course, the local weatherman's giving his typical Ichabod forecast. *Maybe a shower. Maybe not. A chance of lightning if it does rain, but most likely, we'll see patches of sun. It's too early to tell.* For Christ's sake—it's tomorrow! The man couldn't forecast a hurricane if he was standing in the eye of it—"

"Agnes, I have to go," Maggie interrupts. "Sky's here. I'll be here if you change your mind about lunch. Otherwise, I'll see you at the party. I'll bring my flag cake, as usual."

She hangs up and opens her front door. Sky isn't at her

house—but close enough. She can see the two girls walking down Leo's driveway.

She hadn't needed to rush Agnes off the phone. But there was something in Agnes's voice that made her desperate to hang up.

Truthfully, she'd been dreading their lunch together. Dreading it so much that when she'd crossed the street earlier to return a bathing suit Sky had left at her house and Leo told her about Xavier's accident, she'd told him he should go to the city to be with his husband.

She *insisted*.

She hadn't mentioned her lunch plans with Agnes. Not even when Leo said he could probably send Sky to Frankie's house instead.

She doesn't know what's going on with her and Agnes lately, but she does know she's not just irked with her friend.

She's mad as hell. Mad that Agnes makes her feel weak for wanting to save her marriage to Pete. Mad that Agnes makes her feel guilty for watching Sky. Mad because—Oh, she could go on and on in her mind. Tallying up all the things that have made her angry in their long friendship that she never admitted to—never had the guts to tell Agnes.

At fifty years old, she's come to the unfortunate conclusion that she's pitiful at being angry.

She can't remember once in her life saying out loud that she was angry. Even this past year, with the foolishness with Pete and the secretary, she'd only used words like *sad*. *Hurt*. *Disappointed*.

She doesn't know the exact moment she stopped being able to say she was angry. To *show* she was angry.

But a memory from her childhood has been replaying in her mind lately.

She was seven or eight when it happened—she doesn't

remember exactly. Only that it was summer and she'd spent the whole day on the cool cement floor of the garage. She was working on a paint-by-number picture of two puppies sitting in a basket. Her mother didn't like anything messy. Which was why Maggie wasn't allowed to paint inside the house.

She hadn't minded spending the day in the garage. Her father kept it clean, and she'd spread a towel down underneath her, set her paints up right in front of her.

Lying on her stomach, her face close to the painting, she'd spent hours carefully staying within the lines. She was going to hang it on her bedroom wall. Look at it at night before she went to sleep.

She was working on the black tip of the puppy's nose when her brother walked in, two of his friends trailing behind. They'd always gotten along just fine, her and Ben. Then he turned thirteen and decided she was a pain.

Maggie the Maggot, he whispered at the dinner table.

"Go do that inside," Ben said, walking up so close that the toe of his sneaker was on her towel. "We need the garage."

"Give me a second. I'm almost done," she said, pausing to look up at him before she went back to the painting.

"You're almost done?" he asked.

Maybe she should have seen it coming. His voice had an edge to it. But she was too busy touching the thin tip of the brush against the puppy's nose, filling the space with black paint.

Her brother nudged the long handle of the paintbrush with his toe. Her hand jerked. Dark paint smeared across the picture.

It was ruined. Unsalvageable.

She stared at it. Tears formed in her eyes. She stood up, her hands clenched into fists, just as her mother walked into the garage.

She cried, pointed at the picture while her mother shushed her, told Maggie to please—*calm down!*

Later, her father had come home from work and spoken to her brother.

At the dinner table, Ben apologized, but she saw the glint in his eye. The fun of it for him.

Anger burned inside of her. Hot and wild, churning her insides.

Her father had sat down, spread his napkin on his lap. Her face was down, staring at her plate, her cheeks red with rage.

"Kitten," her father said to her. "Look at me. Come on. Where's my girl?"

She looked up, and he reached over and tickled her.

"Be nice, now. Don't ruin dinner," he said. "You're so pretty when you smile. Isn't she, Cin?" he asked her mother, who nodded.

"Of course she is," her mother said. "She's the sweetest, prettiest girl in the world when she wants to be."

Even now, leaning against the door, more than forty years later, Maggie feels her insides clench when she thinks of that night at the table.

How she turned up the corners of her mouth to please her parents. To be the nice girl they wanted her to be.

Sweet Maggie.

All her life that's who she's been.

There's a mirror on the wall next to the door. Maggie looks at her reflection.

She scowls at herself. Allows the lines on her face to deepen. Ugly. That's what her parents would say about her right now.

"Go to hell," she says to the mirror.

The problem is, she doesn't know if she's talking to her parents. Or her reflection.

12

Two things happen in one day that make Sky's life better: Xavier hurts his ankle, so he can't take the ferry over to Ichabod for the Fourth of July weekend, and Frankie's mother throws her back out and has to stay in bed.

Which means Frankie gets to sleep over. All weekend. And Xavier won't be around to pick a fight with Leo about it—or anything else.

So even though she knows her mother would have lectured her about how it's wrong to be happy because of someone else's bad luck, she's looking forward to the weekend.

Which says a lot.

Tomorrow is the Fourth of July. She's been dreading it—thinking about her and Leo and Xavier—the entire weekend stretching out in front of them. What would they even *do*? Apparently, Xavier hates the beach.

And that's where she's spent every Fourth of July for her entire life.

Her mother and father would pack a picnic. They'd go to the beach late in the afternoon, stay until the sky grew dark, and watch the fireworks from their beach chairs.

The memory of it has had her insides twisted up all week. But now that Frankie gets to stay with her and Xavier won't be around, the weekend has her smiling in what seems like the first time in forever. And the truth is, she's tired of crying. Tired of thinking about anything sad.

It's the Fourth of July, and she wants to have fun. Let the colorful explosions and loud booms in the darkness spark something inside of her.

So when Frankie whispers that they should go to the cliff and light off the sparklers she stole from her brothers, it's just about the best idea she's ever heard.

Frankie leans over and says this to her just as Miss Maggie hangs up the phone with Leo. It's the third time he's called to give an update on when he thinks he'll be home. Miss Maggie told him to just stay with Xavier for the night—Sky and Frankie can sleep at her house.

"Well, I'm the lucky one who gets you beauties tonight," Miss Maggie says to them. "Run home and get what you need for the night. I'll start dinner."

"Is it okay if we make a quick stop at the tree house to get the sketchbook I left by accident?" Frankie looks at Sky so she won't open her big mouth and blurt out that no, Frankie didn't leave it there.

It's in her backpack where it always is.

But Miss Maggie's head is in the refrigerator and she calls out that it's fine. Dinner won't be ready for another hour.

"Thanks, Miss Maggie," they say at the same time, opening the back door.

"Girls."

They freeze.

"Do me a favor," Miss Maggie says, standing now. "When you call me that, I feel like I'm back in school. Drop the 'Miss' for the summer. Agreed?"

They nod and slip out the back door, jogging over to Sky's house.

They scatter once they're inside. Frankie to the bedroom to get her backpack and Sky to the hutch in the living room, where she finds a lighter in the drawer.

Outside, they run as fast as they can to the granite slabs at the edge of the cliff.

Frankie puts her backpack down and unzips it while Sky looks around. She's been out here alone plenty of times, usually in the dark. But something feels different.

Behind her, leaves swirl in a sudden breeze. The faraway *BOOM* of a firework makes her jump.

She looks behind her. Once. Then again.

There's nothing but trees, but she shivers, puts her arms around herself, the sharp edge of the lighter digging into her ribs.

"What's wrong?" Frankie asks. She holds a sparkler out to Sky. "Why do you keep looking over your shoulder?"

"I thought I heard something."

Frankie smirks. "It's called a firework. You know—pretty light, big noise."

"Ha ha," she says while Frankie takes the lighter and puts the flame to the tip of Sky's sparkler and then her own.

They stand as close to the edge as they dare. Arms outstretched, a shower of sparkles erupts in front of them, raining down on the jagged rock face of the cliff below.

Frankie cheers, and the sound echoes around them, her voice fading as the last twinkle disappears.

There's a thick gray line sitting over the ocean, the sun almost hidden behind it. The air is suddenly cool. It's not raining yet, but the sky is threatening to split open, and they still have a handful of sparklers left.

"Here," Frankie says, dividing them into two bunches and handing a thick stack to Sky. "Let's light them all together."

Frankie holds out the lighter just as something rustles behind them, a crunch of leaves reaching them.

She whips her head around, looking at the forest. She stops breathing, listens.

"Did you hear that?" she whispers. Frankie nods, slides her eyes over to where Sky is looking.

"It's probably a squirrel or something," Frankie offers unconvincingly. "Why are you so jumpy all of a sudden?"

Sky pulls her eyes away from the trees, looks at Frankie. "It's just this weird feeling I've had all week. Even yesterday when we were at the tree house, it felt like somebody was there. Sort of . . . watching us."

"What? Like a ghost? Maybe your parents?" Frankie's eyes widen in fake horror, and she scans the air around her. "Mr. and Mrs. Pope—is that you? Give us a sign if you can hear us!"

"Okay, cut it out. I didn't say a ghost. That's not what I meant."

"Then what?" Frankie asks, back to normal now. "Like someone spying on us?"

Sky shrugs. "You didn't feel anything?"

Frankie shakes her head. "No, but I was painting while you were goofing around." She rolls her eyes at Sky.

It's true, actually.

Sky had asked Frankie to give her a painting lesson, but when they were set up in the tree house, Sky kept wandering over to the doorway, looking down at the trees. She hadn't told Frankie she felt as though someone was out there. At the time, she couldn't find the words to explain the feeling.

Sky puts her arm out, the thick stack of sparklers in her hand.

"Come on. Hold yours out too. We need to get back."

Everything inside of her is telling her to run, but she stays, waits for Frankie to flick the lighter.

Frankie runs her thumb over the switch, and a flame pops out, yellow and flickering. She lights the two bunches as fast as she can, and they both stick their arms out straight as flashes of white explode in front of them.

The sky ignites at the end of their fingertips. Sparks spurting in all directions. Fire twinkling in the air. A ball of brightness cracking and hissing, warming their faces, their eyes glowing in the reflection.

Sky laughs. Frankie cheers again, louder this time—loud enough that it echoes, bounces off the trees and the sky and the rocks.

Then she hears it. Clapping. Faint, but unmistakable.

Someone is clapping. Someone behind them. Close behind them. So close that a tremble starts in her legs and spreads through her middle, down her arms, up her neck.

She can't move.

Frankie hears it too, and they lock eyes.

The sparklers fizzle out and the clapping stops. The night is dead silent.

She doesn't know who runs first.

All she knows is that Frankie is right on her heels. Both of them sprinting through the forest. Trying to get home.

13

Foolish! That's what she is. Careless and foolish and just . . . stupid. That's what Mac would say. Plain old stupid.

She could blame it on the bottle of champagne she drank. A gift left on her doorstep by Greer, who said it was merely a Fourth of July offering, although she knew it was a thank-you for the picture she'd painted and left in the barn—the horse in the pasture behind the shed had been too beautiful to ignore. And what was she going to do with the painting? Take it to her grave?

But she knew what sent her into the forest didn't come from the bottle. She drank two glasses while the sun hung low in the sky and the air was peppered with the sound of fireworks.

Then she heard voices and knew it was the girl. She crept in the forest, just wanting to look from a distance and remember what it was like to be that age. To be so young and free and wild.

The trees shielded her while she watched the girls light the sparklers. She inched closer when each girl held a thick bunch and kicked herself when leaves crunched under her foot and they turned, startled. She hid behind the tree, held her breath until they looked away.

When they lit the sparklers, the sky exploded with bright twinkles of light so intoxicating and beautiful, her eyes filled with tears. Then she heard it. Laughing and cheering. A celebration between the two girls.

Her hands joined together, and she clapped. Over and over. Powerless to stop. She couldn't stop the tears, or the tremble in her limbs, or the emotion that spread through her.

Joy, in its purest form. So sweet and good she couldn't even feel bad that she'd scared the girls away. She only felt one thing. Thankful.

14

Leo had been looking forward to the Fourth of July. Xavier was coming to the island. They were going to have a leisurely couple of days. See some fireworks. Spend time with Sky as a family.

Then Xavier called from the emergency room to say his ankle was the size of a melon. By the time Leo caught the ferry and reached the mainland, Xavier was already home, icing his injury, angry that he'd had to call a taxi.

It takes Leo another hour in traffic to reach their condo. When he steps out onto the sidewalk in front of his house, his head throbs from the noise of the city, which seems louder than usual today, and he can't help but think it's because he's used to the quiet of the island. A peacefulness that doesn't exist on their crowded, busy block just outside of the financial district.

He forces himself to take a minute to calm down and *breathe* before he walks up the steps to the door.

On the island, the day had been cool, a summer sea breeze floating through the house all morning, salty and fresh. The city is the opposite—stifling and humid, the sun boring a hole in the top of his head.

He unlocks the door and steps in, closes it quietly behind

him. The television is on in the living room. He finds Xavier reclined on the couch, his back against the arm and his leg propped up on a pillow.

There's an open bottle of beer on the coffee table. A half-eaten sandwich in his lap.

"How are you?" Leo asks, crossing the room. "How's your ankle?"

He leans down to kiss Xavier, but he brushes Leo away.

"Don't. I stink from spin class. How am I? Well, my ankle feels like a truck ran over it. I'm eating crappy hospital cafeteria food. And the power went out last night because some drunk jackass ran into the pole with his truck, so my beer is lukewarm." He holds up the bottle. "Here's to kicking off the holiday," he toasts, and takes a swig.

Xavier's anger is a living thing, snaking its way around them both and pulling them into another argument.

"I was hoping you'd just sit tight in the hospital lobby. I was on my way. I could've bought you a real lunch. And a cold beer." He smiles, trying to lighten Xavier's mood.

"I did sit tight," Xavier snaps. "I *sat tight* for two hours before I called a cab. Did you row over in a dinghy from the island? What took you so long?"

It's an absurd thing to ask—the ferry ride is an hour, and by the time he made arrangements for Sky and Frankie, he had to wait another hour to catch the next one off the island.

Never mind the city traffic that he's been trapped in trying to get from the ferry to the condo.

Despite all of this, it's the way Xavier asks him that makes Leo's jaw set.

As though Leo hadn't dropped everything to rush over to help Xavier with what appears to be nothing more than a mild sprain. And looking at it propped up on the pillow, his ankle is nowhere near the size of a melon.

A small clementine, in Leo's opinion.

He clears his throat, willing himself not to blurt this out.

"I had Sky and Frankie at the house," he explains calmly. "Thankfully, Maggie offered to watch them, so I could come here."

"Come *here*? Home, you mean. Right? So you could come *home*." Xavier doesn't say this as much as push it out of his mouth. A sucker punch that slams into Leo, heavy and suffocating.

"All right," Leo says after a minute. "Let's do this now."

He sits in the chair across from Xavier, leans forward with his knees on his elbows, looking straight at his husband.

"Do what now?" Xavier asks, shifting on the couch. Shrinking back, it seems. As if he's gone too far and he knows it.

But it's out there. And Leo can't ignore it.

In the last three months, he can count on one hand the number of times they've been together and not argued. Count on one hand the nice things they've said to each other.

Ever since Sky came into their life.

"I know you're angry," Leo says quietly. "I can't blame you for it—I won't blame you. We said no kids. We agreed to it. And I'm changing that agreement, and you're angry. I wish you weren't, but you are."

Xavier snorts. "So that's it? Sorry you're angry, but suck it up and get over it? Get used to *never* seeing your husband?"

"You can see me whenever you want, Xavier. You can *live* with me. With us. You're a freelance journalist—you work from home—"

"I like the city! I like my life here! Remember here? Right here—where we live?"

"Stop saying that like I have a choice. There is no choice—"

"Of course there is!" Xavier shouts. "You choose me—choose us! Our life together!"

Leo is quiet. Stunned.

"And Sky?" he asks finally. "What do I tell her?"

"You tell her what should have been said the minute you learned you were her guardian!" Xavier throws up his arms, as though this should be obvious to Leo.

Obvious to everyone.

"You tell her that you love her very much, but as a *friend*. You explain that you and your husband"—he points to himself—"aren't prepared to take on the commitment of raising a child—"

"No," he interrupts. Xavier waits for him to speak, but he can't put the words together. Not because he doesn't know what to say. There is too much to say. And none of it wants to come out of his mouth.

Things like: *Is this worth losing me? Losing us?*

"She has a grandmother, Leo! One who took the ferry over to tell you she wants to be part of Sky's future!"

"A grandmother who she doesn't really know—"

"Who cares? It's a *blood* relative! Never mind Maggie, who would raise that girl in a second if she got the chance. You can see the way she looks at Sky. It's not just affection. That's love—"

"I said no."

Xavier stops midsentence and stares at him. "No? Just . . . no?"

"I won't do that to her," Leo says. "It wouldn't be right."

"And *this* is right? You don't know the first thing about kids—how are you even remotely qualified to do this? How do you expect *me* to do this?"

Leo shrugs. "I thought that, at first. That I wouldn't know how to act around her. How to be. But I do. I can't explain it. It just feels right."

"And is it right for her?" Xavier asks. "Have you even asked her if she wants to be raised by us? Have you given *her* the choice?"

"This again. Don't use that as a cop-out, Xavier——"

"What if they tease her because of us? You know kids. They're ruthless."

"And adults aren't? I grew up black on an all-white island. Some of the worst things ever said to me came from adults. She's a tough kid. If her gay parents are the only thing she's teased about, then she's probably lucky."

Xavier is silent, his eyes on the floor.

"You know what happened with my father," Xavier says suddenly. "He was a nasty, worthless alcoholic who liked to call us all—my mother, sisters, and me—the most awful names. Stupid was the favorite for them. Or crazy. *Stupid, crazy bitches*, he'd yell at them after a night of drinking. But he only ever said one thing to me—the same thing. Over and over. That I was an accident. I was the youngest by almost seven years. Every time he was drunk, he'd go on about that—how they never wanted me. How I was a mistake."

He glances up at Leo, who's waiting for him to continue. But Xavier simply looks at him.

"But you know that's not true," Leo says. "Your mother loved you. I was with you when she died. I remember her telling you that you were one of the best things that ever happened to her."

Xavier scowls at him. "Will you listen to me? I'm not talking about my mother. She didn't kick the son of a bitch out of the house until I was almost eighteen! He never remembered what he said after a blackout. And I wasn't brave enough to bring it up——he scared the shit out of me. Hell, he's dead and still does. What I'm saying is, I'm not going to do that to Sky."

Leo squints at him. "What are you talking about? I've seen you drunk maybe twice, and you simply close your eyes and fall asleep. And unless someone kidnaps your body and replaces your brain, you would never behave that way——"

"But I feel that way!" Xavier shouts, leaning forward. "Even if I might not say it to her——I *feel* that way." He stops, picks at the label on his bottle. "I hate to admit, but I do."

Leo pauses, not trusting his voice. "What way?" he finally chokes out.

Xavier studies him. "Like all of this is just a big mistake that I'm going to wake up from. That it's just a bad dream. I want to go back to that day when the phone rang and you found out you were suddenly a parent and just snap my fingers and wake up! Go back to our old life. When it was just me and you. And we slept naked. And made love whenever we wanted to. I miss you. I miss us——"

"I miss us too," Leo cuts in. He stands, walks over, and sits on the coffee table in front of Xavier. "And we'll get to do all those things again, I promise. I'll do a better job at making time for us and getting a babysitter for a weekend night——"

Xavier holds up his hand. "Stop," he whispers.

He looks at Leo, and simply like that, it's over.

Leo sees it in his eyes. They were one of the first things about Xavier that he fell in love with. Deep-set and a thick green the color of a forest at dusk, they also reveal too much.

Xavier doesn't need to say that he's done coming to the island. He's done pretending this parenting thing might just work.

"Go back to the island. I'm staying here."

"Come with me. Please."

"I'm not going to ruin your weekend."

"Maggie is watching Sky overnight. Let's at least enjoy the time—"

"Until when?" Xavier interrupts. "Tomorrow morning, after we've spent the night together and you have to leave, and the house is silent again? Like it is all week. I thought it would get easier when we first started doing this. Me leaving the island every Sunday. Or you stopping in when you come to the city for work—I thought saying goodbye wouldn't be as awful. But it's the opposite."

Leo doesn't have it in him to argue. He hasn't even had a chance to share his bad news with Xavier. That Leo's boss had called him while he was on the ferry to tell him they'd need him in the office more—that this working-from-home thing wasn't working as well as he'd hoped.

It didn't help that the firm had lost the $11.2-million library bid. The one that Leo worked on for months.

All these things are churning up his insides when he stands and turns to leave. He can't turn around again. He's afraid he'll stay. Afraid he'll never go back to the island.

He opens the door and closes it quietly behind him. Then he stands in the hallway and waits.

He listens for the sound of crutches against the wood floor. He listens for any movement at all. He waits for the door to open. For Xavier to tell him he was wrong. Of course they'll make it work.

Five minutes pass. Then ten.

Finally, he walks outside, stands on the sidewalk in front of his house, the one he's called home for more than a decade, feeling more lost than he has in his entire life.

15

The Fourth of July starts with Maggie's own version of fireworks. Not the good kind.

Pete picks a fight with her. Or maybe she picks one with him. It's hard to tell these days who is to blame for their mutual discontent.

Every argument seems to veer off the rails, lurching here and there, until the very thing they started fighting about is so far in the distance, they can't get back to it.

This one starts with Pete passing behind her while she waits for the coffee to brew, pecking her on the back of her head, a kiss that reminds her of how he used to greet Molly, their old retriever, who died years ago.

Pete would come home from work, and the dog would amble over, her tail wagging, bouncing against the low cabinets, and he'd lean down and give her a tight-lipped peck on the head.

"What a good girl you are," he'd say. "Such a silly old girl."

That's how he makes her feel now, with that type of kiss to say goodbye. As though she's just a silly old girl.

He doesn't even wait for her to turn around. Just *peck*, right on the crown of her unwashed head, and off he goes to the front door.

"I'll see you in the morning," he calls over his shoulder.

"What?" She follows him to the foyer. "Where are you going?"

He turns, looks at her. "To work," he says simply.

She glances at her watch. "Now? It's not even eight in the morning."

"I told everyone I'd bring coffee and doughnuts."

Well, how nice of you, she thinks. *How* sweet.

"Did you say you'd see me in the morning? As in tomorrow morning?"

He tilts his head at her and sighs. "I told you I had to work," he says slowly, as though she's daft.

Just a daft, silly old girl.

She knew he was working on the Fourth. They'd talked about it weeks ago. She'd pressed him for details—asked if perhaps he could take some of the night off. He was the police chief, after all. It seemed to her that he'd been working this holiday since he was a rookie. Why didn't some of the younger guys take the shift?

He'd given her vague answers. Not once did he tell her he was working from eight in the morning until the next day.

"You did tell me. But overnight too?"

"I always work overnight on the Fourth. You know that," he tells her irritably, as though she really *should* know it. As though an entire year hasn't passed in which she might have just simply *forgotten*.

Maybe he had worked overnight last year. Maybe she had forgotten.

But that isn't the point.

"Well you might have reminded me," she replies. "I've been asking for weeks if you had to work on the Fourth, and all you said was *yes*." She makes quotes in the air with her fingers.

"Because I do!"

Maggie waves him away. "No—it's as though you try to give me the least amount of information. And then you pretend that

I'm *silly* for not knowing something. Here's silly old Maggie getting all riled up again!"

Pete sighs again. "I never said you were silly."

"You don't have to. It's all over your face."

"Look—what's the big deal? We've never spent the Fourth together. I work. You go to Agnes's party. That's the way it's always been."

"Alone," Maggie points out. "I go alone every year to Agnes's party *because* you're working." She softens her tone as much as she can manage. "I thought this year might be different."

Pete frowns. "Why?"

"Because I asked if things could be different. I've been *asking* if things can be different. I was hoping maybe you could work part of the night. Then we could spend some of it together. You know, to celebrate."

"Celebrate what?" he asks, befuddled.

She waits. He raises an eyebrow.

"The Fourth of July, Pete," she says finally.

He pauses. "Is that a thing? I mean, for folks our age? Adults? Without grandchildren or anything?"

"Yes, it's a thing—I'm going to a party later specifically to celebrate the Fourth of July. An *adult* party."

Silly old girl.

A tear slips down her cheek, hot and fast.

"Jesus, Maggie," Pete says, and steps toward her. "What in the world. Are you crying?"

She wipes the tear away. "It's nothing. Forget I brought it up."

He presses his fingers into his eye sockets, as though she's given him a headache. "It's obviously not nothing. You're crying—"

"Go," she interrupts, and waves him away. "Just go to work. I'll be fine."

He hesitates, but she waves him away again and he opens the door and steps out. He looks back at her. "So we're okay?" he asks.

No, she thinks. *We're not.*

"Yes," she says.

After Pete left, she made her flag cake for the party and left it cooling on top of the stove. Then she went upstairs and showered and dressed, and before she knew it, it was already afternoon.

She thought she'd have Sky and Frankie for a sleepover last night with Leo tending to Xavier in the city, but Leo had shown up unexpectedly after dinner with news that Xavier was fine but had decided to recover in the city for the weekend.

She had been looking forward to the girls' company, as sad and pathetic as that was—a fifty-year-old woman seeking companionship from two ten-year-old girls. But they were easy. Easy to laugh with. Easy to take care of. Easy company.

Now, she's on the patio, drinking a glass of wine before Agnes's party.

She doesn't normally drink during the day. But it's the Fourth of July. It feels like an act of defiance against Pete and his awful attitude. Not that she's fooled anyway.

As the chief of police, Pete would know more than anyone how festive the harbor would be today. How many adults would be lugging coolers and grills to the beach. How many *adults* would be enjoying the holiday. Couples holding hands as fireworks exploded in the sky. Maybe sharing a kiss at the end of the finale.

To be honest, a tiny part of her hoped he'd change his mind. Come back to the house and tell her that, of course he could take *some* of the night off.

Part of it, at least.

Maybe he'd tell her there was nowhere he'd rather be than with her.

This makes her laugh. Snort, actually—the wine almost spilling out of her nose—it's that absurd.

She leans back in her chair and considers this. When had it become absurd to think he might say something like that to her—his wife?

Certainly not when they were first married.

Although it's hard to remember back that far—they had been kids. Both of them just twenty-three years old. A cliché, of course. A shotgun wedding when she was three months pregnant with PJ. Nobody knew except her and Pete. Not even her parents or Agnes.

Not one of the thirty guests had a clue.

They just saw two people in love.

And they were. She and Pete. She knows that. They were in love for a lot of years. Certainly, at their tenth anniversary. Even their twentieth.

And then two things happened. Pete turned forty-eight and two days later, his twin brother dropped dead from a stroke. No warning. Not one symptom.

A perfectly healthy man, Tim was the mirror image of Pete.

Fit and athletic. Married to his high school sweetheart and father to their four kids, Maggie always thought they were the golden family. Sun-kissed and blond in their pictures. The perfect California family.

Except that wasn't the story Pete held on to after Tim died. Not the one he believed to be true.

According to Pete, Tim felt trapped.

"Trapped how?" Maggie remembers asking Pete. "In his marriage?"

"No, not trapped like that," he'd said. "He loved Abigail. Loved the kids. It's just . . . he said he couldn't remember a time in his life when he wasn't expected to be somewhere. To be doing *something*. You know, between work and Abigail and the kids. He had this whole list of things that he wanted to do. Travel. Hobbies. One of them was just a goddamn day when he did what *he* wanted to do. When *he* wanted to do it. Then *poof*! He's dead. Game over."

"Your brother was happy, Pete," she said. "I'm sure he wouldn't have any regrets about how he chose to live his life." She nodded, confident, and waited for him to agree.

But Pete hadn't agreed.

And the following year after Tim died is still a blur in Maggie's head. Their life changed, just like that.

It wasn't even subtle. Almost overnight, Pete pulled away and morphed into someone she no longer recognized.

He did what he wanted when he wanted. Planned weekends away to fish or surf without consulting her—never mind inviting her along.

Oh, she tried to be patient. Give him time. Then a year passed, and nothing changed, even though she talked to him about her feelings.

Talked and talked. Told him she knew what he was going through until she knew if those words passed her lips one more time, she would scream.

Because she had known what he was going through—she lost both her parents in a short amount of time. She understood grief! And this thing with Pete may have started as him grieving his brother, but somewhere along the way, it developed into something different.

She knew it to be true when he cheated on her with his secretary. And then had the audacity—*the nerve*—to deny it. But Maggie had seen it with her own eyes. A text on his phone when Pete was taking out the trash one day. She'd walked by his phone on the kitchen counter and stopped short when she saw the word *sexy*.

Hi sexy, she'd read. She saw the other texts. Scrolled through, scanning them until Pete was back in the kitchen, grabbing the phone out of her hand.

It's police business, he'd mumbled, shoving the evidence in his back pocket. She didn't argue with him. She went upstairs and packed a bag. Only then did he tell her that he was sorry. Admit that he screwed up.

He tried to convince Maggie that it was a professional relationship that had crossed over a line. Inappropriate but nothing sexual, he insisted. He said he didn't know why he did it—it just happened.

As if this was some consolation. It still didn't explain why the secretary had texted him at midnight. Or on Thanksgiving. Or on Sunday mornings. All details that trickled out in therapy, sharp and breathtaking.

Like small cuts to Maggie's soul.

And slowly, in Maggie's mind, she started to think of Pete as a child. An immature, unformed, large child of a man who couldn't control his actions. A person who lacked the desire to understand *why* he did what he did.

Now, sitting on the patio, her glass of wine empty, Maggie stands up abruptly and walks around to the front of the house.

Across the street, Joe is working in his garden. Sky and Frankie are in his yard, running through the sprinkler, the spray soaking their shorts and T-shirts.

Maggie strides over before she changes her mind. By the time she reaches them, Sky and Frankie are flopped on their backs, faces to the sun.

Joe smiles when he sees her. "Well, don't you look pretty," he says, eyeing her dress.

Maggie feels her cheeks warm at the compliment.

She usually wore the same red skirt and white shirt to Agnes's party. But she'd reached into the back of her closet this morning and found a sundress she'd bought on sale at the end of the summer last year. Simple and black, there was nothing festive about it.

"Thank you," she says to Joe, who points to several chairs in the backyard.

"Come sit. I'll get us a drink. I have iced tea. Beer. Wine. Water. Your choice." He smiles, waits for her to answer.

"Will you come with me tonight?" she blurts. "To Agnes's party? I know you don't like her—and I don't blame you. She can be, um . . ." She searches for the word.

"Uppity?" Joe offers.

Maggie nods. "Among other things."

Joe is quiet, studying her. "Well," he says finally. "To tell you the truth, I sort of imagine that party to be just that. A bunch of overdressed uppity-ups from snob hill."

She grins. "Snob hill? I wasn't aware there was such a place on the island."

Joe shrugs. "You get my drift."

"Okay," Maggie says, turning. "I figured you'd say that, but I thought I'd ask."

Joe steps forward, his arm out. "Well, hold on now. I wasn't finished."

She turns, waits.

"I would be honored to go with you. As long as Pete's fine with it. I don't need the chief of police on my case," he jokes.

"He's working as usual. And I just don't feel like making

small talk with people I only see once a year. There will be good food. And beer. You like beer."

Joe nods, and Sky looks up at Maggie.

"We're going too," she says.

"You are?" Maggie asks, surprised.

"Leo bribed us," Sky says. "He said he got on Agnes's bad side and she always wants all of the neighborhood to come and nobody besides you ever does, and if we go for an hour, he'll give us each ten bucks."

Joe laughs, and Maggie eyes him. "It's not that bad of a party," she insists.

He holds up his hands. "I'll take your word for it. I'm the only one she doesn't invite. Glad to go as your guest and get under her skin. Besides," he says, "any party with you by my side is one I want to be at."

She smiles and waves goodbye, says she'll see him in a bit.

Her cheeks are warm again as she crosses the street. She knows Joe's just being playful—she's used to his teasing.

But when she opens her door and shuts it behind her, she catches her reflection in the mirror on the wall.

There's someone looking back at her. A stranger almost. Only a hint of someone she remembers.

A woman in a sexy, black dress. Flushed and happy and smiling.

16

Leo decided to go to Agnes's Fourth of July party at the last minute. The morning of, actually, when he'd found the invitation on the table and noticed that it read *regrets only* for the RSVP, and even though he wasn't overly fond of Agnes, he felt it was just plain rude to cancel the day of the party.

He's promised to take Sky and Frankie to the beach to watch the fireworks show in the harbor after they've made their appearance.

But they're only at the party for fifteen minutes when Leo looks across the yard and regrets coming. Under the tent, sitting at a table, is Lillian.

He remembers then that she'd called earlier in the week and left a voice mail, asking him to return her call.

He hadn't because he knew she was going to ask to see Sky, and he didn't know how to answer her, how to admit that Sky had asked "Do I have to?"

Now, she's not only on the island, she's in Agnes's backyard, less than twenty feet from him and Sky, who is across the yard with Frankie, playing badminton with Joe and Maggie.

Lillian must feel him staring at her because she turns and walks over.

"Well, hello again," she says. Just like that.

As if they're old friends running into each other on the street.

He feels his stomach bottom out. And his temper flare.

Both at the same moment.

Having Sky and Lillian reunite wasn't exactly on his agenda tonight. And after the week he's had—a shitty week, really—he can feel his heart racing, his mouth suddenly dry.

Maybe he's having a heart attack.

There's a hammock strung between two trees off in the distance, and he has an overwhelming urge to walk over and lie down, curl up on his side, and simply fall asleep. Slip into a dream world where his life doesn't involve an estranged grandmother and a resentful husband and a job he's about to lose.

He hears his name and blinks Lillian's face into focus. She's saying something, raising her glass to him.

"I'm sorry," he says. "What?"

"Oh, I was just toasting the Fourth. It's always been one of my favorite holidays—"

"Lillian—can I have a moment with you? In private?" He tilts his head to Agnes's house. He's not going to stand here and make small talk when, at any moment, Sky could walk over.

Lillian follows him. When they're inside, tucked in a corner of the living room, Leo faces her.

"What's going on here?" he asks urgently. "I know you said you wanted to see Sky, but I assumed you'd wait to hear from me. Now you just show up. Without any warning?"

"Warning?" she asks, her eyes wide. "What does *that* mean?"

She looks so shocked that he feels silly, as though he's over-reacting. "Poor choice of words," he says, softening his tone. "I just thought you would have called to say you would be here."

"I did call you. And I didn't hear back."

"I'm sorry for not getting back to you. It's been a hell of a week. Why didn't you just tell me you were coming to the party in the voice mail?"

"I didn't know anything about the party when I called you. I just wanted to make plans to see Sky. Then Agnes got in touch. Said she's been throwing this party for years and would love for me to come. I didn't have any plans. So, I thought, why not?"

"Why not?" he repeats, his voice louder than intended. But he can't believe his ears. "I can give you one very important reason. She's about this tall." He holds his hand up to where Sky's head rests against him when she hugs him good night. "And she has no idea you're here and she's *outside* right now." He glances out the window.

"She is? I can't wait to see her!" She peers out the window, scanning the crowded lawn.

Leo steps in front of her view. "And I understand that, but surprising her is not ideal."

"I don't see the problem. I had no idea Sky would be here tonight. But I'm thrilled. I was going to walk down to your house tomorrow morning anyway."

"Walk down from where?" he asks just as Agnes joins them, a set of keys in her hand.

"Hello, Leo." Agnes smiles, but it's a tight line. "What a surprise. I didn't expect you to come. I always invite the neighborhood. I wish more people would make an effort."

"I'm sure it's nothing personal," Leo offers, even though he knows it is.

The party is exactly what Leo thought it would be.

Ichabod's wealthiest elite. White-haired men in seersucker jackets. Wives in colorful sleeveless, shapeless shifts. Pearls around their necks. Get close enough and you'll get a lesson in history. One of them happy to remind you how their great-

great-grandfather built this island. Made Ichabod what it is today.

Leo came to the party because he somehow ended up on the wrong side of Agnes. And that was never his intention.

He came to make amends. Agnes is his neighbor, after all.

But now, with Lillian standing in front of them, invited here specifically by Agnes, he feels blindsided. He's had the sense that Agnes doesn't approve of him. That she would prefer Lillian as Sky's guardian. And forget about Xavier.

She hasn't remotely tried to hide her feelings about his marriage.

"I didn't know you and Lillian knew each other," Leo says, turning to Agnes. "Ann never mentioned it. Interesting that you've been in touch with her now."

He doesn't mention that Ann didn't like to talk about her mother. He's picking a fight. But it's one worth picking.

"Oh, I wouldn't say interesting," Agnes replies. "Expected, I would think. I'm aware that Ann and Lillian had difficulties. Ann also knew my feelings on the matter. A grandparent should never be denied access to a grandchild. Plus, Lillian is a native of this island, and I'm going to do all I can to make her feel welcome here."

"How nice of you," Leo says. He looks at Lillian, who has been quietly watching them, as though she doesn't have a part in this.

"Speaking of houses, Leo," Agnes says. "Mrs. Pearse passed earlier today." She turns to Lillian. "Mrs. Pearse was Leo's tenant next door. Such a loss for the island—her ancestors were the original settlers on Ichabod."

"I didn't know that. But it explains the cars in the driveway. I'm sorry to hear it. She was a nice woman," he says, even though he didn't know her at all, and his property manager had complained about having to chase her down for the rent every month.

"And perfect for this street," Agnes replies. "She always spoke about how she felt lucky to end up in the part of town that's still historic. The tourists basically ran her out of her old neighborhood." She leans toward Lillian. "She had a quaint house on the water, and some developer hounded her for years to sell it to them. Now it's a hideous time-share. I can't even stand to drive by it."

"Didn't she sell her house for a fortune? Five million dollars or something like that? I remember her house. It was falling down around her," Leo says.

Agnes ignores him.

"I just wanted to give you this." Agnes hands Lillian a key ring. "The gold one is for the front door. The silver is the back. I'd say don't worry about locking it, but with all the tourists here, you never know." Agnes looks at Leo. "I've invited Lillian to stay in my house across the street. As my guest. I'm only telling you this because I've repeatedly asked everyone in the neighborhood to keep an eye on one another's houses, and mine will no longer be vacant. If you see lights on, then you'll know why. Lillian—I'll find you in a bit and give you a tour. Help you get settled."

Agnes turns and walks away.

Leo stares blankly after her, trying to comprehend what just happened.

"You're moving here?" he asks Lillian, finally. Dumbly.

"It just sort of happened," Lillian offers. "Agnes invited me to stay the night. And then earlier we were talking in the kitchen, and I mentioned that I have to find a new place to live—it's a long story—so she graciously offered her house in the interim. I'll have to go home and pack, but I'm hoping to be back in a couple of weeks to stay—"

"But we *agreed* to take it slow. You stood on that dock and said you had Sky's best interest at heart. Didn't you?"

Lillian has her mouth open to answer when she stops, her eyes on something over Leo's shoulder. He turns to see Sky and Frankie walking toward them.

"Can we go soon?" Sky asks.

Before he can answer, Lillian steps out from behind him.

"Skylar—look at you! My gosh, you're so tall!" Lillian exclaims, engulfing the girl in a hug.

Lillian steps back and holds out a hand to Frankie.

"I'm Lillian, Skylar's grandmother," she announces.

Frankie smiles and shakes her hand. "Frankie," she says. "Nice to meet you."

"Oh, it's nice to meet *you*!" Lillian says enthusiastically. "I'm sorry it's been so long, Skylar. I don't want to get into that now though. I'm just so happy to see you. So where are you off to? The fireworks, I hope?"

Sky nods, and Leo holds his breath, wondering if Lillian is going to ask to come. But she reaches out and puts a hand on Sky's and Frankie's shoulders and gives them a quick squeeze.

"Well, you have a blast. I'm staying overnight at Agnes's other house, across the street. My ferry isn't until noon. Can I see you in the morning?"

"We're going surfing tomorrow," Sky says.

"Yes," Leo lies. "We are."

Frankie looks from Sky to Leo, her eyebrow up.

"That's okay," Lillian says cheerily. "I'll be back in a couple of weeks. We'll be neighbors. We can see each other all the time.

Anyway, have fun! See you soon!" She gives Sky a quick hug and disappears through the door onto the lawn.

Sky has a blank look on her face. As though she has no idea what's just happened. She peers through the window after Lillian.

"That was weird," she mutters.

"I'm sorry," Leo says. "I had no idea she was going to be here."

"Wait, *who* is she?" Frankie asks. "I thought your grandmother was dead."

"That's my nana. Dad's mom. She's my mom's mom."

Frankie gives Sky a quizzical look. "Never heard you talk about her."

Sky shifts uncomfortably. "Because I haven't seen her in forever. She and my mom didn't get along."

"She seems nice," Frankie offers.

Sky shrugs. "I don't really remember her. Wait—she's moving here?" She turns to Leo.

"I don't know," he says honestly.

He looks at Sky, tries to figure out what to say to her about all of it.

"Can we go?" she asks. "We need to get there early to get a good spot."

"Read my mind," he answers, ushering them out the back door. Away from the house. Away from Lillian.

Who said she'd move slow and is, instead, moving four doors down the street.

17

The last weeks of July pass in a blur of beach days. She and Frankie go surfing whenever they want, since Leo hardly works anymore.

Xavier hasn't been to the island since he hurt his ankle, which Sky isn't sorry about at all.

It's not as though she misses him.

But she does feel bad that Leo seems upset about it. Then she feels guilty for being happy that it's just her and Leo. She doesn't think about her parents as much. Of course, she misses them. Always will. But she doesn't expect them to come walking through the door anymore.

And being with Leo is different. Her skin has always been darker than just about everyone in her school. On the island, too.

With Leo, when they're out at a restaurant or in a store, she's not the only dark-skinned person in the room.

It's a first for her. Blending in with the person next to her. She kind of likes it.

And now it's going to be just the two of them on the beach, with Frankie leaving for camp for the next few weeks. She tried to talk Frankie out of going, but that was useless because it's art camp and nothing would keep Frankie from her art.

Not even Sky.

This morning, Leo asked her if she wanted to go to the beach. She told him she needed a day out of the sun, but really, surfing by herself all day didn't seem that fun. Leo would come out on his surfboard with her, but he wasn't very good.

Leo had gone downstairs to fix the washing machine. It was hot outside. And humid. According to Leo, as good a day as any to spend in the cool, dark basement and figure out why the floor flooded every time they ran a load of clothes through the washing machine.

Sky had taken a book Frankie had lent her about how to paint animals outside to the patio, but now she's just sitting at the table, staring at nothing after reading the same page four times.

For her, there is only one way to learn. And that's by doing it.

She hears a noise and looks over to see Joe in his yard. She puts the book on the table and walks over to him.

"Hey there, Sport," he says when she reaches him. "Where's your sidekick?"

"Camp. For like, weeks."

"Ah. Hence the glum face."

"The what?"

"Glum. You know—sad."

She nods. "Not really sad. I'm happy for Frankie. She loves it. It's just boring without her."

"Boring?" He leans on his rake, studies her. "You know, when I was a kid and I used that word around my house, two things happened. My mother would tell me to go outside and find my father. And when I did, my father would give me a job. Painting the fence. Washing the mold off the house. Picking weeds from the cracks in the sidewalk out front."

"That sounds awful," Sky says.

"Yup. I wasn't the brightest kid, so it took some time before

I dropped *bored* from my vocabulary. Saved me a lot of grunt work." He smiled. "My roundabout way of saying if you're look-ing for something to do, I've got a list a mile long."

"I want to paint a picture in the woods, but the tree house is too hot. And last time I brought my paints and my sketchbook and got all set up by the cliff, the wind kept knocking everything over. Frankie can paint from her imagination, but I need to see it. I'm not as good as her."

Joe is quiet, studying her. "You need an easel," he says finally. "Then you can paint wherever you want. The kind with clips so the paper stays put."

"Frankie has one. She would have lent it to me, but I forgot to ask."

"Look here—a carpenter has his own tools. A musician plays his own instrument. And an artist like you, my dear, has her own easel." He squints at her. "Know how to swing a hammer?" he asks.

They work through lunch, straight into the middle of the after-noon.

First, Joe brings her into his garage. A large room full of benches and tools and saws. So clean and organized that she takes her time walking around and looking in all the small draw-ers. Whole rows of them labeled *Nails. Screws. Bolts.*

There's a wall full of clamps. Another with every type of wrench or screwdriver you could ever need.

"My father's worktable in the basement doesn't look like this," Sky tells him. "He'd try to build something, and he was always running out to the hardware store because he couldn't find what he was looking for."

Joe laughs. "Pride was your father's problem. I'd offer to

help. No can do. Let's just say I hope you didn't inherit your woodworking skills from him. Okay, Sport—first things first. Safety." He hands her a pair of clear plastic glasses, and she frowns.

"Nonnegotiable," he says, and she rolls her eyes but slips them on.

They pick out the wood next, and she watches Joe use the saw to cut the legs. Then he sets her up at a table and teaches her how to use the electric sander.

Which turns out to be so fun that she gets carried away and sands both of the legs down to what Joe calls toothpicks and they have to start all over again.

Joe doesn't seem to mind. He just cuts two more legs and hands her a piece of sandpaper, shows her what he wants her to do in the same calm voice he always uses.

"You're much nicer than Mr. Craft," she tells him.

"Who is Mr. Craft, and why isn't he nice to you?"

"He teaches woodworking at the high school. He's not nice to anyone. Frankie's brothers are scared of him, and they're not scared of anyone."

"It's a tough job. I'm not sure I could handle a classful of teenagers. I only went through that stage once with my son, and I sure made my share of mistakes."

She looks at him through a cloud of dust that's formed above her hand, the sandpaper hot in her palm. "I didn't know you had a son. How come he never comes over?"

Joe studies her. "He died four years ago. You knew him, actually, but you were just a baby. You just don't remember."

She does the easy math and frowns at him. "I'll be eleven in four months. Four years ago, I was almost seven. I wasn't a baby."

Joe nods, considers this. "Well—you were a baby when

he was . . . himself. There were a lot of years he didn't come home. He had a drug problem. Then my wife got sick, and he started stealing her pain medication. We couldn't allow him in the house anymore."

"Where did he go?" She couldn't imagine not having anywhere to live. "I sleep in the tree house sometimes, but I wouldn't want to live there."

Joe gives her a sad smile. "He wasn't a child like you, Sky. David was twenty-four. An adult. And we didn't just kick him out. We were helping him pay for an apartment in the city. Then I surprised him with a visit and an old woman answered his door. He'd given us a fake address. He was homeless, using the money on drugs." He looks down at the floor, then back at her. "We thought we were helping him, but he wasn't ready for the help. The last thing he told me was to stay out of his life. That I made him feel worse about himself. Then he died of an overdose."

She rubs the wood with the grainy paper. She doesn't want to tell him that she's sorry. That's what everyone says to her about her parents and she never knows what to say back. *Thank you? Me too?*

She glances at Joe, who's running his hand against a wooden leg.

"That's what my mother used to say about her mother. My grandmother," she says. "I'd ask about her—we don't even have one picture of her in our house. My mom said that her mother always made her feel bad about herself. That she didn't want her in our life."

Joe reaches over and takes the sandpaper out of her hand. Hands her a new sheet.

"She's moving down the street. Into Agnes's house."

"Your grandmother? How do you feel about that?"

She shrugs. "My mom liked everyone. So why didn't she like her own mother?"

"I don't have the answers, Sport." He gestures for her to keep sanding. "I don't know what happened between your mother and grandmother. I do know that when David said we made him feel bad about himself, it was the disease talking. He wanted to get better. And then he'd fail and feel awful about himself. Over and over again, he'd try to get sober and fail, and then in his mind, we were the ones making him feel broken. Not the drugs or the alcohol. Not the disease."

They hear a knock on the door, and Leo pokes his head in.

"Hey, Joe. Got a minute? I have an issue I could use your help with." He waves to Sky, holds his thumb up when she holds one of the legs in the air to show him.

"Keep at it," Joe tells her. "I'll be right back."

Joe has the radio set to a talk station, and two men are going on and on about the Red Sox. She tunes them out, concentrates on running the paper evenly over the wood, smooth now under her fingers except for several rough spots.

She wonders what Frankie is doing exactly at this moment. She pictures her out on some rocky cliff, painting the view of the ocean below. She knows this is silly because the camp where Frankie goes is in western Massachusetts and as far as she knows, there's only lakes and ponds out there, and she's thinking about a cliff over the ocean only because that's where she wants to be right now.

Out on the cliff in the woods, painting on her new easel.

She told herself she's only going back in the woods during the day now though, after what happened when they lit the sparklers. She can still hear that clapping.

Frankie had told Sky she was being ridiculous—there was

a farm on the other side of the woods. Obviously the owners were having a party and the clapping just trickled over to them.

Sky had nodded, agreeing. Except she hadn't ever heard any noise from that farm.

Not in all the years she'd walked through the woods. And the clapping hadn't come from the other side of the woods. It had come from behind them. *Right* behind them.

Fifteen minutes later, when it feels like her arm is about to fall off and both the legs are done, she puts down the sandpaper and walks over to her house, looking for Joe.

The basement door is open, voices trickling up the stairs to the kitchen. She skips down the stairs, the wood creaking loudly under her feet, and rounds the corner, bumping straight into Joe's back, who jumps as though she's quietly snuck up on him.

Leo is bent over, leaning into the storage space under the stairs.

"There's more in here. A lot more," he calls out, then steps back and straightens when he sees her, his eyes wide.

There's a cardboard box at Joe's feet, full of empty bottles. All the same size and shape. *Jim Beam* printed in black letters on a white label. The only thing her father drank.

Leo has a bottle in his hand. The brown liquid sloshing, half-full.

He looks at Sky, and she sees him move the bottle out of sight, behind his leg. Then he sighs, puts the bottle on top of the others.

"I was going to make up some lie about your father collecting these. But I get the sense you know that's not true." He looks at her. "Did you know he was drinking?"

She shrugs. "Only because they fought about it. He never drank upstairs."

Leo stares blankly at the bottles. "He was coming up on fifteen years sober. Three weeks before he died, we sat in a bar and watched the game and he had a Coke. I didn't even think about it anymore. I just assumed he didn't either." He nudges the box of bottles with his toe. "There must be thirty here." He looks over to the space under the stairs. "How did I not know? Why didn't Ann say anything?"

She isn't sure if he's asking her, but she knows the answer.

"Because he told her it was nobody's business. Then she'd say that she was going to tell someone. And he'd say that he was going to tell someone she wasn't taking her pills. They fought about it all the time when they thought I was asleep."

Leo squints at her. "What pills? Was your mother sick?"

"I don't know. He'd say that she acted crazy if she didn't take them. That he worried about her taking care of me."

"Were you ever worried?" he asks quietly.

She could probably lie. What would it matter? They were both dead anyway.

"Sometimes. She'd get this look on her face. Like she was a different person. And she'd wear this red lipstick and get all dressed up." She looked over at Joe. "Like the day you fell off the ladder and got hurt."

Joe doesn't answer, but he swallows so hard she can hear it. He doesn't need to say he knows what she's talking about. She sees it all over his face.

18

She finds a holistic therapist in town and pays for the massage with cash. Gives him a fake name. Answers the few questions he asks with lies before she requests that they don't speak. The only thing that's true is how wonderful it feels to be touched. The one thing that makes her feel human while she prepares to die.

After, she puts on her enormous sunglasses, a floppy hat on her head, and sits on a bench by the harbor. Not to be seen. To watch. People. Dogs. Birds. Boats sailing in and ships steaming out.

Life.

How had hers slipped away from her?

She can catalog her bad decisions as if they were entries on a spreadsheet she could print out and shred, make them all disappear.

She can do that. Forget what she's done. Destroy the facts.

Yet the results are here to stay. The scars on her arms from the drugs. The cancer in her lungs. Now liver and brain, from decades of smoking. Her bones brittle from starving herself between photo shoots. Her thinness was a badge of honor. Now her skin hangs, puckered and loose from lack of muscle. Her body tired and starved from the poison she's feasted on her whole life.

Alone, too. That's all she is. That's what happens when you give away everything you should keep. And keep the things that destroy you.

But she feels as though she's a part of something here, on Ichabod.

This is where she's meant to be. Even when the ache in her bones reminds her that she's not long for this earth, she's thankful to sit here on this bench and breathe in the salt air. Let the island wrap its arms around her and pull her close, safe in the harbor surrounded by the sights and sounds that nourished her all those years ago. She never told Mac she'd come and sit for hours in this very spot. Tiny feet rippling across her middle.

She sits until dusk, when the air grows cooler. Back at the shed, she settles in front of the large window overlooking the barn and pasture, the ocean in the distance.

She imagines the life she didn't live. The one she gave away. All the beauty she won't live to see.

This is when she sketches. Pencil in hand, for hours and hours, until the candle on the table burns out, she sits at the table and becomes the woman she's always wanted to be.

19

She hears about Lillian staying in Agnes's house, not from Agnes but from Leo.

They're standing on her front lawn talking about the early August rain that's supposed to pass through when a van drives past, *The Moving Guys* stenciled on the side. It pulls into the driveway of the vacant house three doors down.

Agnes's vacant house.

"I wonder what that's all about?" Maggie asks out loud.

Leo looks at her. "She didn't tell you?"

"Who didn't tell me?"

"Agnes."

She gives him a blank look. "About what?"

"Lillian's now staying in Agnes's house."

Maggie squints. "*Staying* as in moving in?"

"I just assumed Agnes told you. I mean, you guys are close. Lillian was at the party. You didn't meet her?"

Maggie shakes her head.

She hadn't spoken to Agnes at the party after they'd shared a brief hello. Agnes was busy catering to William's law-firm cronies. Plus, Maggie had made it clear to Agnes that she should mind her own business when it came to Leo and Xavier and Sky.

Agnes probably went to great lengths to make sure Maggie didn't know Lillian was there.

Her cheeks turn hot, her heart suddenly pounding. "I thought Lillian told you she was going to move slowly and give Sky some time to adjust. She has enough to deal with right now without this."

"Apparently, she got an offer she couldn't refuse. She's staying for free as Agnes's *guest*." He makes quotes in the air with his fingers, then sighs. "I'm trying not to be paranoid here, but she's just rude to me. Hostile, really. Xavier says she won't even acknowledge him." He looks at Maggie. "You don't think it's because we're gay, do you? I mean, I'm assuming she knows about her own daughter? I was a summer sailing instructor for Grace when she was in the sixth grade, and I could've told you then that she was gay."

"They don't exactly have the best relationship. So yes, I think Agnes knows and chooses to ignore it. Which is probably why Grace never comes to Ichabod."

She stares at the van idling in the driveway. The driver's side window is rolled down, a man's forearm visible, his fingers tapping along to a beat she can't hear.

Down the street, a door slams and Agnes appears, walking toward the van.

"Excuse me, Leo," she says, marching after her.

"Oh, geez," he mutters. Leo doesn't like conflict any more than she does—but there is a buzzing in her head.

A fury building inside of her.

By the time she reaches the end of the driveway, the van driver, a short, stocky man with a baseball hat on backward, is pointing to the clipboard in his hand, explaining something to Agnes, who's bent over to accommodate the height difference.

He stops midsentence when Maggie strides up next to them.

Agnes straightens, gives her a surprised look. "Oh, hi. I was going to call you later to see if—"

"What's going on here?" she interrupts. "Did you invite Lillian to stay here? For free?"

She glances at the driver, who hasn't moved, his eyes wide, his hand still offering the clipboard, which rests in the air between the three of them.

Agnes crosses her arms. "I don't appreciate your tone of voice—"

"Yes or no?"

Agnes tilts her head, studies Maggie. "Yes, I did. And this is why I didn't tell you. I knew you'd act like this. As if it's any of your business."

"My business? Agnes—this is none of *your* business!"

The driver points to his clipboard.

"Ma'am. Sign here for payment. Check these boxes on the waiver," the driver says.

Agnes ignores him. "I invited an old friend to stay in *my* house. I didn't realize I needed to get permission from you. Or Leo."

"Old friend—you don't even know her!"

"Ma'am. Just sign right—"

"Know her? We grew up together. She's a native—"

"Who left the island when she was ten—I know, I know. You told me. If she's such a good friend, why haven't you spoken to her in *forty* years? You and I both know this is about Sky and Leo and Xavier and your desire to stick your big fat nose in the middle of all of it."

The driver chuckles. Agnes glares.

"Can't you be *doing* something?" Agnes barks at him. "Moving things in. You know, like I'm *paying* you to do."

"I can't do anything until you sign the waiver—"

Agnes grabs the pen and scrawls her name. "Jesus! It's clothing and toiletries, not a crystal chandelier." She waves him away.

"Here too." He points to the waiver. "And there and there and there."

Agnes's jaw juts out. The driver raises an eyebrow.

Agnes leans over the clipboard while the driver looks at Maggie and grins, as though he's happy to stand here all day and listen to two middle-aged women scream at each other.

"There," Agnes says. "Do you need a copy of my driver's license too? Maybe my passport?"

"Nope," the driver says cheerily, ignoring Agnes's sarcasm. "Okay if I use the john?"

Agnes doesn't answer him. He holds his hands up, winks at her. "Only number one, I promise."

She turns to Maggie. "You know, I find it interesting that I can barely get you on the phone anymore, but the minute precious Sky is involved, you're over here, shot out of a cannon."

Maggie frowns. "What are you talking about? I talked to you yesterday."

"Because I called you—"

"No. You called me *back*," Maggie points out. "I called you two days ago, and you were in the middle of a phone call with your doctor, so you said you'd call me back."

"Which I did. I called you *back* because apparently it wasn't important enough to you to call me to find out what the doctor said."

She takes a moment to breathe. But it doesn't help. She *had* called Agnes. Agnes had told her she'd call Maggie *right* back. She didn't. Instead, Maggie had called again the next day. And when she asked Agnes what happened with the doctor, Agnes said she didn't want to talk about it. And now, somehow, Agnes was upset with *her*?

"Ma'am?" the driver calls from the front steps, a box in his arms. "This one's not marked. Where do you want it? The waiver says I have to ask."

Agnes sighs.

"It's not my stuff. I don't know. Just anywhere." She faces Maggie.

"In the kitchen or the living room, ma'am? The waiver says unmarked boxes all go in the same room. Homeowner's choice."

"*The waiver says. The waiver says,*" Agnes mimics under her breath, then turns to the driver. "Put them in the foyer. That's the room right when you walk in—"

"I know what a foyer is, ma'am," the driver says, and disappears through the open door.

"I didn't know if the *waiver* said you needed me to explain the rooms," Agnes shouts after him.

"He's just doing his job," Maggie offers, embarrassed by Agnes's rudeness. "And you're paying for this? So you're not just letting her stay for free—you're *paying* for her to come to the island?"

"I'm *helping* her get settled."

She can hardly believe her ears. "What does William have to say about all of this?"

"William? What does he have to do with it?"

"He's a lawyer. I mean, is this even *legal*? Leo was specifically named as Sky's guardian. Ann didn't leave her in the care of Lillian. In fact, we know—and you know—that she hadn't spoken to Lillian in years. And now you're inviting this woman into this child's life and you don't know anything about the situation. Do you?"

"I know Lillian is Sky's *grandmother*. And that's all I need to know—"

"That's not what I asked. I asked why Ann and Lillian were estranged. What happened between them?"

"That's not my business, Maggie—"

"Oh my God! You really don't know? Have you even asked? She could be abusive, for all we know! She could have a drinking problem that she won't get help for. She could be a nutjob. A psychopath. A child molester—I could go on and on."

"Lillian is none of those things. You'll see when you meet her that she's perfectly normal. More normal than what's going on down there." She gestures to Sky's house. "And I heard the boyfriend is out of the picture now too? Talk about a lack of stability for the child."

Maggie swallows hard, tears suddenly in her eyes. "Husband. For the millionth time. Xavier is Leo's husband. And that's a disgusting thing to say. Leo's sexuality has nothing to do with how good a parent—"

"Oh, stop it," Agnes interrupts. "I meant normal as in a person outside of the family raising the child instead of a family member. There's nothing normal about a man—two men— raising a little girl instead of her own grandmother."

"Have you thought of Sky in all of this? I know what you want. And it seems obvious what Lillian wants with moving here and not even consulting Leo about it. But what about Sky?"

"She's a child. She doesn't know what's best for her—"

"And you do?"

Agnes pauses. "I'm not emotionally invested in the situation like you are. Sometimes you have trouble accepting facts when your feelings are involved. Even when it's clear what the right thing to do would be."

The way it's delivered is unmistakable.

Maggie has seen that look on Agnes's face before. She has seen that look on Agnes's face all year long when she talks about Maggie's marriage.

It's a look of pity.

As if Maggie is weak and foolish for trying to save her twenty-seven-year marriage.

"I'm doing what I think is best here—"

"This isn't about you, Agnes! You know what? Don't call me. Don't get in touch. I can't be around you right now," Maggie spits, the words scattering on the driveway between them. She sees the shock on Agnes's face. Disbelief.

Maggie is stunned as well. They've never fought like this— Maggie has never fought with *anyone* like this.

It's always been her job to fix things. To smooth edges and soothe tempers and put a smile on her face.

Nobody likes an angry girl, her father used to say.

Sweet Maggie.

She turns and walks away.

"The MRI was clear," Agnes shouts after her. "In case you were wondering!"

She should turn around. Give Agnes a hug and tell her that's the best news she's heard in a long time.

Instead, she keeps moving in the other direction.

Sweet Maggie echoing in her head on a loop. Her father's voice loud in her thoughts, deafening almost, until she closes her front door behind her and stares in the mirror on the wall.

Stares and stares, refusing to look away while she studies the expression on her face. Takes in every feature. Every frown line and wrinkle.

She lets what's inside of her reflect in the mirror—this time, she won't smile it away.

It hurts to do this. Every part of her wants to look away.

But she stays. She looks at herself. Angry. Furious, actually. Her eyes wide open for what feels like the first time in her life.

20

It's official as of Monday morning. He's unemployed.

Leo knew this after talking to his boss on Friday, but when he opens his eyes on the first workday of the week, it somehow hits him even harder than expected.

It's nothing personal, he knows. He hadn't been fired; his boss *wanted* to make it work. But it was five days in the office— no flexibility. The project he was assigned to required it. Late nights and impromptu client meetings. He knew the drill— he'd been in this business long enough to know he'd have to move back to the city.

And in his mind, that just wasn't an option anymore.

So he quit. The first time he's quit a job in his whole life.

He hasn't even told Xavier. But they've barely spoken these last weeks. A couple of brief conversations. Voices tight and words clipped.

Neither of them willing to give an inch.

Money isn't an issue, but it will be. He went through his finances last night, and he has enough savings to get by for three months, maybe four.

He's paying two mortgages now. His half of the condo and the mortgage on Brian and Ann's house. Neither Brian nor Ann had life insurance. There wasn't much left over in Brian's and

Ann's accounts after the funeral fees. Just enough to pay the bills for a couple of months.

Brian's truck was so old, Leo was thankful when Brian's firefighter buddies offered to take it off his hands. Ann's car wasn't an issue—they were driving it the night they were killed.

Their financial situation didn't surprise Leo. Ann was a teacher's aide at the elementary school, a job she took after she gave up being a midwife. The hours too unpredictable after they adopted Sky. Brian had worked his way up at the fire station, but he was still young, his salary enough to cover the essentials with a little leftover for Sky's sports and camps and the family vacation they took every year to Myrtle Beach.

And Ichabod Island wasn't the same place Leo's parents had moved to all those years ago. Back then, you could get more for your money on Ichabod than on the mainland. Taxes were low, and land was available, and as long as you were willing to work, the island offered an opportunity to have a decent life—a home of your own. A living wage.

Now it was expensive to live on the island. Million-dollar houses were being built. Houses on the water were untouchable unless you were wealthy. The summer crowd that swept through the island from Memorial Day to Labor Day brought in lots of money for rentals, but only for the folks who bought when prices were low.

Folks like Agnes Coffin, whose ancestors were already wealthy when they came here. They came for the opportunity, just like Leo's parents, but in a different form. Leo's parents wanted a house they could afford. Paying jobs.

Agnes's family bought properties all over the island as though they were in a real-life Monopoly game.

It was Agnes who now owned most of the waterfront summer rentals. And she priced out anyone who didn't look or live like her. Those not white and wealthy need not apply.

Which is one of the reasons Xavier doesn't want to move here. He won't listen when Leo explains that the Agnes Coffins of the world are everywhere. Even in Boston, Xavier's beloved city. Leo won't be chased away from his hometown. His island. He knows the heart of this place. The same place that welcomed his parents and gave them a life his mother always called "blessed."

But Leo's not stupid enough to tell Xavier that he doesn't have a job anymore. Not until he has a plan. The next step in place for his future.

He doesn't like lying about it—and in Leo's mind, not telling Xavier *is* lying. But right now, it's one more reason for Xavier to insist that this isn't working.

Leo's lying in bed, running all this through his head, when suddenly he gets up. No sense in letting it overwhelm him. Not when there is something he can do about it. Something he's been thinking about ever since he learned that Mrs. Pearse died and his childhood home is vacant.

The tide waits for no man, he thinks while he brushes his teeth and gets dressed.

Sky's door is shut, so he makes a cup of coffee and walks over to Joe's house, even though it's not yet seven in the morning. Joe is standing in his garden, a mug in one hand. A watering can in the other.

"Ah, welcome to the land of unemployed misfits," Joe says, raising his mug. "How'd it feel waking up a free man?"

"Shitty," Leo replies honestly. "Well, not entirely shitty. I won't miss the city. Or the long hours. I'll miss the work. And the paycheck, of course."

"You're one of those morning people, aren't you? A simple 'good' or 'bad' would've done."

Leo smiles. "You got a minute?" he asks. "I need a professional opinion on the state of this house." He nods in the direction of Ann and Brian's house. Joe puts down the watering can, sighs.

"Absolutely. But I'll tell you right now, it's not going to be good news."

They walk to the back of the house, and Joe points to the roof.

"I'll give you the same bad news that I gave Brian when he asked for a list of what needed fixing. You've got maybe one winter left with the roof before it starts leaking on your head. See the gutters there? They're not pitched right, so ten to one, there's water sitting there from when it rained last night. No good. These windows are the originals, so you're heating the outside in the winter and cooling it if you use AC in the summer."

Joe nods to the front, and Leo follows him around the house.

"See up there?" Joe points to a large portion of the front of the house that's missing shingles, only green construction paper covering the bare wood.

"That's from when I fell off the scaffolding. I told Brian to get someone over here to finish the job, and he didn't. You've also got a boiler on its last leg. An electrical system from the dark ages. And a basement with a foundation issue, which is why you get water. It's not the washing machine. It's the crack the size of a canyon on the north side of the house."

Joe pauses, looks at Leo.

"Is that all?" Leo asks.

Joe shakes his head. "Nope. But I think it's probably enough for now."

"Why is it in such bad condition? I mean, look at the places down the street!" He points to Joe's house. And Maggie's. And his old house, the one he grew up in. "They're all the same house."

"Yup. And the people living in them kept up with the work," Joe says, an edge to his voice. "Don't even get me started. I was on Brian all the time. He'd rather have gone fishing than do anything on this house. He finally let me fix the front. And that was a shit show. Should've left well enough alone and minded my own business."

Something in Joe's voice makes Leo pause and look at him. "A shit show how?"

Joe shrugs, his eyes on the house. "Not worth talking about. They were my friends."

He begins to walk away, back to his own house.

"Hey. Wait a second." Leo jogs until he's walking beside Joe. "That's when you fell, isn't it? When you got hurt."

They're in Joe's backyard again. Leo watches while Joe picks up the watering can and fills it with water from the faucet on the side of the house. He brings the can to the tomato plants and tips it over the green leaves.

"You're not going to answer me?" Leo asks.

"I forgot the question."

"Oh, come on, man. I've known you a long time. You don't just say something like that if it's not bothering you. So what— you fell and Brian didn't pay you for the work?"

"We didn't exchange money. I did work on the house when I was in between jobs. Ann sent dinner over the entire time my wife was sick. Wasn't ever going to take a dollar from them." He puts down the watering can.

When he straightens, Leo steps in close to him, holds his

eyes. "I saw something on Sky's face when we found those empty bottles in the basement. And my best friends went over a cliff and nobody seems to know why. If you know anything about what was going on at their house, tell me. As my friend too."

Joe sighs. "I don't know anything. Look, Leo. I'm just a simple guy. Take people at face value. Brian and Ann were always just good people—"

"What happened?"

Joe looks over his shoulder, back at Leo. "This stays between me and you. Got it?"

Leo motions for him to hurry up. Sky will be up any second, and he doesn't want her to wander outside and hear them.

"I'm up on the scaffolding on the second floor, replacing the shingles. It's the middle of the day. Two, three o'clock. Brian's at work. Ann's somewhere in the house. Sky is at school. I'm in front of that window when something inside catches my eye." He points to the second-floor bathroom window. "I know it's the bathroom, so I move. I mean, Ann knows I'm on the scaffolding. But maybe she forgot or something. The shade is up, so I can see right in, eye level. I sidestep a little. Move out of sight. And that's when I hear it. A knock on the glass. I glance over, and through the window I see Ann waving for me to come closer. Her face right up to the glass." Joe clears his throat, pauses, his cheeks suddenly flushed.

"And?" Leo urges. "Ann taps on the window for you to come closer . . ."

Joe swallows. "And I sort of lean in, my eyes up to the glass, thinking she's going to ask me something. But she backed up. Now she's standing in the middle of the bathroom. Just, um, looking at me." He swallows again. "You know . . . smiling." He shuffles his feet, picks at his fingernail.

"Joe—she was smiling at you? What's the big deal—"

"She was naked," Joe whispers, and looks over his shoulder. "And not just out-of-the-shower naked. High heels, posing for me naked. Waving at me to come inside. *Calling* me inside."

"What? No." He shakes his head. "Ann? Ann Pope? She was like, Mother Teresa." He pauses. "Maybe she thought you were Brian."

Joe scowls. "Yeah, maybe her nickname for him was *Joe*. She was looking right at me. This bright lipstick on. Calling my name."

Leo is silent, considering this. "Well, what did you do?" Leo asks finally.

"I fell off the scaffolding, you idiot." He points to the scar on his leg. "That's what happens when a sixty-year-old man is surprised by a naked lady in high heels. I wasn't aware until then that it was an occupational hazard."

Leo doesn't know what to say. He's not trying to picture Ann naked. He's trying to picture her in high heels and lipstick.

The whole scenario is bizarre.

"What happened when you came home? I mean, did she ever mention it?"

"Nope. She came to the hospital. Brought flowers and muffins." He paused. "This is the weird part. She didn't just not mention it—she didn't seem to even remember it. I could tell when she asked how I fell. She said she was downstairs doing the dishes when she heard a thump outside. Not a hint of anything in her eyes." Joe looks at him. "There was a naked lady calling to me in that bathroom. But it wasn't Ann. Not the one we knew."

They stand in silence, both of them turning to look at the house.

Leo's eyes drift to the second floor where the bathroom sits.

He imagines the window looking out at the street. He squints, staring at the image in his thoughts, as though if he looks hard enough, this naked stranger in high heels and lipstick might somehow reappear.

By the time he returns home, Sky is in the den watching cartoons, a bagel in front of her. She smiles when she sees him, and he plants a light kiss on the top of her head.

"What's up today? Want to beach it?" he asks.

She shakes her head. "My easel is done. I want to go out to the cliff and paint a picture. Can I go when I finish my bagel?"

"Are we talking the edge of the cliff or just near it?"

She rolls her eyes. "I'm not going to fall off the cliff. You worry about the weirdest things."

"Maybe I should come with you. You know, just in case."

"In case of what?"

He shrugs. "I don't know. It's through the woods."

She laughs. "There are thirty trees in between us and the ocean. And my tree house is in the middle. Which is actually in my backyard."

He glances out the window. "They said there's a chance of a shower. What if it rains?"

"Then I'll come home."

"Your easel will get wet."

"It's already set up under a tree with branches. Joe brought it out. And he made this box where I can leave the painting while it dries. I don't have to carry anything."

He starts to argue but decides against it. He roamed all over these parts alone when he was a kid. Why shouldn't she be able to walk a straight line through the wooded backyard?

"I'm going upstairs for a second. Stay put, okay? I want to set some ground rules before you leave."

She nods, and he turns, takes the steps two at a time before he forgets what he wanted to do.

In the bathroom, he locks the door and opens the medicine cabinet. In the basement after he and Joe found the whiskey bottles, Sky had said Brian and Ann argued over pills.

He scans the shelves for a prescription bottle. But there's only toothpaste and floss. A shelf with hairbands, a few tampons, small mouthwash bottles, and nail files. Another with so many tiny jars of cream, his eyes blur. In the corner on the bottom shelf, there's a lone bottle of Advil. He shakes one out into his hand and puts it back when he sees the tiny letters imprinted on the pill.

He closes the cabinet and rifles through the vanity drawers, emptying each one onto the counter, shaking out washcloths and hand towels to make sure nothing is concealed. Under the sink, a large basket holds cleaning products, a hair dryer, and an assortment of curling irons.

The small linen closet in the hallway doesn't offer any clues. Just towels and more towels. The only other upstairs room is Sky's bedroom. From the look on her face when she mentioned the pills it's clear that she had no idea *what* they are. Never mind *where* they are.

He walks downstairs to his bedroom, stands in the doorway and looks around. He's still living out of a suitcase. Brian's and Ann's clothes are still in their respective dressers. The closet filled with their coats and dresses, shirts and shoes.

When Leo moved in, he'd slept on an air mattress in the den for weeks. It was only when Sky mentioned that she'd lost her TV room that he considered sleeping in Brian and Ann's room. Even then, it seemed strange to him.

Then one Saturday morning, he'd packed up the air mattress and put it in the closet, and within the hour, Sky was curled up on the couch in the den watching cartoons. And he realized this was probably her routine.

One she'd lost when he moved in.

It seemed cruel to him. Adding insult to injury. He'd grown up with a den just like this. He remembered watching cartoons in the morning, his parents sipping coffee in the other room. So much had changed for her, so quickly.

He decided then and there to try to put as much of her life back together as he could.

He'd gone into Brian and Ann's room, taken a deep breath, and stripped the bed straight down to the bare mattress. He was afraid to breathe. Afraid some scent would trigger a memory. Maybe the cigars Brian smoked. Or the perfume Ann wore.

He threw everything in a trash bag and took it to the dump. Hauled the mattress and the metal frame there too.

Xavier was the shopper between the two of them, and by that night, they had a new queen mattress with freshly washed sheets and brand-new pillows. Of course, Leo was the only one who slept there.

Xavier wouldn't budge from the couch. Not until they had the *talk* with Sky. The one Xavier insisted on having to explain that they were married. And sleeping together.

Leo refused. He couldn't imagine anything more uncomfortable. She knew they were gay. She was the flower girl at their wedding.

Xavier rolled his eyes when Leo said this. "That's it? That's all you have? That doesn't mean she knows we sleep together. That we have *sex*."

"What? Xavier—this is crazy. First of all— there is a *door* on the bedroom. One that locks. Look—she has enough to deal with right now without us giving her the sex talk. You can go there if you want, but I'm out."

"*I* can go there? Oh, that's ripe. *I* have zero experience with kids. No—less than zero—negative. Negative experience. I wasn't even good with kids when I *was* a kid! You see what happens. Sky comes in the room, and I freeze. I have no idea what to say to her. What do ten-year-old girls even *do*? I mean—we have nothing in common."

"You're a person. She is too. Start with that," he told him.

It had been the wrong thing to say. Leo knew it when it passed his lips.

But he had been tired and stressed and overwhelmed. Normally, Leo could handle Xavier's anxiety. Manage his husband's tendency to overanalyze every situation. But there was nothing normal about *this* situation.

After he said it, Xavier had shut down right in front of him. His face went blank, and he turned and walked away. Leo had thought they might talk about it again.

But they never did.

Sky's voice breaks the silence, startling him. He blinks, and she's standing next to him in the bedroom doorway. She looks at him and scans the room.

"Why are you just standing here?" she asks.

He pauses, looks at his suitcase in the corner, open and overflowing.

"We need to talk," he says.

She turns her head slightly, as though she's listening.

Problem is, he has no idea what to say.

21

She follows Leo down the street, waiting for him to say something. He hasn't spoken since they stood in the bedroom doorway and he said, "Come with me."

She thought they might sit at the kitchen table and talk about whatever he wanted to talk about.

Instead, he walked right out the front door, down to the street, and turned left.

Now their footsteps match each other's as they walk.

They pass Joe's house in silence. A sprinkler is on across the street at Maggie's house and Sky skips over, runs through it, the cold water making her gasp.

When she joins Leo again, he reaches out, tugs on a strand of her hair.

"Give me half your energy," he says.

There's a car in the driveway of the house where nobody lives, and she points to it. "Is she here?"

He nods. "I think so," he says, and then steps around Sky so he's on the inside of the sidewalk. Between her and the house. She glances up at him, but his eyes are on the sidewalk, as if nothing happened.

She's not sure what to think about her grandmother living

down the street. Which seems weird to her. It's her *grandmother*.
But she barely remembers her.

"It's weird that she's living there," she says out loud. It feels
good to say it. She doesn't want to pretend it's *not* weird. "How
does she know Mrs. Coffin?"

Leo shrugs. "They're friends, I guess," he says.

"I thought Maggie was her only friend," Sky whispers. She
doesn't like Mrs. Coffin. Never has.

"Speak of the devil," Leo says as Mrs. Coffin backs out of the
driveway of her house across the street.

Leo puts his hand in the air to her, but Mrs. Coffin drives
away without acknowledging him.

"Why didn't she wave back?" she asks.

Leo glances at her. "Maybe she just didn't see me."

She snorts. "She looked right at you."

Leo shoves his hands in his pockets and kicks a pebble out of
the way. "You don't miss a trick."

"My father said she's racist."

Leo stops, faces her. "He said that? To you?"

"No. He said it to my mother once. They got in a fight about
it. My mother said she worked with Mrs. Coffin and she would
know if she was racist. And my father said all she needed to do
was open her eyes to know it."

"Has she ever said anything to you? You know . . . that made
you feel bad?" he asks, walking again.

"No. She's nice to me. Frankie hates her though. She got called
down to the nurse's office because of some form her mother forgot to send in. But when she got there, Mrs. Coffin brought her
in the office alone and shut the door behind them and told Frankie
she should stop dressing like a boy if she didn't want to get teased."

"Frankie gets teased at school?" he asks, stopping again.

Sky laughs. "Frankie? Are you kidding? *Everyone* likes Frankie."

"Why did Agnes—Mrs. Coffin—say that, then?"

"I don't know. I guess she doesn't like the way she dresses."

Leo sighs, starts walking again.

"So Mrs. Coffin invited her to the island?" she asks.

Leo looks over at her. "You know, Sky—I'm going to be honest. I think Mrs. Coffin would like your grandmother to be in your life. I'm not saying it's right or wrong. It just is. I don't know what happened between your mother and grandmother. But I do know that we have to see your grandmother at some point. Like soon. I could be there the whole time. I won't leave. Even if she wants me to."

"How much do I have to see her?"

"Not all the time. I'll call her and we'll see her. Then you call the shots from there. Deal?"

She nods. "Where are we going anyway?" she asks, looking around.

They're at the end of the street, standing in front of the last house on the dead end.

Leo looks at her then at the house in front of them. "Here, actually."

"Mrs. Pearse's house?"

"It's my house. I was renting it to Mrs. Pearse. Come on, let's go in." He starts to walk up the path but stops when he notices she isn't next to him.

She's still standing on the sidewalk.

"What's wrong?" he asks her.

"I'm not going in there."

He looks at the house, then at her. "Why?"

"Me and Frankie don't even come here on Halloween. Mrs.

Pearse would sit on the porch in her rocking chair like a real live witch. It's probably haunted."

Leo laughs, waves for her to come with him. But she crosses her arms and stays where she is.

"You're not afraid of anything," he says.

"Except Mrs. Pearse's ghost. She was mean when she was alive. Who knows what she's like dead?"

Leo tilts his head, waits.

She steps back and leans against the tree behind her.

"All right," he says finally. "Will you walk around back with me? Can I at least show you something?"

She eyes him. "Is it inside?"

"You don't have to step foot in the house. I promise." He waves for her to follow him, and she walks up the steps, makes a wide path around the house to the backyard.

Leo has his back to her, looking at something in the distance. The lawn is overgrown, tall grass stretching out and sloping down to a line of trees. She can't stop looking over her shoulder at the old house.

"Come here," Leo says, and she walks forward to where he's standing, still glancing behind her.

When she's right next to him, she turns.

The view in front of her makes her blink. The ocean sparkles in the distance, only visible from their spot on the lawn.

She doesn't know what to say. The ocean has always done that to her. Left her with a loss for words.

Leo looks down at her. "For years, I wanted to knock this place down and build something for my parents. The back of the house all glass, so you can always see the ocean."

"Why didn't you?"

"Lots of reasons. Money, for one. And my father was a stubborn old goat." He smiles. "He liked his house the way it was. I'd say, what about the view, Dad? And he'd look at my mother and tell me that she was the only view he needed."

She looks back at the house now too. Suddenly, it doesn't seem so scary.

"You can build it now," she says.

"If you want, *we* can build it now. But it's not that simple—"

She turns and looks at the ocean while he talks. She's only half listening because she already knows what he's going to say. That they either move here or stay in her home. The only one she's ever known.

They can't live in both. It's one or the other.

Leo says that he's sorry she has to choose. She thinks it's the craziest thing to apologize for.

For the first time in her whole life, she gets to decide what happens next.

After they eat lunch, she convinces Leo to let her go to the cliff to paint. The air is cool even though it's the middle of August, the sun only peeking out now and then from behind thick white clouds.

The backpack on her shoulder is heavy as she walks past the tree house and sees the first glimpse of blue water far off in the distance. Leaves snap under her footsteps, and her heart speeds up, remembering the strange clapping that had startled her and Frankie the night they'd lit the sparklers.

They hadn't talked about it again. After Frankie said it was nothing. And it was nothing.

Nothing at all.

She repeats this in her mind as she walks. Makes a song out of it that she steps in time to until she's suddenly at the end of the path, a wide rock ledge spreading out in front of her. She and Joe had set up the easel earlier in the week. Joe had secured it to a tree set back from the ledge, the tall, thick branches above creating her very own canopy.

There's a wooden box on the ground at the base of the tree. After they'd put the last coat of stain on the easel, Joe had a million questions. How was she going to carry her paints to the cliff? Where would the painting dry? What about paintbrushes?

She wasn't able to answer him. In her mind, the easel was the first thing she needed. And that was still drying in the corner.

The next day, they met in his garage. Joe had told her he'd help her set up the easel on the cliff. But when she walked over to where he was standing, he pointed to a box on the worktable. It was wooden. The size of a briefcase.

When he opened it, the lid rested straight on its hinges.

"What do you think? It's an old humidor I picked up some-where. Thought it was kind of neat, but I don't smoke, so it's just been sitting out here. After you left, I was thinking about how you were going to get a wet painting back to your house and I saw this. Put a couple coats of stain on it so it'll stand up to some light weather. But I figure if we tuck it under a tree, won't be a problem." He closed the lid, ran his hand over the smooth top. "What do you think?"

Sky touched the box, lifted the lid, put her nose to the wood, and breathed in.

"I think it's great," she said after a minute.

Joe lifted an eyebrow. "Great? Shucks—I was only going for not bad." He clapped once. "All right. We've got work to do."

Before he could walk away, she leaned forward, rested her head against his shirt, and put an arm around his back.

"Thanks, Joe," she said.

"You're doing me a favor putting this to good use. No thanks necessary," he told her, straightening under her arm. But she didn't move, and he put his hand on the back of her head, his fingers gently tapping her braid in a way that reminded her of a mother comforting a baby.

A drop of rain lands on her shoulder, and she looks up, waits for the next one. But the sun slips out from behind a cloud, and the day is suddenly bright again.

She gets started before the rain changes its mind and returns.

She reaches into the backpack and pulls out the supplies Frankie lent her before she left for camp. Small tubes of paint, a handful of paintbrushes, a small water bucket, and an oval wooden palette. She digs out a water bottle and pours some in the bucket, then pulls out a pad of paper and clips a fresh sheet to the easel.

Next, she squeezes a circle of each paint color on the palette, chooses the right size paintbrush, and looks at the blank paper.

She takes in the view in front of her. The harbor off to the left, way down where the ferry's come in. So far off in the distance, the boats are only specks in the water. There's the lighthouse to her right. The outline of a seagull perched on the railing.

But she's not good enough to paint that. Not yet. Not the way she wants to, with the water and the sky not blending to make a blue mess, which is what happened when she tried to paint it earlier in the summer when Frankie brought her paints to the tree house and they'd walked out to the cliff for inspiration.

"What am I doing wrong?" she'd whined to Frankie.

Frankie had glanced over at the painting. "Start smaller. Like, one thing. Not the whole ocean with a big boat in the middle."

"It's a lighthouse. Not a boat. And that's the sky on top. Not the ocean. Why would I paint the ocean in the sky?"

Frankie took the pad from her, flipped the page, and handed it back to her. "Pick one. Ocean. Sky. Lighthouse. Just one."

Now she looks out at the water, dips her paintbrush and begins.

By the time she's done, the sun is low on the horizon, and her stomach is growling. There's a lighthouse on the paper in front of her. Not a great one, but not a boat either. She can't get the color right—the shade of the red stripe through the middle looks pink—and the more she plays with it, the worse it gets.

She puts the painting in the box to dry and cleans up her mess, using the water to wash the paint off the palette and wrapping it in the small towel she brought with her.

It's not until she's walking home, past the tree house, that a shiver goes through her, a feeling suddenly that she's not alone. She keeps walking, turns in a circle, but there's nothing but trees and bushes.

Not a single sound besides her own footsteps.

22

She tells herself she's going to stay away. Promises herself! And then, as if drawn by an irresistible force, she finds herself among the trees.

Waiting. Watching.

It's not hard to be invisible.

A thick line of arborvitae runs the length of the property. Even when she slips through the massive green hedge, there's a forest between her and the tree house. Scrub oak and blueberry bushes, wild and overgrown, line the path where the girls walk. Tall spruce and wide-trunked elms conceal her—not difficult these days. She's thinner than she's ever been in her life. Even when she was in her modeling heyday, she still had breasts. Skin on her bones.

Now she's a skeleton in the mirror. A ghost walking the earth.

But she still has some strength. She'll know when it's time to end her life. It's why she's here. She'll do it her way. It's just a matter of when. She'll choose when she steps off the cliff. She won't let herself get too weak.

She wants to see the girl again. She leaves the house in the afternoon, hides in her spot by the tree house. But nothing. Just her and the birds. She sits and waits, but the mosquitoes chase her away. So she retraces her steps, walks on the farm property to the cliff, leans against the massive tree on the edge, and looks out at the water.

It would be easy to step off the cliff right now, fall through the air to her end. But she's not ready yet. Then she hears it. A noise down the path. She ducks behind the trees, follows the sound.

When she finally sees the girl, the sight brings her to her knees. She crawls quietly behind a large holly bush, the sharp leaves nipping her hand when she peers through.

But she doesn't care.

The view in front of her is all that matters.

23

August is the month of reckoning. That's how she comes to think of it.

Just her and her miserable self, trying to sort out what's become of her life.

With Leo out of work, she doesn't see Sky as much. Pete's on a surfing vacation in Costa Rica. Without her, of course.

A guys' trip is what he called it. She hasn't spoken to Agnes since they argued in the driveway.

As the middle of August settles in, Maggie's alone. She's always hated to be alone.

The first day Pete left, she fidgeted. Tried to think of ways to fill her time.

Then she went to the beach, but it wasn't very much fun without Sky or Joe. She'd asked them to come, but they were in the middle of a woodworking project.

She went for walks then stopped when they felt like a chore. All her body really wanted to do was lie down. She tried to force herself out of her awful mood. She picked up a handful of books at the library, but when she sat to read, her mind wandered, and she found herself on the same page twenty minutes later.

She could have argued that she was depressed. Had her doctor give her some meds. And she probably was depressed. But there was a reason behind it. She could feel it just waiting there, begging for her to name it.

Finally she gave in. Forced herself to just sit with her thoughts and face the unpleasant reality that she was unhappy.

That's where she stays as the August heat descends on Ichabod.

Her first thought when she opens her eyes in the morning is that she's unhappy. With her marriage. Her life.

Herself.

Sweet Maggie.

This is the person she frowns at now in the mirror. Stares at until the serious look on her face doesn't make her insides squirm.

Angry is ugly. Unladylike, the voice in her head insists.

Still, she looks at her reflection. Allows the words to fill the room until they fade.

By the time Pete is supposed to come home, she's worked through some of her anger. There's a whole pad of paper with stuff she'd like to discuss with him.

Maybe they can fix things.

Or that's what she's thinking when she gets out of bed on Friday.

Pete's landing on the mainland late this afternoon. It will take him several hours to get home from the city. Which is fine with her. She's not even sure what she wants to say to him. Or she knows what to say, but not a clue how to say it so he'll hear her.

She walks downstairs, makes coffee and opens the windows. The day is warm, but she's tired of the AC. The hum is too loud for her already distracted mind.

She opens the front door, grabs the newspaper from the stoop, and walks to the mailbox. She's sorting through the mail, the paper tucked under her arm, when she hears someone shout her name.

She jumps and turns to see a woman walking over to her.

"You must be Maggie," the woman says in a softer voice when she reaches her.

She knows it's Lillian.

Yet she's not what Maggie expected. Ann had been so blond. So preppy. The woman has dark hair and tanned skin. She's dressed casually in jeans and flip-flops with some sort of stone medallion around her neck that glints in the sunlight. *Artsy* is the first word that comes to mind.

"I am," she says. "I'm guessing you're Lillian?"

"Yes. I didn't mean to startle you. It's so quiet here; I'm used to shouting in the city." She laughs self-consciously while Maggie tries to reconcile this Lillian with the Lillian she'd conjured in her mind.

She pictured a mean old lady. Uptight and rigid, wearing pearls around a high-necked, old-fashioned, shapeless dress.

"You're Agnes's friend, right? She said you went to college together."

Maggie doesn't answer. Instead, she thinks about how to say what she wants to say. It's best to just say it. Pretending everything is fine when it's not is what she did with Pete all last year. And look where they are now.

"I'm very close to Sky. And Leo. I don't feel right standing here making small talk without telling you that I think it was wrong of you to come here."

She braces herself for Lillian's response. Expects to see the woman's expression turn from placid to something else. Indignant. Offended. Possibly even angry.

Lillian simply nods. "I know you're upset that I'm here," she says. "Agnes mentioned it."

Maggie snorts. "I'm sure she did. Though I wouldn't know. We haven't spoken since we argued about it."

Lillian winces. "That makes me feel worse. Especially since I've been avoiding Agnes." She lowers her voice, glances at Agnes's house. "I didn't realize when I accepted her offer to stay here that it was conditional. As in—she would pop in *all the time*. She kept talking about me being born here and how I had a right to the island and how we were connected because of our ancestors. I haven't lived here since I was ten. The island has changed so much. Honestly, I don't even really remember it. Anyway—I have to run. I just wanted to say that I hope you'll give me a chance. I'm not here to cause any harm. And I hope you work it out with Agnes. I've had a couple of people in my life slip away from me that I regret letting go."

Maggie wonders if she's talking about Ann.

"I know you and Ann had difficulties. I'm sure it must be hard now that she's gone. You must want to take back those years."

Lillian is turning to leave, but she stops, looks at her. "That wasn't my choice. Sometimes even our children make decisions that we don't support. Can't support without changing who we are as a person. No—I regret a lot of things that happened between me and Ann, but I can't take responsibility for her absence in my life." She puts up a hand as a goodbye. Turns and walks away.

Maggie blinks, and watches her go, wondering when it was exactly that her life decided to become a puzzle. One that spilled from the box onto the table. Pieces scattering everywhere. Perhaps never to be found.

*   *   *

Back inside the house, she takes a cup of coffee and the paper to the table on the patio. She sits, blows on the coffee, too hot to take a sip, and spreads the paper in front of her.

The front page makes her blink in disbelief. Not at the headline: "Summer in Full Swing on Ichabod."

No—it's the collage of photos below that draw her in. One in particular.

One of Pete.

He's on the ferry, leaning over the snack bar counter with a young woman's wrist in his hand. She's obviously the galley help. A name tag on her shirt Maggie can't make out.

The caption below the picture reads: *Police Chief Pete Thompson to the rescue after a galley staff member, Anna, cuts her finger.*

Maggie brings the paper closer to her face, studies the picture. Anna is obviously okay despite her injury—a coy smile on her face, directed at Pete. She's a young woman—early twenties perhaps. Pretty and fresh-faced.

Her arm is being held in the air by Pete, who's leaning over the counter in such a way that his lips are nearly touching Anna's neck.

The picture is familiar, even though she's never seen it before.

She closes her eyes, remembers the last day of school and her conversation with Agnes. How Agnes had wanted to show her a picture of Pete on the ferry.

There had been a rainbow.

She opens her eyes. Studies the photo. Sure enough, there it is. Hazy and faded, a rainbow directly over Pete's shoulder.

Weeks ago, Maggie had seen an open call for pictures from residents for this feature.

Send in your fun-in-the-sun shots!

There is nothing fun about this picture. Not one person would notice the rainbow—even Maggie has a hard time making it out.

She knows that Agnes sent in the picture. Confirms it when she sees who wrote the feature. *Amelia Dickinson.* She recognizes the woman's name. She's heard more than once from Agnes how Amelia sings beautifully at the church services.

She pulls the paper so close it almost grazes her reading glasses, her eyes on Pete.

The look on her husband's face as he gazes at Anna. She knows that look, and it guts her.

She's been married to her husband for twenty-seven years. She knows every one of his looks. Although this one she hasn't seen in years.

A decade, maybe.

Pete's looking at Anna with desire. So raw and feral, it jumps off the page and lands on Maggie, claws at her until she's ripped open, torn apart, the assault too damaging to ignore.

More damaging than the affair that *wasn't really an affair* with his secretary. Or perhaps it's just the thing that pushes her too far—the thing that makes her get up from the table.

In the spare bedroom, she digs a suitcase out of the closet, the largest one she can find.

Then it's to the master, where she carefully empties his dresser, packing each item in the suitcase carefully, methodically, as though she's sending a child off to camp. One of her sons off to college.

Sweet Maggie.

But inside, a fury has unleashed.

One that's been waiting to be free all her life.

*　　　*　　　*

It's dark when she hears the car pull in the driveway. She's at the kitchen table with a glass of champagne in front of her. She found the bottle in the refrigerator when she was making dinner.

She'd bought it to celebrate their anniversary months ago. Then Pete had called to say he had to work late. Apparently, they hadn't found a reason to open it since.

Now, it seems fitting to drink it alone.

She hears the side door open and close. Pete walks into the kitchen, puts his bag down when he sees her.

"Why is it so dark in here?" he asks, flipping on the switch. She blinks, holds her hand up. He doesn't bother to turn the knob to dim the light. "What are you doing sitting in the dark?"

Hello, she thinks. *Nice to see you too.*

"Drinking," she replies. She takes a gulp and notices her glass is almost empty. She picks up the bottle, refills the flute until the liquid threatens to spill over the top.

Pete stands in the corner and doesn't speak.

There was a time he would have walked into this scene and joined her. She remembers the days when the kids were younger, and she'd finally get them to bed and she'd sit in the kitchen with a glass of wine, a candle on the table. He'd sit across from her, take her leg and put it on his lap, work his fingers into the soles of her feet.

Then the kids were teenagers, out late every weekend, and Pete would come home from work and they'd sit at the table, one eye on the clock while they sipped a beer and talked.

Now, they haven't seen each other in weeks. They've talked on the phone a handful of times. Halting, strained conversations that made her wish she hadn't called him.

She knows from his expression, his posture, that he's wary of what she's going to say.

"Come sit," she says.

He walks over, pulls out the chair, and perches on the edge, as though he might want to make a quick exit.

"I'd kiss you, but you seem sort of . . ."

"Sort of what?" Maggie asks.

"I don't know. Bothered."

She smiles at the word. Pete doesn't use the word *angry* when it comes to her. *Upset*, he'll say. *Bothered* is acceptable. *Angry* is too much. Always has been.

"You made the paper," she tells him, points to his picture on the front page.

He frowns, looks down at it, then up at her. "You'd think they could find something more interesting than that."

"I find it interesting," Maggie says, then pauses.

How to say this?

"Have you kissed her?" she asks calmly, pointedly.

His head snaps up. "Have I—what?"

"Have you kissed her?"

"Maggie. You're acting crazy. That's a silly thing to ask."

Silly old Maggie. Such a good girl.

"Yes or no?"

"I'm not going to justify that with an answer. She works for me!"

Maggie laughs. She can't *not* laugh. "Your secretary worked for you too."

"I can't do this tonight—"

She slams the paper on the table so hard, the legs shake. Pete freezes.

She holds the paper up. "Have you kissed her?" she asks again.

It's not what she planned to ask him. Nothing has gone as planned since he walked in the door. She wanted to stay calm. But she's shaking with anger, her hands trembling when she sets the paper on the table.

"What do you want to hear, Maggie? That I had sex with my secretary? And kissed this girl—hell, had sex with her too. Why not? I'm that much of a scumbag. Well, I didn't. And I'm not. And this picture. Christ. It's just me and some girl who—"

"Who you're obviously attracted to! Look at your face! I remember that look. Granted I'm not some young, perky thing like she is. But I was once. And I remember that look. I remember it very well."

Pete puts his head in his hands. His forearms are tanned, thick. A part of her wants to run her hands over his muscled back. A part of her will always want the man she married.

But he's not sitting in front of her.

Pete sits up. Something catches his eye and he turns. Looks at the suitcase in the doorway.

"Is that mine?" he asks, and she nods.

Her insides are twisted. Her voice caught.

He stands up, throws his bag over his shoulder. He walks over and picks up the suitcase. Then he's gone. Crossing the kitchen and out the door, closing it gently behind him.

As though leaving has been on his mind for quite some time.

24

Leo doesn't bring up selling the house again. He can't even settle on the right decision.

The small Cape is a money pit. But it's also Sky's childhood home. The one that holds memories of her parents. Who is he to ask her to do anything more than what she's already done?

Which is to put one step in front of the other. Try not to get buried under the weight of everything she's lost.

He wishes he could talk about it with Xavier. But he still hasn't told him he's out of work. They speak on the phone. Text here and there. But it's all mundane conversation. Xavier replies with one-word answers—if he even replies at all.

How are you? *Fine.*

Good day? *Yup.*

Miss you.

That one never gets a reply. Still, Leo texts it. Because he does miss him. So much it feels as though a part of him is missing.

He's made it clear to Xavier that living on Ichabod is permanent—at least until Sky graduates from high school. But even he knows that renovating his childhood home—moving there with Sky—is life changing.

He can't deny his heart pumps faster when he thinks about it.

It's a dream, really.

One he'd given up on after his father died and he pretended to be someone he wasn't. With a woman he didn't even know. Right there, in his childhood bed.

He doesn't remember her name. Only that she was a childhood friend of Ann's, visiting for the weekend. Brian hadn't even met her before. And they all got drunk after the funeral. And he woke up the next morning, hungover and naked and at a loss for what to say to this beautiful creature lying against him.

He ended up telling her the truth. That he was who he was. And he knew what he wanted. And even though the sex had been great (he actually didn't remember it)—he was in love with another person.

A man, to be exact.

She laughed. Said it was no big deal. And then she left, and he never saw her again. Never even told Brian and Ann about it, he was so ashamed.

But it was a big deal to Leo.

He felt as though he'd dishonored his parents. The two people who loved and accepted him for who he was. The first people he'd come out to when he was in college. The ones who had looked at him, so concerned across the table, while tears slipped down his face and he'd blurted out that he was gay.

"Is that all?" his father had said. A hand to his chest. "You scared the life out of me—I thought you were sick or something!"

He'd asked so much of them and given so little in return. He knew they'd wanted grandchildren. But it wasn't part of Leo's plan. Everyone knew that it wasn't part of Leo's plan. Brian and Ann never even asked him to babysit. They'd tease him—say they didn't want to cramp his style.

He finds it mystifying now that they've left their only child to him. But he knows it's probably a matter of who was left to do the job. Brian's parents were dead. His only brother was an economics professor in Germany. Ann was an only child. Her father died when she was a toddler. And she hadn't spoken to her mother in years.

Crazy Lillian, he calls her now in his head. Even though that isn't fair. He doesn't know her. Still, the fact that she moved here at all, free house or not, makes him uneasy.

He's been avoiding dealing with it, but just minutes ago, she'd driven past him while he got the mail and waved at him, all smiles, as though they were old pals.

Now or never, he thought to himself.

The tide waits for no man.

He'd gone inside and told Sky to stay put—he'd be back in a couple of minutes. She was watching TV and didn't take her eyes off the screen, just nodded to show she heard him. He walked out of the house and down the street before he changed his mind.

Now he's listening to the doorbell chime, wondering what the hell he's going to say when he hears footsteps, and a minute later, the door swings open.

But it's not Lillian in front of him. It's Agnes. She raises her eyebrows, pulls the door closer to her body, shielding his view of the interior of the house.

"Leo," she says, and stops, as if that's all the greeting she can possibly muster.

"Agnes," he replies. "Is Lillian here?"

"Is she expecting you?" she asks in a scolding tone of voice. As though she knows perfectly well that Lillian is not expecting him.

"Nope," he tells her, and smiles. But inside, his heart speeds up. This woman unnerves him. Maybe because she was the school nurse when he was Sky's age and she always seemed terrifyingly large and deeply angry. He remembers going to her office to get a Band-Aid for a paper cut, and she'd sighed, a long, bothered noise.

"Be more careful next time," she lectured, holding out the thin bandage as though it weighed more than she could hold. "Who knew a nursing degree would mean I get to spend my days dealing with phantom stomachaches, runny noses, and paper cuts?" she muttered, waving him out of her office.

She hasn't changed much since then. The same pursed lips. Haughty demeanor.

"She's busy unpacking," Agnes tells him. "I don't want to disturb her."

"It won't take long," he insists. "Plus, you're not disturbing her. I am."

She doesn't move, just frowns deeper at him. Leo's wondering if she's going to slam the door in his face when he hears a voice coming from behind Agnes. Lillian's face appears in the small space between Agnes's body and the door frame.

"Leo—come in," she says brightly. "I was hoping you'd stop by." She steps closer, but Agnes refuses to move.

There's an awkward moment when nobody speaks while Lillian peers at him over Agnes's shoulder.

"Agnes. Open the door," Lillian says in a voice that reminds him of the tone she'd used the day he'd met her on the dock, and she told him she wasn't interested in the past. Just the future.

Agnes opens the door, brushes past him, stomps down the steps and turns. "Of course, I want you to feel welcome to have visitors, Lillian. But please remember there are valuables—island artifacts—throughout the home."

"Of course," Lillian says. "Although I don't think Leo's here to trash the place." She smiles, but there's a flash of irritation on her face. If Agnes notices, she doesn't show it.

"Obviously," Agnes says. "It's just that I've been asked to be the town historian with Mrs. Pearse passing away. It's my job to make sure the island's history is preserved."

He watches her turn and stomp away. "Bye," he calls out, but she doesn't respond.

"Please, come in. I feel like I should apologize even though it's not my house," Lillian says over her shoulder as he follows her down the hallway and into the kitchen. "Agnes has me afraid to touch anything. I've never lived in a historic house."

"There's nothing historic about it. I grew up next door. They're all just old capes built in the forties. She thinks it's historic because she's kept it a shrine to her parents. Besides the church and the women's club, you're the only one who's been in here since they died."

"That's pretty obvious." She looks around the dated kitchen. "I insisted on paying a rental fee after it became clear that *free* to Agnes means she can pop in whenever she wants. At least now, she knocks before she comes over. Three times a day. Would you like some tea? I have muffins too. That bakery in town is to die for. Delicious but deadly on the waistline." She grins, winks at him.

This is not what Leo had expected. He's not sure what he expected. Perhaps that she would be influenced by Agnes because she's a guest in her house. That Agnes would convince her that Sky shouldn't be with Leo. He had mentally prepared for this to be a contentious discussion.

"No, thank you. I only have a minute. Look—Lillian. Can we back up here? We agreed to meet on the dock, and frankly, you seemed great. And you seemed to understand that I wanted to

move slow. And then, just like that, you're here. On this street."
He leans against the counter, folds his arms. "I didn't get a clear
answer at the Fourth of July party as to how this came about.
Explain it to me, please."

She gives him a half smile that fades quickly. "I'm not sure
I can."

He waits. He's not leaving until he gets an answer. There's a
girl watching cartoons down the street who needs him to be the
type of man who won't leave without an answer.

"I feel like you think it's some sinister plot." Lillian pulls out a
chair from the kitchen table and plops down. "And you know—
it's not. If anything, it's pathetic."

She runs her hands through her hair and sighs, looks at him.
"First, I lost my job. I was a counselor at a house for girls with
mental-health issues. There was a girl in the overnight program.
A teenager. But older—wiser. Manipulative. She reminded me
so much of my own dau—" She pauses, shakes her head. "Of a
younger Ann. I wanted to get this kid to see what her choices
were doing to the people around her. Her poor parents. It was
unprofessional of me." She threw up her hands. "And then it was
like dominoes. Lose the job. Landlord hikes the rent. Boyfriend
decides he's not into monogamy, as it turns out. And out of the
blue, I get a call from Agnes, inviting me to a Fourth of July party.
When I got here, we started talking. She asked me about my life,
and it all just came out. She asked if I wanted to stay here for a
bit. To get back on my feet. I've always wanted to come back
here. And I actually thought it was a nice offer. A genuine offer."

"And now?"

Lillian closes one eye. "Let's just say I'm feeling as though
I was invited here under false pretenses. She's not exactly shy
about telling me I should be Sky's legal guardian."

"Because you're her grandmother?" He stands up straighter, crosses his arms. "Or because you're not gay? Or black?"

Lillian doesn't flinch at the question. Her expression tells him she's asked herself these same things. "I don't know. She's never said anything to me. But then again, I made it clear when I moved in that I thought you were wonderful—I think you're wonderful."

"But still, you're here, Lillian. You must have known this would complicate things."

"They're already complicated, Leo."

"I find it hard to believe that you didn't come here to be closer to Sky—"

"Of course I did. I came to be closer to Sky and the daughter I wanted to be close to but wasn't. I want to see what her life *looked* like with my very own eyes. Ann didn't want me here. But I wanted to be here. I wanted things to be different between us."

He wants to leave it alone. But he has to know what happens next. "And what about what Sky wants? Have you thought of that?"

"Yes, I have. And it's simple. I'd like her to get to know me. And I'd like to get to know her."

"Which is exactly the problem, Lillian. Sky doesn't feel the same way. She's asked me to be with you when you see her. And if you think I'm going to force her to see you alone, you're mistaken."

Lillian stands, puts her arms across her body. "I don't have a problem with that. I think when she gets to know me, she'll change her mind," she says confidently. "I'm glad she feels as close to you as she does."

He nods. "The two of us have settled in. We're good."

Lillian tilts her head. "The two of you? I thought you were married?"

"I am." He clears this throat. "I meant the three of us. Me, Xavier, and Sky. We're all doing good."

She nods slowly, but he can tell she doesn't believe him. Or maybe it's just that he doesn't like to lie.

"So you're taking the summer off?" he asks, changing the subject.

"Off? Oh, no. I'd go crazy if I didn't work. I actually just heard about a job at a pet-boarding place in town. In the large-dog room. Hopefully the barking doesn't make me crazy."

He looks up when she says crazy, remembering what he'd wanted to ask her.

"I know you said you don't like to talk about the past. But Sky overheard Brian say that Ann wasn't taking her medication. Not that it matters—I mean, she's gone. But at some point, I don't know if Sky will want to talk about it. The more information I have, the better. Do you know if she was sick?"

Lillian blinks. Her face blank. He doesn't think she's going to answer him when she shakes her head.

"I wouldn't know," she says quietly. "I'm sorry."

He nods. "Right. I should get back to Sky," he says and turns to leave.

"Wait. Maybe you guys can come for dinner? I make a mean lasagna." She gives him a hopeful look.

He hesitates. "Look—Sky is my first concern. I think it's best if you see her on her own turf. I want her to feel safe. And comfortable. Keep it casual. I'll do a cookout at our house."

"Of course," Lillian says. "I think we both want the same things. But if Sky asks to see me, I hope you won't stand in the way. I'm sure I have some rights. Legally. I'm not expecting it will come to that."

She says this politely. But there's a hint of that tone in her voice again. The resolve.

He says goodbye, leaves her standing in the kitchen. His hand is on the knob when he hears his name.

He turns to see her standing in the hallway.

"I wasn't a very good mother. When Ann was Sky's age, I was always out somewhere. She was left with babysitters often. I got sober when she was in high school. But I missed a lot. Probably didn't notice things that I should have." She leans her head against the wall, closes her eyes. When she looks at him, her eyes are wet. "I'm looking forward to a do-over. Sober this time. Anyway. I'm sorry I'm not more help to you about Ann. I'm really sorry."

He nods, slips out the door. Not entirely sure if she is apologizing to him. Or her late daughter.

The one whose life she came here to see with her very own eyes.

25

It's another week before she can go back to the cliff to finish her painting. The rain kept her away two days. Then Leo made her go for her checkups at the doctor and the dentist the next day, and by the time they got home, she wasn't exactly feeling all that creative.

Then she decided she might as well wait for Frankie to come home so they could go out to the cliff together.

Which is only one of the reasons her heart sinks when Frankie's mother's car pulls in the driveway and she opens the front door, waving wildly even though she can't actually see Frankie through the tinted windows of the huge SUV.

Then Frankie gets out and it takes her a minute to see that Frankie is missing an arm.

Or not exactly missing. It's just not hanging by her side where it should be. Instead, it's in a sling across her body.

"I broke it, and I don't want to talk about it, so don't ask," Frankie grumbles, walking past her into the house.

"What do you mean, *don't ask*? Are you crazy—that's your painting hand!" She follows Frankie to her bedroom and shuts the door.

Frankie plops on the bed, her body bouncing off the mattress.

"Exactly. Don't remind me." After a minute, Frankie sits up, looks at Sky, forces a smile. "Hi, by the way. I missed you."

"Yeah, me too. Now talk. There's no way you're not telling me what happened."

Frankie sighs. "That's the thing. There's nothing to tell. It's not some great story."

"Who says it has to be a great story?"

"Maybe not great. But at least not embarrassing." Frankie plops down again, throws her good arm over her face.

Sky sits on the bed next to her, speechless. Frankie doesn't get embarrassed. Or not that Sky's ever seen.

"Like on a scale of one to ten. How embarrassing?"

"Eleven and a half. Maybe a twelve." Frankie sits up. "I fell out of my bunk."

"I thought you weren't allowed to be on the top bunk anymore."

"I wasn't! It was the stupid lower bunk. My feet must have caught in the sheet or something. I woke up, and I was flat on my face, my arm underneath me."

Sky winces, imagining it. She's lost count of Frankie injuries from sleepwalking. Last year, she came home from camp with a concussion because she'd fallen out of the top bunk. The year before that, a fat lip and a chipped tooth. Then they got smart and put her on the bottom bunk.

Apparently, that was just as dangerous.

"Now I can't paint. Can't surf. I'm not even allowed to go in the water." Frankie is close to tears. Sky is disappointed too—she's been waiting all month to go surfing with Frankie. But she forces her voice to be light and cheery.

"The waves have been awful," she lies. Truthfully, they've been the best she's ever seen. "Besides, I've been dying to show you something. Come on."

She stands and motions for Frankie to follow her. Frankie stares at her before she finally stands up, and trudges behind Sky.

They walk outside to the path leading to the tree house. Frankie is quiet while they walk through the woods. Sky fills in the silence, telling her everything that's happened since she left.

How Xavier hasn't been back to the island since Frankie left, and Joe and Leo found a bunch of her father's empty bottles down in the basement, and Leo seemed surprised that her parents fought, and now Leo wants to sell the house and build a new one down the street where he grew up—

"Wait—what house?" Frankie interrupts.

"Old Mrs. Pearse's. It's Leo's."

Frankie stops. "The haunted one? You told him no, right? Because if you move there, we're having every sleepover at my house. No way I'm stepping foot in there."

"He said we'd knock it down. Plus, you can see the water out back."

"I'm skipping camp next year. All I did was learn how to draw noses and fall out of my bunk and break my arm."

"Noses like on your face?"

Frankie starts walking again. "What other kind is there?"

"I don't know. Maybe an animal's nose. Like a dog or a bird."

"A dog has a snout. Birds have beaks." Frankie laughs.

She rolls her eyes. "At least you're smiling now. Know-it-all."

"Where are we going?" Frankie asks.

They're at the cliff now, and Sky steps onto the path that runs along the rocky edge.

"Look." She points to the tree, the easel leaning against it.

Frankie's eyes light up. She walks over and runs her hand down the wood, looks at Sky.

"Joe?" she asks, and Sky nods.

"He also made a box so we can leave our paintings out here to dry."

Sky leans down and flips open the top of the box, relieved that the painting wasn't ruined in the storm earlier this week. Joe said it was weather-tight, but the wind and rain had almost blown the shutters off the house, and she worried the box had flown away in the gusts.

She picks it up and turns the painting to face Frankie before she even looks at it. It's not very good—she remembers she'd painted only the lighthouse and even then, the railing wasn't quite right. But she wants to get better. And Frankie can help her.

"See?" she says to Frankie. "I followed your advice. Started with just one thing."

Frankie stares at the painting, glances up at Sky, then back down at the paper. "Wow. That's um—you're really . . ." Her voice trails off.

Sky sighs. "You said to keep trying. So, I'm trying—"

"Talented," Frankie interrupts. "I was about to say talented."

Sky lets out a snort. "Don't be sarcastic." She shoves the painting in the box and reaches in her backpack, digging out a fresh piece of paper. "That's why I have you to teach me. And what's better is that your arm is broken, so you can't just do it for me like you usually do—"

She stands, speechless.

Frankie has dug her painting out of the box and is holding it up. But it's not Sky's picture. Not all of it, at least.

The lighthouse is the only thing she recognizes. And even that is different—the railing the perfect shade.

Now there is an ocean surrounding the lighthouse, so deep and layered, she wants to reach out and touch it. She can almost feel the water slipping through her fingers. The salt air on her skin.

Clouds hang above, and she instinctively looks up, and yes—they are as real on the paper as they are before her eyes. Brilliant white in shapes that change and shift depending on how she gazes at the picture.

She can't find her voice. She just looks at Frankie and swallows.

"What?" Frankie says, looking from Sky to the painting. "I'm not kidding. You're really talented. This is really good."

Sky shakes her head.

"Oh, all right. I get it. You think I'm jealous or something. Look—it's amazing, okay. I always knew you had it in you—"

"That's not mine," Sky whispers. Her head is spinning. She leans over, puts her hands on her knees, breathes deep.

"What do you mean it's not yours?"

Sky straightens. "I mean *this* is mine." She points to the lighthouse. "That's all I painted. And I couldn't get it right—the railing was off, and the colors were wrong. So, I put it in the box. I haven't been out here since."

Frankie screws up her face. "Maybe Joe did it," she offers.

"Joe helped me make the easel. He kept saying he can't draw a straight line."

"Leo?" Frankie asks, but Sky can already tell Frankie knows he didn't do it.

Something occurs to Sky, and a shiver runs through her.

"Remember that clapping we heard?" she whispers, stepping closer to Frankie. "What if it's him. Or her. Them! What if they're *watching* us?"

Frankie looks over her shoulder. "Cut it out with the creepy voice. You're freaking me out."

"*I'm* freaking you out? There's someone following us, and you're blaming me?"

"Okay, stop. First of all—nobody is following anyone. You always have to go to the worst-case scenario—"

"Everyone who gets chopped into pieces in a horror movie acts like nothing is wrong—"

Frankie slaps a hand over Sky's mouth and glares at her. "We're not going to talk about anyone getting chopped up. Okay? Calm down and listen. If I take my hand away, you're going to stay quiet. Yes?"

Sky nods, and Frankie drops her hand.

"What I was trying to say was that whoever is doing this isn't exactly a serial killer. They're fixing a painting! Let's just relax about it."

Sky folds her arms across her body, looks over her shoulder again. "It's still creepy."

"I don't know. I think it's kind of cool." Frankie studies the painting. "I think we should see if it happens again."

She takes a sheet of paper out of the backpack with her good arm and hands it to Sky.

"What do you want to paint?" she asks while Sky clips the paper to the easel.

"Oh, let's see. Chainsaw murderer chasing two girls through the woods. Because that's going to be us."

Frankie ignores her, hands her a paintbrush, and reaches into the bag for the paints.

"Let's see how good this mystery artist really is. Is this your school backpack?" she asks, and Sky nods. Frankie unzips the front pocket, reaches in, and straightens.

"Ever do a portrait?" she asks, holding up Sky's school ID.

"I can't do a lighthouse. You think I can paint myself?"

"Nope. And that's what I'm counting on. Clip it to the top."
She hands Sky the picture. "We're only going to paint the shape
of your face and your hair. Nothing else. I can sketch it with my
left hand but you're going to paint. The mystery artist can do
the rest."

They spend the next hour on the painting. Frankie tracing it
lightly in pencil. Sky going over it with paint.

When they're done, she packs up the paints but leaves the
picture and the school ID right where they are on the easel.

They're walking away when Sky stops, looks back at the
painting.

"Bye, unfinished me," she says to the picture, and Frankie
laughs, pulls her away. As they walk through the woods, the
image stays in Sky's mind.

The outline of her head. The brown loose curls. Features that
are missing. Her very own face, waiting to become whole.

26

She knows they know. Heard every word they said from where she hid, safely tucked away in a massive scrub bush.

She heard them walking through the woods from her chair in front of the shed. She knew where they were going—she'd only finished the painting early this morning, while the sun was barely a sliver on the horizon.

She'd brought the painting back to her house when she first found it. She'd just wanted to study it. Be as close as she could to the small hands that had held the picture. Then she couldn't stop from putting a little of herself on the paper. Her only chance to be with the girl in any real way. Even if it was just through both of them sharing the same vision.

She wanted to sign the painting when she was done. To leave proof that she existed. But she'd promised her best friend all those years ago. Told Mac that she'd never tell their secret.

She's never kept any promises. Ever. Except this one.

Which is why she puts the picture back when it's done. No initials. No signature. Just the faceless, nameless touch of a woman clinging to the last thread of her existence.

Now, she slips soundlessly to the easel when she knows the girls are gone. She carefully removes the picture and holds it gently to her middle. It's what she's holding in her other hand that has her heart racing, her breath caught.

She brings it to her face, presses it to her lips before she tucks it in her back pocket.

The only thing on her mind this morning was death.

Tonight, she'll light a candle. Set the paper on the table. Wet her brushes and arrange her paints.

And look at the face on the small laminated ID card until she can draw each feature by memory. She won't look away until it's a living thing inside of her. Filling her body, breathing her air.

Until finally, she's complete.

27

She's setting up her classroom on Thursday, getting ready for the kids to come back to school when there's a knock on the door.

Maggie looks up to see the assistant principal standing in the doorway.

"Hi, Lori," Maggie says, forcing a smile. She's kept to herself since Pete left. She let the battery on her phone drain. Shut the shades. Disconnected from the world, ignoring her laptop on the counter. More than one day, she just stayed on the couch in her pajamas, a pillow wedged under her head and the television on, mindlessly watching home-renovations shows.

They were pleasing somehow, these shows. Turning something old and worn into something new and fresh. Something desirable.

More than once she found herself wishing it were as simple as hiring a crew to come in and work their magic on *her*. Remodel her into a different version of herself. Someone who didn't feel so useless. So discarded.

"How was summer camp?" she asks cheerfully. Maybe if she pretends, the feeling will follow. "Must be hard to put your assistant principal hat back on."

Lori smiles. "Feels like every summer goes by a little bit quicker."

"Sure does. But it's good to be back. Hopefully the weather turns. Hot as heck out there."

"Oh, I know. Never good to start the year during a heat wave."

Maggie nods, moves a stack of books onto a shelf, expecting the assistant principal to say goodbye. She likes Lori, but they're not overly close. This is the sort of small talk they've shared for years.

She's surprised when she looks up to see that Lori isn't in the doorway but right in front of her desk.

"I don't want to overstep. I just wanted to stop by and see how you're doing," she says sympathetically. "You know, with everything." She lowers her voice when she asks this, glancing back at the doorway briefly, as though she doesn't want to be overheard.

Maggie cranes her neck forward. "With everything?"

"It's okay if you don't want to talk about it," Lori says quickly. "I just want you to know that I'm here for you. I know we're not that close, but I actually have some experience with this. You know. Personally." Her cheeks redden, two bright spots appearing on each cheekbone.

Experience with this?

"I'm sorry, Lori—what exactly are you talking about?"

Lori walks around the desk and stands next to Maggie, as though the object between them might be causing the confusion.

"The picture," she whispers. "I just don't want you to feel alone. I mean, not that you would—I'm sure you have a million friends to support you. But, you know, you can never have too many." She smiles self-consciously.

"Picture? What picture?" Maggie asks irritably, frustrated now with all this posturing.

Lori's eyes are wide. "Oh gosh. I just assumed—forget I said anything." She turns to walk away, but Maggie grabs her arm.

"What is going on? Lori—what picture?"

"In the paper. You know, of your husband." Lori sighs. "I'm sorry it's become sort of . . . a *thing*." She winces.

Maggie stares at her.

"It was in the paper—"

"I saw it—what do you mean it's a *thing*?"

She hasn't spoken to anyone besides Pete about the picture. And sure, she noticed how he was looking at the girl. But there was nothing inappropriate about the actual photograph—she hadn't even considered someone else noticing Pete's expression. She swallows, her head swirling.

"I follow the town page. On social media. The paper posted the feature. You know, all the photos people sent in and—well, there were some—comments."

Maggie's body trembles. She wants to leave the room. Walk out of this life. But she needs to know. Right now.

"Comments about what?"

Lori backs away from her. "I feel like such an idiot right now. This is *so* none of my business. I just—my boyfriend, well ex now, but we were together for, like, six years—anyway he was fired for sexually harassing women at work, and I literally had no idea, and I remember feeling so alone. And then this weekend, I saw all these posts about your—well, you know. I'm going to go. Okay—bye," she says, nearly running into the door on the way out.

Maggie walks calmly over to her desk and grabs her pocketbook. She turns off the light on the way out.

In the car on the way home, she concentrates on driving. The school is less than a mile away from her house, and by the time she pulls in the driveway and shuts off the car, the tremble she felt in her body in the classroom has escalated to a visible shake—her hand barely able to get the key in the door.

She drops her purse on the floor and grabs the laptop from the counter. She clicks on the blue icon and waits for the page to load, searches for the town page. She has to scroll down to find it.

The post is a screenshot of the photo collage. The four pictures that were featured on the front page. She clicks on the comments, scans through the first ten or so, things like *Great shots! Ichabod rules! Go summer!*

Then she sees it. *Lol. Chief Pete up to his old tricks.* She clicks on the profile picture and it's a man she doesn't recognize. In his fifties, maybe older, from the wife and grown kids standing next to him.

She clicks back and reads the first response. *Not so funny when you're the target.* The profile picture is a woman in her thirties, young and pretty, leaning against an ambulance, dressed in an EMT uniform.

It's this comment that seems to be the one that kicks off all the rest. Too many to count—her eyes blur as she reads them.

He should've been canned years ago. #Metoo

Complained over and over. Nothing ever done. Finally quit.

She reads until she can't breathe. Then slams the laptop shut, suddenly nauseous. She staggers to the sink, holds her head over the lip, and runs the water, splashes some on her face, the room spinning.

There's a knock on the side door. She grabs a towel, presses it to her lips, planning to ignore whoever is outside when there's a second knock, this time more urgent.

She walks over and opens the door. Pete is standing on the

step, looking as though he hasn't slept in days. Maybe he hasn't. She wouldn't know. They haven't spoken since he left.

"I just got put on administrative leave," he says, and walks past her into the house before she has a chance to speak.

As though she doesn't have anything to say about him coming back home. As though it's her role to fix whatever mess he's made.

Of course he thinks that. It's what she's been doing her whole goddamn life.

Sweet Maggie, she thinks, as she closes the door behind her. *Silly old girl*.

28

He decides to come clean to Xavier about losing his job when he can't take it anymore. He's never been a good liar. His sleep is disturbed. Appetite gone.

When Sky asked him last night if he was feeling all right after he'd pushed his dinner around on his plate until it was cold, he promised himself that he'd call Xavier first thing in the morning and tell him everything.

But now it's almost ten in the morning, and the phone is in his hand, and he's pacing in the backyard, trying to figure out *exactly* what he's going to say.

"So, I have news," he says out loud to a tree. "I'm looking for a new job." He changes direction.

That's actually another lie. He's not looking for a job. Hasn't even considered it yet.

He has his finger on Xavier's name on his cell phone screen. He almost presses it. Instead, he shoves the phone into his back pocket, changes direction again, picking up the pace.

"What are you doing?"

He looks up to see Sky in the open window over the patio. She's peering through the screen, a glass of water in her hand.

"Nothing. Walking. Thinking." He smiles sheepishly.

"Is it okay if Frankie comes over?"

He nods. "Of course." He shifts when his back pocket vibrates, a ringtone filling the air. He pulls out his phone and sees Xavier's name on the screen.

"I have to take this," he says to Sky, but she's already gone, the window empty.

He breathes out, presses the screen.

"Hi," he says brightly. "I was just about to call you."

"You just did," Xavier says. "A minute ago. You pocket-dialed me."

He closes his eyes. Not exactly how he wanted to start the conversation.

"So. What are you thinking about?" Xavier asks.

"What?"

"You told someone you were walking. Thinking. You don't usually pace unless it's serious."

He feels a lump form in his throat. His love for this man making him blink back tears. How comforting it is to be known so well by another person. He wishes Xavier were standing in front of him. That he didn't have to deliver this news through a phone line. Mostly he wishes he didn't have to tell him what he's about to tell him.

"I lost my job. I've been pacing the backyard for the last half hour trying to frame it in the best possible light. But the truth is that they wanted me in the office, and I said no."

He waits for Xavier to tell him this is exactly why none of this was ever going to work. Why Leo should cut his losses now and come back to the city. Why he should tell Sky she should go live with her grandmother.

"I know," Xavier says. "I've known for weeks. Shelly is my yoga instructor."

How had he forgotten? His boss's wife was a trainer at Xavier's gym.

"Why didn't you say anything?"

"You're kidding, right? Why didn't *you* say anything?"

"I'm sorry—I should've told you the day it happened. It's just that I didn't want to make this even more complicated."

"Well, then you're going to love my news."

Leo presses the phone firmly to his ear, waiting.

"I'm doing the story on post-Weinstein-era Hollywood. *Esquire*'s interested."

"Wow—congratulations!"

"Thanks," Xavier grumbles.

"I thought you'd be happy. You've been pitching this for over a year."

There's a long pause on the other end. Leo looks at the phone to make sure he didn't lose the call.

"They want a bigger scope. Lots of interviews," Xavier is saying when he presses the phone back to his ear. "It's not something I can do from here. They want me there. In LA."

Leo swallows, clears his throat. "For how long?"

"I don't really want to get into this right now—"

"How long?" he presses.

The line goes silent. He can hear Xavier breathing.

"A couple of months. Maybe more."

The ground shifts under his feet. He leans against the edge of the patio table, steadying himself. LA? A couple of months? The thought of Xavier across the country makes his insides feel hollow. "And when were you going to tell me? After you checked in to the Beverly Hills Hotel?"

"I wouldn't call you from there. That place is a shithole," Xavier jokes.

Leo doesn't respond. He can feel Xavier slipping away from him.

"Look—I don't leave until October. We have time to figure this out."

"Come here this weekend," Leo blurts, not bothering to hide the desperation in his voice. He has to *try*. "Please. Or I'll come there. Whatever you want."

Xavier is silent. "What about Sky?"

"She's going camping with Frankie. She'll be gone the whole weekend. We'll have three days to ourselves."

"I'll come there," Xavier says. Just like that.

"Yeah? Are you sure? I can come to you—"

"I've been cooped up here with this damn ankle and the walls are closing in. You know it's bad when that island starts looking good to me."

"What? I thought you were off the crutches."

"I was. Then I ignored the doctor and went to spin class and now it's twice the size it was before. Serves me right, I guess."

Leo laughs. "Well, I'm sorry about the ankle. But happy it's bringing you here."

"You better pick me up at the dock though. If I have to crutch on cobblestones, I'm going to be pissed," Xavier growls, but Leo isn't listening.

He's too busy grinning at the phone.

Later, he's in the kitchen making lunch when Frankie and Sky hurry in from the other room, as though they're in a rush.

"Whoa," he says. "Where's the fire?"

"We have an idea," Sky announces. Frankie nods, looks at Leo expectantly.

"Why do I get the feeling that I'm part of this idea?" He narrows his eyes at them.

"We should camp in the backyard tonight. You know, in like, tents." Sky holds her hands up when she sees his expression. "Come on—you won't have to do anything. We'll set up both tents—it'll be practice for the weekend. Please?" she begs.

Leo sighs. "Fine. But I want the air mattress in my tent. I'm too old to sleep on the ground." He looks out the window. "And make sure you don't put the tents under the cherry tree. I don't trust that huge branch."

Sky looks at Frankie, then at Leo.

"What?" he asks.

"We wanted to camp at the other house. Down the street. I told Frankie we're going to move there, and she doesn't believe me."

"I didn't say that," Frankie corrects. "I said you're too scared to even walk by the house, never mind go inside it—"

"Wait," Leo interrupts, turning to Sky. "Is that what you want? To move there?"

His pulse quickens, but he keeps his voice even. There's nothing he wants more than to put a For Sale sign in this front yard.

A new beginning for both of them.

But it's her choice. He doesn't want to influence her decision.

Sky studies him. "You said we could tear it down, right? Build a whole new house. Make it whatever we want."

"Within reason, of course. There are zoning issues that we need to follow. Keep the size of the plot the same, but we could go up. Add some height. Open it up. Take advantage of the view out back. We can't do everything. Some of the money we get from this house is for your college fund."

"I didn't know I had a college fund."

Leo smiles. "You don't. Not yet at least."

"Do it," Frankie urges. "Then I can sleep over all the time."

"You don't have to decide right now," Leo adds. "It's a big decision—"

"Can you draw something? So I can see what it will look like?" Sky asks.

Leo considers this. Why hadn't he thought of that? But he knows the answer. Drawing the house—seeing it on paper—would make it real.

That much harder to walk away.

Sky is waiting for him to answer, a hopeful expression on her face.

"Set up the tents," he tells them. "I'll start working on a sketch."

29

There's something wrong with her. Maybe she's broken inside. Unable to feel what Leo wants her to feel.

It's a huge decision, he keeps telling her. *Your childhood home. Full of memories. The only house you've ever known.*

She pretends to be wrestling with the decision. Torn up about it.

Truth is, ever since Leo brought her down the street and they walked in the backyard and she looked out at the ocean, she hasn't been able to stop thinking about it.

She spends hours dreaming about her new room. Wondering if she'll be able to see the water from her bed. Then she feels guilty.

Her parents are gone, and all she can think about is selling the house they all lived in together.

The one full of happy memories.

Except, for the last year, her house had become a war zone. Her parents fighting all the time. The basement filling up with her father's empty bottles. Her mother's mood swings making her tiptoe through the house.

"But what about the tree house?" Frankie asks. "What if a family buys the house and it belongs to some other kid?"

Sky hasn't thought of that.

Now, it's the only thing that keeps her from telling Leo she wants to move. She's hoping the picture he draws of the new house will be so good—so real—that she'll be able to give up the tree house.

But every time she thinks of it not belonging to her, she can't imagine it. The thought of it makes her insides feel hollow.

Especially now that she's planning on decorating the walls with her paintings. She has a hammer and nails in her backpack, the lighthouse painting rolled up and tucked carefully next to her paints.

After she and Frankie set up the tents in the backyard, they cut through Joe's backyard and into the woods.

They walk straight past the tree house, to the cliff, Sky's heart racing the closer they get. Frankie walks along beside her, chewing on her nail distractedly, as though she doesn't have a care in the world.

"How can you be so calm? What if we're being watched?" She lowers her voice, looks over her shoulder. "Like, *right now.*"

Frankie glances around in mock horror. "The mystery artist strikes again. Run for your life!"

Sky grabs her arm, yanks her back.

"Stop fooling around." She scowls, and Frankie laughs, steps in time with her again. "Seriously. Aren't you freaked out at all?"

"About what? That someone finished your painting?"

She gives Frankie a look, as though this should be obvious.

"It's probably just some show-off staying at the studio on Crow Farm. My art teacher at the co-op stays there sometimes. The way he talks about himself, you'd think he was Picasso."

The easel is just around the corner. She can see the legs peeking out from under a long tree branch.

She swallows, lets Frankie walk ahead of her. They step out

of the woods, onto the path together, but Frankie is in front of her, blocking the easel.

"Holy crap," she hears her say.

Sky steps up, stands next to Frankie. Blinks. Once. Then again.

Someone has finished what she and Frankie had left undone.

She's looking at an exact replica of herself, her features perfectly drawn on the painting. Chills run up her spine. She stands close enough to Frankie that their shoulders touch.

"Holy crap is right," Sky says. "It's really good." She studies the painting, amazed at the detail, how strange it is to see herself looking back at her.

"No." Frankie shakes her head, steps up to the painting. "Holy crap, it's gone. The picture of you that we left isn't here." She points to the empty clip. The one that held her school ID. Frankie bends down and looks in the box, then back at Sky.

"It's empty," she says, her eyes darting around them.

"Maybe it just fell," Sky says, searching the ground.

"Or maybe you have an admirer." Frankie raises an eyebrow. "*Now* this just got interesting."

"Interesting? Try weird. And creepy." She stands facing the woods, searching the trees. "Let's just go." She pulls the picture from the easel, rolls it up, and shoves it in her bag.

"Oh, relax, will you? It's a school ID—not like you're naked or something."

Sky slings her backpack over her shoulder and walks past Frankie, heading back through the woods.

"Wait a second, will you?" Frankie says, scrambling after her.

When she finally catches up, they're on the path in the woods, the tree house in front of them.

"Sky, wait!" Frankie tugs on her arm, stopping her.

"No way. You stay if you want. I'm leaving." She turns, and Frankie tugs on her arm again.

"No. Look!" Frankie points to the ground.

She glances down. Her school ID is lying there, her face staring up at them.

"See," Frankie says. "It probably just blew away. Okay?"

She's ready to turn, walk away, out of the woods, but she pauses. Frankie holds out the picture reassuringly.

"So?" she whispers. "Someone still painted me. My whole *face*!"

"Which we *wanted* them to do! I mean, we left the school ID—it's not like whoever it is knows what you look like. It's no different than the view that they finished for you. It was right in front of them!"

"But why?" She looks around. "And who?"

Frankie shrugs, unzips the side pocket on Sky's backpack, and tucks the school ID away.

"Who knows? It's a game. Not like we have anything better going on." She looks at Sky. "I say we keep playing."

"Playing how?"

"Let's go back and leave another picture. You know, like bait. I have a plan." Frankie smiles at her.

"No way. You go. I'll be up in the tree house. Knock twice when you get back or I'm not opening the door." She hands Frankie the backpack, takes out the paintings, and the hammer and nails.

"I can't climb up there with my arm. I'll just call up." Frankie slings the strap over her shoulder and turns.

"Chicken," she calls over her back.

"Lunatic," Sky answers, and scurries up the ladder.

On the landing, she opens the door and pokes her head in,

surveying the room. She shuts the door behind her, throws the latch.

There's a camping mattress in the corner, her pillow and goose-feather blanket folded on top. She'd begged her parents to let her sleep in the tree house for months, and they'd only agreed under three conditions. That she have bedding to keep her warm, Frankie had to stay with her, and her father would sleep in a tent at the base of the tree house.

After they died, she knew she was breaking the rules sleeping in the tree house alone. But she felt more at home up here than anywhere. Especially those first nights when Xavier slept over, looking around her small house as though he'd rather be anywhere else in the world.

The walls are bare, something she's been meaning to fix. By the time she nails the painting to the walls, she hears someone calling her name.

"Is that you?" she yells. "Frankie?"

"No," Frankie calls backs.

She opens the door and steps out, looks down at Frankie, who's smiling up at her.

"You ready for my plan?" Frankie asks.

She doesn't answer. She's known Frankie long enough to know she's going to hear the plan, like it or not.

She begs Frankie to stay for the cookout. But she can't. She made a deal with her mother that she'd go home for dinner and then she could come back to sleep in the backyard with Sky and Leo.

"It makes no sense," Sky argues. "You're already *here*. What's the big deal?"

They're waiting outside Sky's house for Frankie's mother, who's running late as usual from one of Frankie's brothers' games.

"What's the big deal about having a hamburger with your *grandmother*? You act like she's scary or something."

"I don't even know what to call her."

"How about Grandma?" Frankie raises an eyebrow.

"Easy for you to say. Your grandmother lives a mile away. You see her all the time. I don't even remember the last time I saw her. *Grandma* just sounds weird."

"You *saw* her at the Fourth of July party. And spoke to her. If you don't like Grandma, call her Lillian. That's what she told me to call her."

She sighs. "I think you should just stay."

Frankie's mother pulls in to the driveway and waves at Frankie to hurry up.

"And I think you should stop overthinking it," Frankie says over her shoulder. "See you at eight."

She sits on the front step and watches the black Suburban drive away. Then she walks inside and into the kitchen.

Leo is forming meat into hamburger patties, and he gestures for her to sit at the counter.

"What time is dinner?" she asks.

He glances at the clock. "Five minutes ago," he says just as she hears Joe announce from the patio that he's here and watering Leo's tomatoes that are clearly about to perish.

"I didn't know Joe was coming," she says, relieved.

"Maggie too." Leo winks. "Just a casual cookout with friends."

"And the grandmother I don't know." She sighs, puts her chin in her hand. "Frankie said I should stop overthinking it."

They hear women's voices from the patio, and Leo takes a

deep breath, lets it out. "Good advice. Ready?" he asks, and she follows him to the backyard.

She hates being the center of attention, and ever since Leo told her about the cookout, she's been dreading it. She's expecting all eyes to be on her when she steps through the door, especially Lillian's.

But Maggie and Joe are turned away from her, looking at Lillian, who is standing in front of them with an enormous dog on a leash. The dog is sitting on the patio, gazing lovingly up at Maggie, who's rubbing his large, furry head.

Sky walks over to them, and the dog looks at her and sweeps the ground with his tail, wagging it back and forth in lazy strokes.

"Meet George," Lillian says.

"He looks exactly like Beethoven. From the movie," Sky says, burying her hand in his soft fur. He leans into her fingers while she scratches his neck.

"I hope you don't mind that I brought him," Lillian says over Sky's head to Leo, who's putting hamburgers on the grill. "I was just leaving my shift when his owner called to say they were delayed getting back to the island. The mom was so upset because George hates the kennel and it was only supposed to be for the day and they were going to have to leave him overnight with the late ferry. I told her I'd take him with me and drop him at her house later."

"Of course not," Leo says. But there's something in his voice that makes Sky watch him a second longer than Lillian, and when he looks back at the grill, Sky sees him roll his eyes.

She doesn't know why Leo is rolling his eyes, but she doesn't really care, because the dog is here, and her mother was allergic and only let Sky have stuffed animals that looked like dogs, and suddenly the dinner has turned from a thing she wanted to skip to a thing with an actual *live* dog standing in front of her.

"I'll get him some water," she tells Lillian, and hurries to the kitchen where she fills up a deep plastic bowl and carries it as gently as she can back to George without the water sloshing over the sides. When she puts it in front of him, his head disappears inside of it. She smiles at the sound of his tongue slapping against the water.

"I should probably take him for a walk," Lillian says. "I'm sure he has some business to do."

"There's a path in the woods," she says. "I can show you if you want."

"I'd love that—" Lillian stops talking and looks at Leo, who's watching them from the grill. "But I don't know if Leo needs your help getting ready for dinner."

She turns to Leo, who blinks. Once. Twice. "Can I go?"

"Go." He sighs, waves at her. "Tell George not to poop on the lawn."

Lillian is waiting for her, and she holds out the leash. "Do you want to walk him?"

She nods and slips her hand through the soft leather handle. George is already standing, and he walks easily beside her, his fur brushing her leg.

"He's so good. Frankie's dog pulls us all over the place when we try to walk him." She loosens her grip on the leash while George stops to sniff at the ground.

"He sounds like the dog we had when your mother was young."

She looks up at Lillian. "I didn't know she had a dog."

"Ann might not have remembered him. She was very young at the time. And we didn't have the dog long. Only a couple of weeks."

She follows behind George, thinks about how sad it would be to get a dog only to have him for a couple of weeks. "What was his name?"

"Her name. Ella. Short for Cinderella." She laughs when Sky wrinkles her nose. "That's what happens when you let a four-year-old girl name a dog."

"She said you couldn't have a dog because you and her were allergic. How come you're not allergic to George?"

"I'm not allergic to dogs. Ann just thought I was." Lillian smiles and shrugs. "We had Ella for a week or two before I noticed Ann had a cold she couldn't seem to get over. Turns out it wasn't a cold. It was Ella's fur."

Sky stops, her mouth open. "You had to give her away? That's awful."

"It was awful. Ann was so upset. We got some fish, but she cried every night for weeks. She was mad as heck at me. I told her it was my fault. My allergies."

She squints. Her mother knew she was allergic to dogs. It's why they couldn't have one. "But she knew she was allergic. When did she find out?"

"I told her when she was older. Old enough to start going over to friends' houses where there might be pets. She'd forgotten about Ella by then. Of course, she was still mad at me. She thought she'd inherited the allergy from me. I never fessed up that I wasn't allergic to anything. It was just sort of this lie that kept growing, and then it was too late to fix it. What a mess, right?" Lillian shakes her head and laughs.

Sky raises an eyebrow, grins. "You should've told her the truth from the start."

Lillian nods. "You're exactly right." She pauses, distracted by something behind Sky. "That's your tree house, right?"

She turns to where Lillian is pointing. "Yeah. Joe built it last year. Me and Frankie come out here all the time."

"Can I?" she asks in a hopeful voice, walking to the ladder. "I've never been in a real live tree house."

She nods, swallows a laugh at Lillian's excitement. It's funny to see a grown woman so excited about a wooden box in the trees.

George tugs on the leash, and she follows him over to a bush and waits while he lifts a leg. When she looks up again, Lillian pokes her head out the door. "The paintings look wonderful in here. I figured you were the artist when I saw the easel."

She stares up at Lillian. Speechless.

How does she know about the easel? And she'd forgotten about the paintings. But Lillian had said they look wonderful, like she'd seen them before. The lighthouse and the self-portrait she'd nailed to the wall.

"The easel?" She stops. Waits.

"By the cliff," Lillian says. "I was exploring out behind Agnes's house and there's a path. I followed it and it brought me to the easel, then past the tree house. I turned around when I ended up looking at the back of your house and Joe's house. I didn't want *exploring* to become *trespassing*." She smiles, climbs down the ladder, and walks over to Sky.

"We should head back. I don't want to make us late for dinner."

She nods, glances at Lillian while they walk, and thinks about the paintings in the tree house. The ones somebody else finished.

The ones *Lillian* finished? Was she the mystery artist?

She could just ask her. But she can't make the words come out of her mouth.

"Do you paint too?" she asks finally, and holds her breath.

George stops, sniffs at a large stump on the path. Lillian opens her mouth to answer when a voice breaks the silence.

"There you are," Maggie shouts from up ahead, waving to them from the entrance of the path. "Dinner's ready."

"Oh, let's hurry," Lillian says, clapping several times. "Come on, George. Let's go!" She's walking so fast that Sky starts to jog to keep up with her. "Some dinner guest I am. Brings a dog without asking *and* makes everyone wait to eat!"

She hurries behind her grandmother, her question lost in the rush to return. The sound of her grandmother clapping ringing in her ears. She holds on to it. Perhaps she can remember it later. Place it in her head next to the sound of the clapping the night she and Frankie lit the sparklers.

See if they sound the same.

30

She heard their voices while she was putting the finished picture on the easel. She didn't even stop to think, just took long, silent strides in the other direction, slipping quietly off the path into a massive tangle of brush, thorns scraping at her arms and legs. She deserved it—cutting it that close!

She only panicked when she heard the girls talking about the school ID—heard the tremble in Sky's voice—and looked down to see the picture still in her hand. She hadn't put it back on the clip like she'd planned. And now the girl was scared. She'd scared the girl!

It was unacceptable. Heartbreaking.

Which is why she didn't even feel the thorns ripping her skin as she fought her way through the woods. Running as quickly and silently as she could. When she was almost at the tree house, she glanced around frantically. Where to leave it so they'd see it? Not too obvious! But she wanted them to find it. She dropped it right where she stood.

Let it settle just like it fell, as though the wind had carried it.

Then she ran. Ran as fast as she could back to the studio and slammed the door behind her, collapsed on the small bed, her limbs bloody and scraped, several thorns still lodged in her skin.

That was it. She was done with all of this. She hadn't come here to harm anyone. To scare anyone! She'd only come for closure. To see one thing in this world she would be leaving behind.

She looks over at the wall to the picture of the girl. She'd painted a second one for herself. So when she takes her last breath, steps off the cliff, she'll be looking in her daughter's eyes.

31

They have variations of the same argument for almost twenty-four hours. Maggie asks what the hell he was thinking, and Pete denies any wrongdoing.

Or at least the first night he's back, that's how it goes.

Then he disappears into the bedroom. She doesn't move from the couch—no way in hell she's sleeping next to him in their bed.

The next morning, she phrases her question differently, asks why he thinks all these women are *wrong* and he's somehow *right*.

"It's not about wrong or right," he tells her. And she merely looks at him quizzically, because she can't imagine how there's any other way to look at it.

"They're talking about me joking around! Hey—I'm not claiming to be an altar boy, but I've never *touched* anyone. And it's not *all* these women, Maggie. It's two people who sucked at their jobs and got fired and now they're coming after me."

"Coming after you? Did someone file a complaint?" she asks, dumbfounded. The minute she says it, she feels foolish. He wouldn't be on leave for rumors.

"Why the hell do you think I'm on leave? It's a two-week

investigation. Dean thinks it'll be done by the end of the week. One of them has already changed her story a bunch of times."

Maggie simply stares at him. Of course John Dean would want it to be over by the end of the week. Rookies together when they first joined the force and Pete's surfing buddy, they're practically brothers.

Two women? She looks at her husband and feels her stomach turn, her face grow hot. All of the social media comments she'd read about him running through her head.

She won't get the truth out of him. The details of exactly what happened will be withheld. Even if he tells her his version, the facts will be skewed to make him appear innocent. His involvement will be downplayed until he has her believing that, somehow, he's the victim.

She's suddenly so tired, she could lie on the floor. Right here and now.

"I want you to leave," she says instead, surprised by the strength of her voice. The steadiness with which the sentence is delivered.

"What? Enough of this, Maggie. I'm sorry you thought the picture in the paper was something more than it was. Let's just move on."

She's not going to argue with him. It always ends the same. With her in tears, feeling ridiculous. Overly emotional. *Crazy*, he's even called her.

She simply walks over to the counter and picks up her pocketbook. Then she turns and walks out the door, closes it calmly behind her, as though she's stepping out to the store for milk. Or eggs. Or bread. Instead of what she knows she's really doing.

Ending her insufferable marriage.

*   *   *

She gets as far as the sidewalk before she realizes she doesn't know where to go. She's not ready to see Agnes. They've managed to avoid each other for weeks now. Anger boils up when she thinks of the picture Agnes sent to the newspaper.

No, she's not ready to forgive. Perhaps she never will be.

It's sort of freeing, this thought. As though a weight has lifted off her. This past year, she's agonized over her marriage. Pete and the secretary always in the back of her mind. And Agnes, with her judgment.

Who knew she could simply stop? Stop agonizing. Stop worrying. Stop all of it!

She hears her name and looks up.

Joe is standing in his garden, waving her over. She crosses the street, walks onto his lawn, and joins him in the side yard.

"Look," he says, pointing to the ground. "They're ready."

"What are?" she asks, scanning the garden. "You know I don't have a green thumb."

"Beets. I planted them for you."

"For me?"

He nods. "You like them, right?"

"Well, yeah. I like them a lot. That was nice of you."

"You said they were your favorite. Right after I said I can't stand them. So, I figured, maybe you can teach an old dog new tricks. Maybe I just haven't given them a fair shot."

She tilts her head at him, her eyes suddenly wet. *You're a remarkably kind person* is what she wants to tell him.

"No time like the present," she says instead.

*   *   *

They're sitting at the outdoor table on Joe's patio under a large umbrella.

Maggie has prepared the beets the way she likes them. Roasted, with a drizzle of olive oil. Salt and pepper. Joe also had a block of hard cheese in his refrigerator, and she shaved some off and added it to the bowl with some lettuce from the garden. She topped it off with a light dressing and chunks of a baguette she found on the counter.

She watches him take a bite and chew. He doesn't wince, and she considers this a success.

"Delicious?" she asks.

"How about not bad? Delicious I save for things that can be delivered to my door. Chinese. Pizza. Subs."

"Come on. You've got a pretty well-stocked kitchen for a single guy. And this garden is impressive."

"Growing I can do. It's the cooking that's out of my league. Suzy did all of that. After she passed, I stuck to grilling and take-out. I end up giving most of this stuff away." He gestures to the garden. "It's just a hobby."

Maggie was never close to Suzy, but she remembers her well. A quiet, dark-haired woman who worked part-time in the school library, always quick with a smile. She seemed to be healthy one minute and gone the next.

Joe doesn't talk about her very often, other than a passing remark. His son, David, had died six months after Suzy passed, and Maggie remembers sitting with him after the services. She hadn't known what to say, so she was making small talk about something when he looked over at her.

"It's probably awful that I'm relieved that if this was going to happen, that it did now," he said.

She nodded slowly, even though she had no idea what he was talking about.

"It would have killed Suzy. I'm glad she went first. She had enough pain. She didn't need this on top of it."

He said it with such care that it had stuck with her.

"You must miss her," she says now. "David too."

She doesn't want to make him uncomfortable, but it feels rude not to acknowledge her death now that he's brought it up.

If he's uncomfortable, he doesn't show it. He just nods, as though missing them is a fact of his life.

"The first year was awful. Then little by little, it was less raw. I used to go to a group," he offers. "Bunch of guys who lost someone. A kid or a wife. That helped for a while, and then it just got old. Or I stopped feeling so awful. Not sure which."

"Maybe both." She pauses. "I started seeing a therapist too." She doesn't know why this pops out. But it does. She spears a beet with her fork, pops it in her mouth, and chews.

"Oh?"

"I'm not really through the feeling-awful part though."

He looks at her, sits back in his chair, and waits. She knows that he knows something is going on. Pete hasn't been parked in the driveway all week. Hadn't been home until just last night.

"You know, Suzy and I had a good marriage. Doesn't mean we didn't fight. Marriage is—"

"Over. Mine is, at least. My marriage is over." She sits up straighter, breathes.

This is the first time she's said it out loud.

"Don't say that. You and Pete will work—"

"Joe. Look at me. Are you my friend?"

His eyes go wide. "Of course I'm your friend."

"I know you like Pete. But if I'm going to sit here as your friend and talk about my marriage—how I want to *leave*—then I need to know—" She stops. She doesn't even know what she's trying to say.

"You want me to pick a side," Joe says after a moment.

"Yes." She meets his eyes.

He smiles, winks at her. "I don't grow beets for just anyone, you know."

32

The girls have fun camping in the backyard, but Leo can barely walk when an old back injury from his days playing basketball flares up. Most likely because he'd slept on the hard ground, the air mattress underneath him flat when he woke up in the middle of the night from a dull pain radiating from his tailbone to his shoulders.

It's the last thing he needs right now, with Xavier coming to the island for the Labor Day weekend. He'd dropped Sky at Frankie's house earlier in the day, planning to go to the grocery store, the liquor store, the butcher, and the fish shop all before noon.

But it's after three in the afternoon, and he's just now pulling in the driveway, his back throbbing, as though someone has taken a sledgehammer to his spine. Getting out of the car seems daunting—he's already done it a handful of times with all his errands, and each time was progressively worse.

He rests his head against the steering wheel, trying to summon the courage to get out of the car and unload the grocery bags and bottles of wine piled in the trunk. He wants this weekend to be perfect.

He hasn't spoken to Xavier since the night of the cookout, when he'd called after everyone had left.

"How'd it go?" Xavier asked. "Did you get the casual *Don't be freaked out your estranged grandmother is here* vibe you were going for?"

"I did, wiseass. But that's because Lillian decided to show up with a dog. And not just any dog. The type that wears a barrel around its neck. Like some dog model in a commercial about the Swiss Alps. Such an obvious bribe. I'm surprised she didn't show up with a truckload of presents. Why not buy Sky's affection!"

Xavier was quiet. "You sound nuts," he said finally.

"*I* sound nuts? She didn't even ask if she could bring it!"

"How gauche. A dog at a backyard cookout. The nerve."

"All right. Knock it off. You get my point."

"What I get is that you have a grandmother who is offering to be involved. Why are you so against this? Don't you think you should at least consider that Sky might be better off with her? She's her *grandmother*!"

"A grandmother who Sky doesn't even know—"

"Who she can get to know!"

Leo sighed into the phone. "I don't want to argue. Let's talk about something else."

They stayed on the phone another five minutes or so. But they never got back on track. And they hung up annoyed with each other.

He doesn't know how long he's been sitting with the AC blowing cold air at him when there's a knock on the window. He opens his eyes to see Joe and Maggie standing outside the car, looking at him with concerned expressions.

He turns off the engine and opens the door. They shuffle back when he swings his legs out and tries to stand, one arm gripping the steering wheel and the other pressed to his back, praying it doesn't give out.

"I thought it was a strange place to take a nap. Guess you were right," Joe says to Maggie, who puts her hand on Leo's arm.

"I knew something was wrong. We were having lunch outside

and saw you pull in, and then you just sat here." She peers around to where his hand is jammed against his lower back, a frightened look on her face, as though she isn't sure what she might find.

"It's fine—just a strain. I let the girls talk me into camping in the backyard and I'm paying for it." He takes a small step, pain exploding up his spine and into his head. He lets out a string of curses and grabs the door again.

"Definitely seems fine," Joe says. "You need to get yourself to the emergency room before you do more damage and end up in bed for weeks. I say this from personal experience."

"I have to get Xavier at the ferry. There's groceries to unload. And wine to chill. A dinner to cook—" He slumps back against the seat, lowering himself as gently as he can. His face is damp with sweat. He feels disoriented, nauseous.

When he looks up again, Joe has the trunk open, his arms loaded with bags.

"I'm taking you to the hospital," Maggie declares, in the teacher voice he remembers from when he was a child in her class.

"Stay right here," she tells him, and walks down the drive-away.

"I'm fine, really," he calls after her.

Joe chuckles from behind the car. "We can tell. Sit tight. I'll get this stuff put away."

He wants to argue, but he's bent over, hands on his knees, unable to straighten. A minute later, Maggie pulls up to where he's standing. She gets out from behind the wheel, walks to where he is hunched over, and opens the back door of her car.

"How do you want to do this?" she asks. "Maybe just shuffle over and put a knee in, and just . . . lie down."

The thought of moving makes him tense up. But Xavier will be at the dock in fifteen minutes. He doesn't have time for this.

"Maybe it's just a spasm," he offers. "I could take something. See if it goes away."

He tries to straighten. A stabbing pain rips through him. He winces and Maggie folds her arms across her body.

"Ready?" she asks, and he nods, defeated.

Somehow, he manages to slide headfirst into the car, preparing for the pain to worsen with the movement, but when he's on the seat, curled with his knees to his chest, it somehow soothes the ache.

He feels ridiculous, childlike, but the relief is so overwhelming, he just closes his eyes and breathes.

"I'd drop you off and get Xavier, but we're probably better off getting him first and then going to the hospital," Maggie says when she's back in the car. She reverses and pulls onto the street, the slight shift making his breath catch.

"Or not," she says, glancing in the mirror. "Let's take you first. I'll call Xavier and ask him to wait."

"No! The last thing he said to me was 'Don't make me do these cobblestones on crutches!'"

Leo thinks about the surf-and-turf dinner he was going to make. The hours he and Xavier would have had stretching out in front of them. Alone. Sky not due back from camping until the end of Labor Day weekend. Three whole nights to talk. Go to bed. Make love. Wake up and do it all over again.

And now he's ruined it.

"Okay, here's the plan. I'm going to pull in one of the handicapped spaces. Leave the car running and find Xavier. Then we'll go to the emergency room. I'm sure Xavier will want to stay with you. Then I'll follow Joe over with your car."

"He's mad at me already. He might take one look at this mess and get on the next ferry home."

Maggie adjusts the mirror, straightening in the seat to meet his eyes with the way he's lying down. "Well, that will be his loss," she says gently. "You know, Leo, a lot of men would have simply walked away. Given someone else the job of raising her."

"Yeah, well. I'm stubborn. If there's a job I can do poorly, I'll at least make sure I screw it up to the end."

"Stop it. I've been working with kids Sky's age for the last thirty years. Through awful situations. A parent dying. Or a sibling. You can tell when these kids have nobody to talk to—no one to help them." She holds his gaze in the mirror. "She's happy with you, Leo. I see it. *Anyone* who knows her can see it."

"Xavier thinks I should let Lillian raise her."

"I think the only one who gets a say in who raises Sky is Sky. Have you asked her what she wants?"

He shakes his head. What if she got to know Lillian and said yes to living with her? What then? The thought of it makes his chest tight.

Maggie pulls into the space, puts the hazards on, and scans the crowded pier. "Hold tight," she says. "I'm off to get invalid number two."

He closes his eyes again. He'd give anything to sit up so he doesn't look so pathetic, but it's not an option.

Minutes later, there's a light tapping noise outside of the car. He opens one eye to see raindrops dot the windshield, then the sky opens, and a torrent of rain slams down around him.

He pushes up on an elbow, trying to see out the window, when the car doors open and Maggie and Xavier pile in. Xavier wrestles his crutches into the car, and frantically slams the door, but his backpack is wedged in between. When he finally shoves it to his feet and manages to click the door shut, he's drenched. He turns, a wild look on his face.

"What is *wrong* with this place? It was just eighty and sunny!"

Maggie is running her hands through her wet hair in the driver's seat. "They knew the rain was coming. But it was supposed to be later tonight."

The crutches have landed awkwardly between the seats, now partially blocking his view of Xavier. Which is fine because he's not at all sure he wants to see Xavier's expression.

He's come all this way on crutches because Leo asked him to—and now Leo will spend the weekend in a hospital bed, hopped up on meds. This happened once before, and it was three days before he could sit up straight.

His disappointment is a crushing weight, making it difficult to breathe.

Xavier shifts the crutches and turns in his seat. Leo expects to see him frowning down at him. Instead, Xavier reaches out and takes Leo's hand. "Squeeze my hand if we hit a bump," he says while Maggie reverses out of the space.

It's the first time they've touched in what feels like an eternity. Leo holds on as tight as he can.

Afraid to let go.

They spend the night in a private room in the hospital. Lucky for Leo, it was a slow afternoon in the ER, the holiday just kicking off. The nurses assured him it was only temporary. That by the morning, potential disasters still on the distant horizon would have struck and beds would be full and he'd most likely be transferred to a smaller, shared room.

But when he opens his eyes for the first time, it's already midmorning and he's still in his corner room with a private bathroom and a distant view of the water.

Or so Leo is told.

He hasn't moved from being flat on his back since he arrived. Xavier slept in the recliner chair and positioned it next to him so they could at least see each other. Talking was more difficult because of the drugs. He slipped in and out of consciousness while Xavier watched television and ate some sort of concoction from the cafeteria.

Then he simply fell into a deep sleep, and the night passed in a blink.

Now, Xavier is sipping a cup of coffee, looking as though he didn't sleep at all. Leo shifts slightly, feels a tightening in his back but not the sharp stabs he felt last night.

"I'm going to try to sit up a little," he announces.

Xavier puts his coffee on the side table, digs the hospital bed remote from under the blankets. "Are you sure? Maybe we should wait for the nurse."

"No—go ahead. Just slow though."

"I don't think it has speeds. It's up or down."

"Don't be a wiseass. Just do a little at a time. You know what I mean."

"Ready?"

He nods, and the bed rises slightly. He feels a twinge, but it passes.

"More," he says, and Xavier presses the button again.

Leo raises his head when he's at a slight incline, just enough that he can actually see the room.

"Good?" Xavier asks.

Leo waits for his back to complain, but all he feels is a small ache. "Better. Definitely better."

"Joanie said to let her know when you wanted breakfast."

"Joanie?"

"The day nurse. Barb's shift ended while you were sleeping. She said to tell you that your husband is wickedly handsome."

"Good old Barb." Leo shifts, winces when his back spasms. He doesn't remember who Barb is. "Such a joker," he chokes out.

Xavier's smile fades. "Maybe you should lie back down again."

Leo nods, presses his eyes shut. He listens to the noise while Xavier presses the remote, and then he's lying flat again.

"Well that was fun for a minute." He sighs, gritting his teeth through the pain. When the spasm passes, he opens his eyes, but Xavier is gone.

A minute later, he returns, a young girl in blue scrubs by his side. She looks as though she's in high school, her brown hair pulled back in a ponytail off her freckled face.

"Joanie," Xavier says, pointing to the girl. "She's just recently received her driver's license."

"He knows I'm twenty-six." Joanie grins, and rolls her eyes. "Is he always this fresh?"

"Yes. But some might use a different word."

Joanie checks the monitor above his bed. "Well, he took good care of you last night. Barb said she was going to offer him a job."

"You guys can't afford me," Xavier jokes.

"Feel free to kick him out. You have my permission."

"Don't listen to him," Xavier says. "It's the drugs talking."

"Didn't you just come to the desk, asking me to give him more? He said you were in pain. *Are* you in pain?"

"Yes," Leo replies. "I want to be tough and say no, but—"

"You don't get points for being tough in this place," Joanie tells him.

"How about funny?" Xavier asks. "Charming and handsome?"

"Definitely," Joanie says. "If you know anyone who fits that description, let me know."

Xavier gives the nurse an impressed look. "Touché, my youthful health practitioner. Touché."

He stands, leans down, and pecks Leo on the forehead. "I'm going back to the house to take a shower. Change my clothes. I'll bring you some as well."

"Don't rush back," Joanie says, replacing the plastic bag on the stand above Leo. "He's going to be fast asleep in a minute."

"Want anything else from the outside?"

"A new back?" Leo jokes, then picks up his head and looks at Xavier, blinking at him. "Wait—where are your crutches? Maggie said she had to leave the car in the farthest lot."

"I haven't used them since last night. Barb got tired of me complaining about how I couldn't get an earlier appointment with my asshole doctor and she gave me this." He lifts up his left foot, now in a walking boot. "Apparently there is one thing about this island that I like."

Joanie snorts. "Yeah. The ocean and the beaches totally stink. Boot cast? Awesome!"

Xavier stares at her, stone-faced. "I liked you better when I thought you were just a vapid, prepubescent person."

"And I liked you better when I thought you were leaving," Joanie replies, equally stone-faced.

Xavier looks at Leo, before he turns and hobbles out.

"Well done," he says to Joanie, impressed.

She shrugs, smiles. "He's a sweetheart. Paid for the coffee shop in town to deliver muffins and platters of fruit to the nurses' station. But I'm not telling you anything. He's your husband, right?"

He doesn't answer. Just closes his eyes, waits for the drugs to enter his body and take his mind to another world.

One where a simple question like that doesn't leave him speechless, searching for the answer.

33

It starts raining the minute they get the tents up.

She and Frankie were looking forward to spending three days on the island campground. They begged Frankie's mother to take them, and she only said yes because it was Labor Day weekend, and Frankie's father said he wasn't in the mood to fork over a grand for their annual cookout, and camping might be fun if they got another couple to join them.

They brought Mr. and Mrs. Emerson; a middle-aged couple dressed as though they'd just stepped off the golf course. Both in matching shorts scattered with tiny whales.

"Isn't this just *darling*?" Mrs. Emerson kept saying as soon as they arrived at the campsite, in a voice that didn't sound as sure as the words, her eyes wide and smile fixed.

Sky and Frankie set up their own tent, then Frankie's parents' tent. They gather branches and use the newspapers and firewood Frankie's father brought from home to get a fire going in the pit while the adults sit at the picnic table and drink cocktails out of fancy plastic glasses Frankie's mother bought just for the occasion.

It's Frankie's mother's first time camping because if she's going to pay to sleep somewhere, why not make it a five-star hotel?

She keeps announcing this, laughing as though it's the funniest thing she's ever heard while Frankie's father and Mr. Emerson discuss the best place to set up the Emersons' tent, which is still sitting on the ground in the bag, tags hanging off it.

Mr. Emerson walks down the slight incline to a spot in the rear of the campsite and announces that this is where he's going to put it.

"You're going to drown if it keeps raining," Frankie points out. "It's downhill."

Both of the men ignore her, and an hour later, the rain turns from a light sprinkle to a downpour.

Dinner was supposed to be kabobs on the grill, but the fire goes out and Frankie's parents start arguing about the weather forecast—she *told* him it was going to rain, and he *never* listens. Mrs. Emerson insists the rain is even more of an *adventure* and pulls sandwich meat and rolls out of the cooler under the table, chatting loudly about how a picnic for dinner is just perfect, but Sky can tell she just wants Frankie's parents to be quiet.

Frankie and Sky had set their tent on a high spot, and they take a bag of chips and two sandwiches inside and put their lantern on low.

Sky tells Frankie she thinks Lillian might be the mystery artist.

"What is with you and this woman?" Frankie shakes her head. "First you're afraid to have a hamburger with her and now she's sneaking around finishing your paintings? I think you're paranoid."

"Why do you think it's *not* her?"

"The better question is why you think it *is* her."

"She knew where the easel was. And she went in the tree house and said she liked the paintings. And later on, she clapped. It sounded just like the clapping we heard that night."

Frankie stares at her.

Sky shrugs. "Fine. It's a stretch. But we're going over to her house. Unannounced. If she has paints lying around, you won't think I'm so *paranoid*."

When they wake up the next morning, it's still pouring, and Mr. and Mrs. Emerson are gone. They left in the middle of the night when they woke up nearly underwater, a foot of muddy runoff in their tent.

Frankie's father is packing the SUV, not even bothering to put their tent back in the bag. He just folds it and throws it in the trunk, muttering about what a piece of crap it is. His hair is matted to his head, and his T-shirt is soaked through, and she's never seen eyes so red in her life.

"Pack it up, girls," he says. "We're out of here."

"We're supposed to be here until Monday—that's two more nights!" Frankie argues.

"Did you notice the weather? Come on, get moving."

"It's just rain." Frankie holds up her palms, letting the drops collect in her hand. "We were supposed to go swimming. You were going to get *wet* anyway!"

They leave in a hurry. Frankie's mother is already in the front seat, fixing her makeup in the visor mirror. Nobody speaks on the way home until they pull up in Sky's driveway and Frankie's mother turns and looks at Sky.

"I just realized I never checked with your . . . caretaker. I don't see a car," she says, scanning the driveway.

"His name is Leo. And he's her *parent*." Frankie gives Sky a sorry look.

"He probably just went to the store. No worries. Thank you!" She shuts the door, hurrying inside, drops of rain pelting her head.

Inside, she goes room to room, but Leo isn't anywhere.

She showers and puts on warm clothes. Then settles in the den in front of the television, her head on the pillow.

She feels her eyes closing and wonders if she should get up and call Leo. He has no idea she's home.

But the couch is too comfortable. The pillow so soft.

She wakes up to the front door slamming, startling her out of sleep. She sits up, looks out the front window at Leo's car in the driveway.

There are footsteps in the hallway coming toward her. Heavy and uneven on the wood floor, as though the person walking toward her has a limp. A figure passes the doorway, taller and thicker than Leo.

And white.

His pale profile there, then gone, heading toward Leo's room.

She freezes, shrinks back in the couch, holding her breath. The footsteps stop. Then reverse.

She blinks when a body fills the doorway.

It's Xavier. His eyes as wide as her own.

"I wasn't expecting you to be here," he says, as though she doesn't actually live here.

He hadn't expected *her*. She hadn't expected *him*. Leo told her that he wasn't doing anything all weekend.

Just me and myself, he'd said.

She doesn't answer, and Xavier clears his throat.

"I mean, Leo said you were camping until Monday. Aren't you supposed to be camping?" He shifts nervously in the doorway, clears his throat again.

She points to the window. "I was. Then it started raining. Now, I'm home."

"Right. Sure. That makes sense." He nods, glances down the hallway as though he's looking for someone to rescue him.

He looks back at her and stands awkwardly in the doorway. Not that she's surprised. He's always awkward with her.

She unfolds from the couch, walks toward him. He quickly shuffles out of the way. She turns the corner, expecting to find Leo in the kitchen, but it's empty.

Xavier has followed her, and now he's lingering in the doorway again. She wonders if he has something against being in the same room with her.

"Where's Leo?" she asks, turning on the faucet and filling a glass with water.

"Leo? Oh right, duh. You were already gone when he went to the hospital."

She freezes, the glass midway to her lips, and he flinches.

"Oh, sorry—he's fine! He has a back injury from years ago that flared up again. I didn't mean to scare you."

She brings the glass of water over to the table, sits heavily in the chair. "It's actually my fault. Me and Frankie asked him to camp with us at the other house. He said he had a bad back, and I made him come anyway. Is he okay?"

"Yeah. Drugged up. Sleeping a lot. But he'll be fine." Xavier's eyes shift to the wall and back at her. "What other house?"

She squints at him.

"Leo's. The one he grew up in. Down the street."

"I thought some old lady lived there?"

"She died. Like two months ago." She tilts her head at him, wondering why he doesn't know this. He looks blankly at her, as if he's wondering the same thing.

"When is Leo coming home?"

"The nurse thought probably tomorrow. I was just going to

shower and change. Then go back." He pauses. "We thought you were camping."

She doesn't know what to say. They've already gone over this. She *was* camping. It rained. She's home. It seems a simple thing, but he's looking at her as though he doesn't understand.

"I'll go over to Maggie's. She won't care if I stay there until Leo comes home."

Xavier straightens in the doorway. "Well, that's not necessary. I mean—you could stay here." He hesitates. "With me."

She walks to the sink, washes her glass, and puts it in the cabinet. Slowly. How can she say no politely? She doesn't want to stay here. Alone. With him.

He doesn't even *like* her.

"That's okay. I know you probably want to get back to the hospital. I wasn't supposed to be home anyway."

He steps into the same room as her for the first time. "Look, Sky—I'd like you to stay. He'll be home tomorrow. Monday, worst-case scenario."

"Why?" she blurts out.

"Well, they might keep him—"

"No—why do you want me to stay? You came here to see Leo. Not me."

He twists the wedding band on his finger. "Fair enough," he says.

She waits for him to say something else, but he just leans back against the doorframe.

She folds her arms across her body. "Why don't you come here anymore? Leo said it was because of work."

"Well, work is . . ." His voice trails off. "I guess I haven't wanted to interfere. I just—I don't want to make your life any harder than it already is. Or has been."

"Why would you make my life hard?"

"Just by being me. I mean us. You know, me and Leo."

She raises an eyebrow.

"We're married, obviously. Which means we're . . ." He clears his throat.

"Gay?" she offers, and he shifts his weight.

"I didn't know at what age you might know about something like that."

"I'm ten. Not, like, five."

"No, of course." His face colors, and he stares at a spot on the wall over her shoulder. "I guess I don't know many kids your age. Well, any really. I mean kids. I don't know any kids."

"So you'd make my life hard because you're gay? I don't get it."

"Well, maybe . . . indirectly. You know, teasing at school. Bullying."

"That wouldn't happen." She shakes her head. "No way."

"Well, it might. You don't know that it wouldn't," he says defensively.

"Yes, I do. Hanna Karbo is in my gym class, and she has two moms, and nobody cares." She tilts her head, challenging him.

"I'm actually shocked to hear you know someone who's gay."

"We live on an island. Not on Mars. There's tons of gay people here."

"Tons? There's not even tons of people on the island."

"Okay, well maybe not tons. But some. Ms. Sunder is gay."

"Who's she?"

"My gym teacher."

He waves her away as though this doesn't count.

"And Mr. Web, the high school swim coach. And Frankie's brother," she says, then regrets it. She doesn't know what she's trying to prove. "Don't tell anybody though. Frankie saw him kissing one of the other players on the football team in their basement one night, but she made me swear I wouldn't tell anyone. He has a girlfriend. Like, a serious one. They've been together since middle school."

Xavier starts to speak, but there's a knock on the back door. The door cracks open, and Maggie's face appears. She smiles at Xavier. Tilts her head when she notices Sky.

"I didn't expect to see you," Maggie says. "Did the rain chase you out of the campground?"

Sky frowns. "No. It chased Frankie's parents out. They made us come home."

Maggie gives her a sympathetic look. She steps in the kitchen, a bouquet of flowers in her arms. She puts them on the counter and walks to the cabinet where the vases are, patting Sky's arm as she passes.

"Well, that's no fun. But neither is getting drenched all weekend. Forecast has this sticking around until Tuesday."

"Figures it's going to rain until the first day of school." She scowls at the window. The rain has stopped, but from the dark color of the sky, it's just waiting to start again.

"Look at the bright side," Maggie tells her. "You could be Leo. Flat on your back in the hospital." She arranges the flowers and places the vase in the middle of the counter. "I was actually surprised to see the car in the driveway," she says to Xavier. "You were so adamant about not leaving him yesterday."

"I really just came back to shower and change. And then Sky was here. I thought she was camping."

"He didn't expect me to be here," Sky finishes.

Xavier sighs, shoves his hands in his pockets. "But I'm glad you are. I'm glad to see you," he insists.

There's an awkward silence in the room. Maggie fiddles with the flowers, plucking petals off a white rose until it's half its size.

"You know," she says, turning to Sky, "I actually stopped over because Leo bought a ton of food, and he doesn't want it to go to waste. Let's have a sleepover at my house. We can make dinner there. You can invite Frankie if you want. Go grab some pajamas and a toothbrush while I pack up."

Sky looks at Xavier. Waits for him to tell Maggie that he wants her to sleep here. That he wants to spend time with her.

But Xavier looks at his watch, glances at both of them.

"I should hop in the shower and head back to the hospital. Maybe I'll see you before I go?" he asks Sky.

She shrugs, moves to the doorway, and he jumps back when she walks past him.

"Tell Leo I hope he feels better," she says, and walks to her bedroom, shuts the door behind her before the tears come. Hot and fast down her face. She wipes them away before Maggie comes in and asks why she's crying.

She doesn't have the answer. She only knows she wanted Xavier to tell Maggie he wanted to stay. He wanted *Sky* to stay. But he hadn't. And now her insides feel empty. And another tear spills out of her eye.

For reasons she can't explain.

34

Maggie has to bribe Sky into the house. Literally.

She couldn't tell her she was staying at Leo's other house with Xavier in the room. Leo had asked her not to tell him. Not before he had a chance to tell Xavier his plans for renovating the house.

They're in the car when she tells Sky she has a surprise for her.

"We're sleeping at Leo's old house," she announces. "I'm going to help him clean out the basement. Pictures and memorabilia and—"

"You're staying at Leo's house?" Sky interrupts, gaping at her. "Like inside? Actually inside the house?"

Maggie nods.

"I'm not going in there. It's definitely haunted."

"Don't be silly." Maggie laughs. "I stayed there last night. Didn't see a single ghost. There's actually something that might be fun. A surprise I think you'll like."

She parks the car on the street, walks up the front stairs and opens the door, thinking Sky is behind her, but when she turns, Sky is still on the sidewalk, her backpack at her feet.

"Sky. This is silly. I told you there's nothing scary about this house. Come up here and see for yourself," she says in the most convincing voice she can muster.

Sky doesn't move. "Why can't we just sleep at your house? Or my house?"

"Because I told Leo I would help him. Come in. Look—it's starting to rain again."

Sky looks up as a drop lands on her forehead. She looks back at Maggie, unfazed.

"All right," Maggie sighs. "How about this? If you come inside, we'll work for an hour or so. Then I'll take you to Pier Two."

Her eyes light up. Pier 2 is the roller rink on the other side of the island. Maggie's least favorite place on the island. Sky's favorite.

"Can Frankie come?"

Maggie nods. "But we're leaving before the disco thing starts. It gives me a headache."

Sky shrugs, slings her backpack over her shoulder, and walks up the stairs toward her.

"That's fine. Frankie hates that part too. It's all couples holding hands." She wrinkles her nose and steps into the house.

Sky studies the room. Maggie is thankful she spent the previous night sprucing things up.

Mrs. Pearse's family had moved all her belongings out of the house after she died, but they hadn't exactly *cleaned*.

There was dust on every surface.

A rug in the middle of the room that looked as though it hadn't been vacuumed in years. Maggie had started in one corner and worked to the other. Vacuuming first. The rug wasn't salvageable, so she'd rolled it up and stood it leaning against the side of the house next to the trash barrels. Then she mopped the floor. Threw out the faded, old curtains and washed the windows.

Now, the wood floor gleams and the musty smell in the room is finally gone.

"Not as scary as you thought, is it?"

Sky lifts her shoulders, lowers them slowly. "It's empty though."

Maggie moves to the middle of the room. "That's the surprise. Picture a tent." She spreads her arms over the floor. "A little indoor camping experience for you and Frankie. And there's a projector downstairs. Some old movies. I don't know if I can get it to work, but it could be fun."

"If it doesn't, we can just watch a movie on my laptop. Can I call Frankie?"

Maggie nods. "Tell her to come over quick. We don't have much time if you want to go to Pier Two."

"Oh, we don't have to do that," Sky says. "This is better anyway."

Maggie walks into the kitchen and gives a small clap. Success on two fronts. Sky's inside the house, and Maggie doesn't have to deal with the hell that is Pier 2.

After she unloads the groceries, she walks through the house, opening doors and poking her head in before moving to the next room. It's empty, just as Leo had told her. Like all the houses on Winding Way, it's the same layout as Maggie's house except it's a one-story, just two low-ceilinged storage spaces on the second floor.

She'd set up an air mattress in the smaller of the two bedrooms on the first floor. Yesterday, she'd planned to stay at the inn in town even though the summer rates would be ridiculous. Then they were waiting in the emergency room when Leo mentioned this house.

It was really just dumb luck that it came up at all.

She was sitting in a chair next to Leo's hospital bed. They were waiting for the doctor when Xavier left for the restroom and Leo picked up his head, waved her over frantically.

She stood over him, leaned down. "Are you okay?" she asked.

"Did Joe tell you I'm thinking about knocking down my old house. Building a new one?" he asked quickly, glancing at the door.

"No," she said. "But that's so exciting—"

"Shh," he hissed, his eyes still on the doorway. "I'll tell you about it later, but Xavier doesn't know! And I've been lying here thinking you're going to say something. So don't say anything!"

She nodded dumbly, an idea popping into her mind. "Do you care if I stay there this weekend?" she whispered. "Don't ask why. Just—is it okay?"

He screwed up his face. "Why the hell would you want to—" He paused. "Don't ask. Okay—it's a mess. Empty. Dirty. I don't think Mrs. Pearse could see very well in her last years."

"I'll clean it," she offered.

"I'm knocking it down anyway. It's the basement that's the problem. It's all my childhood stuff. Pictures and whatever. I threw it all in a corner in bags years ago. Sort of forgot about it until I went down there a couple of weeks ago. It was so over-whelming, I left."

"I'll make you a deal. Let me stay there for the weekend and I'll organize. Sound good?"

"Sounds good to me," he said, just as Xavier walked through the door.

"What sounds good?" he asked, and Leo looked blankly at Maggie.

Maggie had to think quickly.

"My beet recipe—I was just telling him how Joe raved about

it," she said, smiling sweetly, as though she hadn't just told two lies in one sentence.

Now she hears her cell phone ringing from the other room. By the time she walks through the house and picks it up, she's missed the call. Pete's name is on the screen.

They haven't spoken since she walked out of the house. She doesn't know if he saw her walk across the street to Joe's. She'd stayed for almost the entire afternoon. Pete's truck had been in the driveway when she'd hurried to get her own car to drive Leo to the hospital.

Hours later, Joe had delivered Leo's car to the hospital and she'd driven them both back to Winding Way, dropping Joe at his house and driving straight down the street to Leo's old house.

She thinks about calling him back, has a moment of panic that he's calling about one of the boys. Maybe something has happened and she's over here, clueless.

But that's absurd.

PJ sent her a text yesterday morning that he was spending the holiday weekend with his girlfriend in Seattle, and Michael had rushed her off the phone earlier in the week when he was hurrying to catch a plane somewhere for work.

Her phone dings, and a text appears on the screen. Then another. And another. It's Pete. Asking where she is. When she's coming home. What this is all about.

She places the phone on the mantel and walks away. She's been trying to talk to him for an entire year.

Now, she's simply out of words. Or the desire to speak to him.

Maybe both.

*   *   *

By nightfall, the tent is up in the living room and the girls are in sleeping bags, the light from the laptop showing through the thin fabric.

Maggie was listening to them argue about what movie they were going to put on while she cleaned up the paper plates from their dinner and brought them outside to the trash barrel. By the time she came back, they were quiet. Only the muted voices of whatever they'd chosen to watch coming from inside the tent.

She wanders the house, restless.

She brought a book, but the overhead light in the bedroom is blindingly bright above the air mattress, and there's not another piece of furniture to sit on while she reads.

Instead, she goes back downstairs to the basement. There are three bins she's labeled and arranged on the cement floor.

Throwaway. Keep. Undecided.

Leo didn't give her any instructions, but she has two sons of her own. She was the one who packed up their rooms once they were grown. She'd kept *everything*. Report cards. Trophies. Posters. Toys. Team pictures—on and on and on. She sorted it for them. Carefully packed all of it in bins.

They wanted next to nothing. A stack of pictures. Yearbooks. Each of them taking a small box, throwing the rest in the back of the truck to go to the dump.

Now, she sorts Leo's things with this in mind.

She puts all the pictures in the *Keep* bin, sorting them in piles by year as best as she can. Leo as a baby. A teenager. The high school years and beyond.

There's a picture of Leo at his college graduation, and Maggie holds it up, smiles at the familiar faces of Leo's parents. She hadn't known them very well. They hadn't been familiar enough for her to call them anything but Mr. and Mrs. Irving—they'd always seemed so much older than her.

When she'd moved to Winding Way in her early twenties, PJ was just a baby. Leo was already a young boy, whizzing by on his bike or playing street hockey in front of her house with Brian. Then she'd started teaching, and Leo was in her class.

Her face still burns when she thinks of her first-parent teacher conference with his parents.

They'd arrived from work. A striking couple even in uniform. Mr. Irving, *Harbormaster* printed in block letters on his shirt, wore a hat, most likely to protect his pale skin from the sun. Fair and freckled, he was the polar opposite of his wife. Brown skin and dark-eyed, Mrs. Irving was stunningly beautiful, even in her baggy nurse scrubs.

She hadn't known anything about the couple other than what Leo had told the class. He said his mother was from "the islands," where Leo was born. Maggie wasn't even sure which island.

"Welcome," she'd said as they sat down and looked at her across the desk. "I can't say enough good things about your son. He's a delight, really. Polite. Works well with others. Does great on projects." She dug a worksheet out of a pile, glanced down at it. "This is his most recent one on heritage. So what island are you from?" she asked curiously, smiling at Leo's mother.

Mrs. Irving studied her, as though Maggie might be joking in some way.

"I'm from New York," she said finally, clearing her throat.

Maggie's face flamed. She realized she'd expected Leo's mother to have an accent. "Oh my gosh—I'm sorry." She looked at the worksheet. Leo's precise handwriting on the page.

"We did a class presentation and the students talked about

where they were born. And where their parents and grandparents were from. Leo wrote he was born in the Caribbean Islands. That you were born and raised there as well," she said to Mrs. Irving, pointing to the paper, offering proof.

"Where am I from?" Mr. Irving asked, amused apparently, from the smirk on his face.

Maggie glanced down. "Rhode Island," she said meekly.

"Well at least he didn't lie about that," he said.

"He shouldn't be lying about any of it," Mrs. Irving hissed. "Leo was born on Ichabod. Right up at that hospital I just came from. I have no idea why he told you that."

"It's not hard to figure out," Mr. Irving said, frowning. "How many black kids do you have in this class?" he asked Maggie.

"Just Leo," Maggie replied.

"Right," he said. "And how many black kids in the school? Kindergarten all the way through twelfth grade?"

Maggie swallowed. "Oh, I don't . . . I wouldn't have that sort of information—"

"Four," Mr. Irving said gently. "There are four kids in the entire Ichabod Island school system that look like my son. And that's even not really true, because his skin is lighter. But what I'm saying is—he looks different. He's used to being asked *why* he looks different." He pauses, looks over at his wife. "Put yourself in his shoes. You're a ten-year-old kid being asked to explain why you look different. Do you give a real answer? Or do you say you're from somewhere faraway? Somewhere exotic. A place where maybe everyone looks like him."

Mrs. Irving folded her arms, scowled at her husband. "Yeah, well, it's still lying. And he's going to hear it from me when we get home."

Mr. Irving had smiled, reached over, and squeezed his wife's shoulder while Maggie considered crawling under the desk, never coming out.

Even now, she winces looking at the picture. She'd never brought it up to Leo. Never knew if his parents had mentioned it. But it stayed with Maggie. The shame of that night.

How she hadn't even *thought* about any of it.

She moves the picture aside and picks up the next one. It's of a newborn baby, swaddled in a blanket. She brings it closer, realizes it's Sky, remembering back all of those years when Brian and Ann had first adopted her. She puts it in her pocket to show the girls, walks up the stairs and shuts the basement light.

The girls are still watching the movie in the tent. Maggie walks over to the opening, bends, and peers in, blinking at the bright screen.

"What are you watching?" she whispers.

"*Moana*," Sky whispers back.

"Again!" Maggie laughs, digging the picture out of her pocket. "I found this downstairs. It's you as a baby. I thought you might want to see it."

Sky takes the picture, but she's distracted, her eyes on the screen.

Maggie hears a faint knocking from the front of the house. She straightens, squinting at the front door, her eyes adjusting to the dark.

She walks to the door and opens it to see Xavier standing in front of her. He startles, as though she's scared him.

"Oh, you're up," he says. "I didn't want to wake you or Sky. I knocked once, but nobody answered."

"I was in the basement," she said, glancing at her watch. "It's only eight o'clock. I'm old but not that old."

"I was thinking Sky might be in bed. But that's silly, right?

She's ten." He blows a breath out. "Exactly why I can't do this. Zero knowledge of kids."

She suddenly remembers Leo. And the house. Their secret.

"How did you know I was here?" she asks cautiously.

"Leo told me. He's feeling better. Up and walking. He should be home tomorrow morning."

"Well, that's great news," she says, and waits. She's not sure why Xavier is here. Leo has her number. He could have easily called. "Is everything all right—"

"You're a good friend to Leo. And Sky," Xavier says. He looks down at his shoes, then back at her. "When I was first here, it seemed like maybe everyone was meddling. But I was wrong."

"Well, you weren't wrong about everyone," she says, sliding her eyes over to Agnes's house. "Do you want to come in? Sky and Frankie are watching a movie. But we could have a glass of wine."

"Thank you, but I can't. I have to go." He doesn't move though. Just looks at his feet, then back at her.

There's a tension between them that makes the hair on her arms stand up. She steps out and pulls the door shut behind her.

"Xavier, did something happen—"

"Leo told me about the house. What he wants to build. It's terrific, but it's just—I'm leaving," he says quietly. "On the last ferry tonight."

"Oh. I thought you were here until Monday—"

"I don't belong here," he says. "There's nothing about this place that makes me feel like I fit in."

She doesn't know what to say. What is there to say? She's a fourth-grade teacher. Half her life has been spent drying the tears of the kids who didn't fit in. And lecturing others about including *everyone*.

And then there are always the kids who don't seem to notice if they fit in or not.

Or care.

Nothing she says will make Xavier feel as though he belongs. But she tries anyway.

"You fit in just fine with Leo. And you will with Sky. Just give it time."

He smiles, nods dismissively, as though she couldn't possibly understand. "That's what Leo said."

He turns before she can speak and disappears into the dark. Vanishing in front of her.

So quickly and silently, it's as though he was never there at all.

35

She keeps an eye on her strength. Makes sure she'll have enough left to step off the cliff. To push her body into the air. Though it won't be hard. There's hardly anything left of her. She barely eats anymore. The groceries she had delivered last week are more than enough to last her weeks. More time than she needs.

She won't go in the forest again. Won't take that chance. Instead, she paints.

She starts in the beginning. Two girls huddled together. One of them crying, the round bump of her middle the focus of the picture. Her and Mac. She paints her desperation. Colors it in with fear and self-loathing.

Even then, the picture can't tell it all. Not how she felt trapped. Hopeless. She didn't want it. Would never either. Not with her modeling career. Not with her insane family—she wouldn't do that to her worst enemy, never mind a child. Her child.

She puts it aside to dry. Moves on to the next picture. She looks at the bed in the corner, the fireplace. Remembers the storm raging outside. Her body racked with pain that came wave after wave. And Mac. So calm. So confident.

"You're my best friend in the world," she'd told Mac while a contraction ripped through her. Mac had laughed, patted her belly.

"Tonight, I'm your midwife," she said. She doesn't paint all that.

Only the fire. And the hurricane outside the window. The two things she prayed to when she thought the pain might kill her. Might kill her baby too. Take away everything she promised Mac could have. Would have! A happy life. A family.

A baby of her own.

36

The first thing Sky asks him when he walks in the door from the hospital is the last thing he wants to talk about.

"Can my bedroom be on the second floor?" she blurts, having just skipped into the living room, Frankie on her heels. "Like in the back of the house. Looking out at the water?"

Maggie is in the kitchen, reading the newspaper at the counter, and she glances at him over the half wall separating the two rooms, gives him a baffled look.

"This was not my doing," she says, and looks back at the newspaper.

"I've only just started drawing the plans. I was sort of waiting to see what you wanted—"

"I want to move," she announces. "We slept there last night, and it's definitely not haunted. We even went in the basement in the middle of the night, and it wasn't even that scary."

"You did?" Maggie looks over. "Why?"

The girls shrug. "We just wanted to," Sky says vaguely.

Maggie stands, tucks the paper under her arm.

"On that note—I want a hot shower. Leo, call me if you need anything. Girls—I'll see you bright and early on Tuesday at school." She waves, disappears through the back door.

Frankie groans. "She had to remind us."

"When can we start working on the plans?" Sky asks.

"How about we start with me putting my keys down. Maybe getting a cup of coffee. Taking a shower."

"Fine," Sky tells him. "But after that, we're starting."

He doesn't answer. Just watches the two of them pile into the kitchen. Cereal boxes appear on the counter. The sound of spoons clinking together rings through the room. He considers walking into the kitchen and explaining that he might have changed his mind.

Instead, he goes into the bedroom, sits on the edge of the bed. Of course he can't tell her that—he doesn't even know if it's true.

He's barely processed what happened with Xavier. How he'd woken up from his drug daze at the hospital and decided to tell his husband about his plans before he lost his nerve.

Xavier had listened. And then stood up.

"The surprises just keep coming," he said. "How long have you been thinking about this?"

Leo shrugged. "Since July, I guess. Right after Mrs. Pearse died. It wasn't an option until then. I mean, I wasn't going to kick an old woman out of the house."

"No, right. That would be inconsiderate," Xavier said sarcastically.

"What's that mean?" Leo sat up straighter, ignored the twinge in his back.

"We're supposed to spend this great weekend together—the first time we've seen each other in months. And we end up here. In this shitty room. And then I stop at the house and Sky's there, catching me totally by surprise—"

"Wait. Sky's home? Why didn't you tell me?"

Xavier looked at him as though he might be insane. "You just woke up ten minutes ago! I leave to take a leak and come back and here you are, wide awake. Apparently ready to share the news about where we're moving next!"

Leo paused, aware that this was not going as he'd hoped. But it was out there in the open now. He wanted to explain.

"Look—I'm sorry. It's not the best time. But I can't lie to you anymore. And I'm lying to you because it's on the tip of my tongue when we talk, and I don't say anything! Regardless of the fact that I *really* want to do this is also the fact that Sky's house is a money pit. And small and old and full of memories that don't belong to us. We sell it. Start fresh." He reached for Xavier. "Say yes."

Xavier stepped back. "Who will start fresh? You and Sky? Am I even part of this equation anymore?"

The question startled him. He needed Xavier to understand how much he wanted him in his life. Needed him in his life. "Of course you are. Look—I know you have to go to LA. I'm not asking you not to. We can keep the condo if you want. We'll make it work. I'll come see you. You can spend time on the island—"

"I can't believe you want to live here!"

Leo flinched, stunned.

"I've walked around this town, Leo. I'm not kidding when I say you're pretty much the only black guy on the island. And gay? Sky swears there are gay people here, but not like where we live. We *fit in* where we live, Leo. Here? I don't fit in. At all."

There were so many things he wanted to say. He could've talked about the years and years of his life that he'd tried to blend in and then, finally, the freedom that came when he stopped caring if he did.

He thought of his father. How many times he'd told Leo

to be himself—to be comfortable in his own skin. Leo never listened.

Until one day, he did.

He looked at Xavier. "The only people you need to fit in with is us. Me and Sky," he said.

Xavier walked toward him. Leo leaned in for an embrace, but Xavier stopped, kissed Leo on the forehead.

"Goodbye," he said, and turned and walked out the door.

A piercing noise makes him jump. The smoke alarm in the kitchen is beeping, and he stands up from the bed, walks to the door. Sky peeks around the corner of the kitchen, yells that it's fine. They're making pancakes and one burned.

He nods, shuts the bedroom door behind him. He should take a shower. Start on the house plans. Look for a job.

Instead, he sits back down on the bed. Lowers his body until his head is on the pillow. He stares at the wall, concentrates on the pattern in the wallpaper, traces the circles with his eyes.

Anything to keep his mind off the fact that he has no idea how to live the rest of his life without his husband.

On Tuesday, he gets Sky off to her first day of school. For the next several hours, he has no idea what to do with his time.

Or his emotions.

When he was younger and he felt like this, he'd put on his running shoes and go for a jog. Let whatever was eating him up inside escape through his pores; he'd be sweat-drenched by the time he was done but less tense.

But he's on doctor's orders to take it slow. His lower back is still stiff, making him walk as though he's an old man.

So now he's stuck with this feeling boiling up inside of him.

He doesn't have any idea how to make it go away. The image of Xavier walking out of the hospital room replaying over and over in his mind.

Each time, he grows angrier. More convinced that moving ahead with his plan is exactly what he needs to do.

Then he changes his mind. Wonders if he should even be on this island anymore. He could just leave. Go back to his life with Xavier.

He woke up this morning with this thought. Then he drove Sky to school, and she leaned over in the car and kissed him goodbye. A peck on the cheek, as though it were the most natural thing in the world.

After she got out of the car, he drove back to Winding Way and straight over to his childhood home. He got out of the car and walked to the middle of the lawn, squinted at the old house. A picture of the new house forming in his head.

Now, it's almost lunchtime when he sits down at his drafting table. He's just hung up the phone with Joe. Hired him as the builder.

"You ready to get back to work?" Leo asked.

"You give me the go-ahead and that house will be history by the end of the week. Maybe sooner," Joe said.

After they hung up, Leo put a clean sheet of paper on the table, sharpened his pencil, and closed his eyes.

And imagined the possibilities of what could be.

37

Her new teacher isn't as nice as Miss Maggie, so the only thing that makes the first week of fifth grade fun at all is that Frankie gets her cast off so she can finally climb up the ladder to the tree house.

Which means their plan is on.

Frankie came up with the idea to spend the night in the tree house. She'd left another picture on the easel, hoping the mystery artist would finish it. But it rained all through Labor Day weekend, and when they went to the easel after school today, the painting was on the ground, a soggy, crumpled-up ball of paper.

They hadn't bothered to leave another one with the sky dark and gloomy, a light drizzle in the forecast.

Instead, they went back to Sky's house, made hot chocolate, and locked themselves in Sky's bedroom so Leo wouldn't overhear them talking about their plan.

Now, Frankie is stretched out on her bed, making a list of things they'll need.

"I think that's it," she says, sitting up. "You have snacks, water, and a lantern. I have a sleeping bag, a pillow, and binoculars." She looks up at Sky. "Should I add night goggles?"

"Night goggles?"

"My brothers got them for Christmas one year. They're on a shelf in the basement. I don't know if they work though."

"My teacher said there's supposed to be a full moon this weekend. Plus, it's a clear view from the tree house to the easel. There's a lantern out there already for when we shut the door to sleep."

Frankie shrugs. "If you say so. So here's the plan. We leave a painting on the easel in the late afternoon. We'll tell Leo we're sleeping at my house. My parents are away, so I'll tell my grandmother I'm sleeping here. She'll never know the difference anyway. She goes to bed while I'm eating dinner."

Frankie's been staying at her grandmother's house all week while her parents get her brothers settled at college. She's about to ask what they should do if Leo wants to talk to Frankie's mother. But she decides not to. He hasn't checked up on her once.

"Then we go to the tree house and wait. The easel isn't far. We'll hear someone walking through the woods. Plus, we can take turns with the binoculars. See if our mystery artist shows up."

"Why don't we just walk over to that artist studio you keep talking about and ask whoever's staying there if it's them?"

Frankie rolls her eyes. "And you think they'll be all, oh yeah—that's me. I did that. It's like painting 101 that you don't mess with someone else's work."

She sighs. She doesn't like lying to Leo.

He made her promise that if she wanted to stay overnight in the tree house, he would sleep in a tent down below, just like her father used to do. But now with his back still bothering him, he can't do that. Plus, they can't have him there anyway.

Not if they want to stake out the easel from the landing of the tree house.

Still she's making Frankie tell Leo. In her mind, it's not actually *her* lie.

"Come on," Frankie says. "It'll be our last summer adventure. We deserve it after camping got rained out."

"Let's go ask," she says to Frankie. "No sense planning all of this if he says I can't sleep over your house. Remember—you ask. It's your plan anyway. But first we're stopping at Lillian's. If she's home, we're going in. I still think it's her."

Frankie stands up, and heads for the door. "You want it to be her because you're afraid the mystery artist is really a psycho. An axe murderer luring us into the woods so he can chop us up in tiny pieces!" She whips around, shrinking back in horror.

Sky walks past Frankie, rolls her eyes as though she's not fazed.

She doesn't admit that a small part of her is thinking just that.

Lillian answers on the first knock. Sky and Frankie had agreed they'd ask to use the bathroom, tell some lie about the plumber working on Sky's bathroom. But they don't even have time to speak before Lillian opens the door wide.

"Come in!" she gushes. "This is kismet because I baked this morning and I never bake. But I had a craving for homemade chocolate chip cookies. Come help me eat them before I gain ten pounds."

"What's kismet?" Frankie asks, stepping into the house. Sky follows, scanning the walls for paintings. But the only thing she sees are gold-framed pictures of unsmiling women in lace bonnets and men who all look like Benjamin Franklin.

"Fate. Destiny. The universe bringing us together by chance but also at the perfect time."

"Oh," Frankie says, sitting at the table. "Do you paint?"

Sky glares at her. Frankie takes a cookie off the plate and pretends she doesn't notice the way Sky's eyes are burning a hole in her forehead.

"Paint?" Lillian takes glasses out of the cabinet and puts them on the table. She fills a pitcher with water and places it next to the plate of cookies. "Yes, actually. I do."

Sky glances at Frankie, raises an eyebrow.

"Mostly landscapes. A portrait here and there. I know Sky paints. Do you too?"

"Can we see one?" Frankie asks.

"I didn't bring any with me. They're all in storage."

"You haven't painted since you've been here?" Frankie presses.

"I've dabbled a little. Nothing serious though," Lillian says vaguely. "No more about me—tell me how camping was. The two of you were going to sleep in the backyard, right?"

Sky nods. "We did, but Leo hurt his back—"

"We're painting by the cliff later," Frankie blurts. "But I don't know if we'll finish. We'll probably just leave it and finish it in the morning. Great view out there, isn't it?"

There's a buzzing noise from the counter, and Lillian stands, picks up her phone.

"I'm sorry, girls. This is work. They were going to call if they needed me. Do you want to take some cookies to go?" she asks.

"No, we're fine. Thank you!" Sky stands and grabs Frankie's arm, yanks it before she can open her mouth again.

"Come back soon," Lillian calls out as they walk through the house and out the door.

"What?" Frankie says when they're on the sidewalk. "Stop looking at me like that. You said you wanted to see if it was her."

She has no idea if the mystery artist is Lillian. Thanks to the way Frankie practically came right out and accused her. "I thought we might figure it out without being so obvious."

"What I told her is only obvious if she's the one who's doing it. I wasn't going to leave it to you. You probably would've asked her to start clapping."

"You're hilarious. Come on, there's Leo. You can ask him about tonight." She points to where Leo is standing on the front lawn of his old house, except there is no house anymore.

He turns when he hears them walk up the steps to where he's standing.

"What do you think?" he asks. "They just took away the last dumpster from the demolition. Sort of surreal, isn't it?"

She looks at Frankie, then back at Leo. "If surreal means good, then yes. When do they start building it? Walls and stuff."

"Next week, I think. Joe told me he was going to move fast. I guess he wasn't kidding."

"Oh, ye of little faith," Joe says, suddenly appearing on the grass next to them. "Sign these." He hands a clipboard to Leo. "I might be on the bottom of the social ladder on this island, but I'm the top dog when it comes to pulling permits." He winks at Sky and Frankie. "Helps when your poker-night buddies are the town inspectors."

Leo glances up, his pen in the air. "These are legit, right? I don't want to cut any corners."

Joe frowns, taps the clipboard. "Whose name is under general contractor?"

Leo looks down. "Armstrong Incorporated," he says.

"That's right. *Joe* Armstrong Incorporated. Never cut a corner in my life. Not about to start now. I build. You design. Got it?"

Leo scribbles on the page, hands the pen and the clipboard

back to Joe. "Want to come over for burgers tomorrow night? Have a beer or two? I'll show you the final plans."

"Can I bring a plus one? Maggie's coming over for a drink. How about we bring a side dish and walk over around seven thirty?"

Leo nods as Joe hands him a piece of paper. "It's the bill for everything up until now. Hate to say it but get used to these. See you later, Sport One and Sport Two," he says, tapping Sky then Frankie on the head with the clipboard.

After he's gone, Sky nudges Frankie with her arm. They lock eyes, and Sky tips her chin in Leo's direction.

"So, Mr. Irving," Frankie begins. "Do you mind if Sky sleeps at my house tomorrow night?"

Leo's looking down at the bill, and he glances up at her, distracted. "Huh?"

"Sky," Frankie says. "Can she stay over? On Saturday night?"

Leo glances down at the paper again. "What? Yeah. Whatever. Just make sure it's okay with your parents. Give me a second, girls. I need to look at this," he says, walking away from them.

"Well, that was easy," Frankie whispers as they turn and hurry down the steps.

Sky just swallows, nods. Wondering what she's gotten herself into.

38

Tomorrow is her last day on this earth. She's ready. She still has her strength but the pain is worse. All week she's painted and slept. Nothing else.

Now, she lies in bed. Looks around the studio. Her paintings surround her. Held up on the walls by thumbtacks she found in a drawer. The last one she painted was something she hadn't seen with her own eyes. Only heard it from Mac.

The storm was raging when Mac had carried the baby from the shed to the truck just outside the door, already warmed and running. Mac had driven to the fire station and stuck her head in, leaving the newborn alone in the car for a brief moment. Just long enough to put a casserole dish on the table. Long enough to make sure the station was empty. Which Mac knew it was—she'd been on the phone with her husband when the fire alarm screeched, and he'd told her there was a fire on the waterfront.

Then Mac drove to the hospital. Rushed inside with the newborn. The story rolling off her tongue as the nurses tended to the baby. How Mac had only gone to the fire station to drop off dinner for her husband. Instead, she'd found a baby in the empty kitchen. A newborn wrapped in blankets. Safe and warm in a basket on the table.

The painting on the wall was of that scene. A baby in a basket on a long, wooden table. She remembers the basket. Remembers Mac swaddling the baby expertly. Placing the small bundle in a deep, cloth-covered basket, so deep the newborn disappeared before her eyes.

Only to be seen again through pictures Mac sent her over the years. Of a girl. Happy and smiling. And loved.

39

Maggie avoided the house as long as she could. She finally went home on Monday of Labor Day weekend, only to find the driveway empty, Pete's truck not parked in his usual spot.

She found a note on the table that said he'd gone to Dean's cabin for the weekend and her phone must be broken or lost because he'd tried to call and text her and she hadn't answered.

She waited all Labor Day for him to show up. Finally, she called him when the sun went down, shadows lurking in the corners of the house.

He picked up on the second ring, as though he was expecting her call.

"So, it's not broken or lost," he said. "I had a feeling."

"You're intuitive like that," she snapped, and then felt bad about it.

But she didn't apologize.

She couldn't muster the words or the feeling inside her. There was just anger. And disappointment.

"I'm just calling to say that we need some time apart. Longer than a weekend. Your note didn't say if you were planning on coming—" She paused. She didn't want to say *home*. "Back," she finished finally, after a moment.

"For how long?" he asked.

Forever, she thought. "I don't know," she said.

The line was quiet. "Do you still love me, Maggie?" Pete asked.

She nodded, her eyes welling up. She didn't trust her voice. She did love him. But somewhere along the way, their love had turned into something that made her feel lonely and broken and not enough.

"I guess that's my answer," Pete said quietly. "Dean said I can stay here for as long as I need. For the record, I love you, Maggie." The phone line went dead, and she sat in the dark, wondering when those words had simply become words.

Something to be said. And heard. She closed her eyes and tried to feel the emotion behind them.

I love you, Maggie.

But there was nothing inside of her except an empty space.

One she could no longer ignore.

On Friday, she's leaving the teachers' lounge, pushing the door open while glancing at her watch when she nearly hits someone on the other side.

"Oops—sorry!" she says. "My fault!"

Agnes pulls the door open wider, giving Maggie room to pass. "Well, I'm glad it wasn't on purpose," she says tightly.

They simply look at each other. They haven't spoken in almost two months. The longest they've gone without speaking since they first became roommates freshman year of college.

Agnes's face looks thin. Thinner than she's ever looked, even though she's always had a wispy, slender frame. Dark half-moons hang under her eyes.

Maggie steps back into the empty teachers' lounge, gestures for Agnes to follow her.

"Are you okay?" she asks after the door closes behind them.

Agnes frowns. "Of course I'm not okay. We haven't spoken in forever——"

"No, I mean health-wise," Maggie interrupts. "You look like you've lost weight. Which would be a compliment if someone said it to me, but you didn't have any to lose."

Agnes is silent. There's suddenly a pressure on Maggie's chest, making it difficult to breathe.

"You said all your tests were clear. In your driveway. Lillian's driveway—or whatever it is now. Has that changed? I mean, you would have called if something changed!"

Maggie's heart is racing. She waits for Agnes to answer. But Agnes simply stares at her, a blank look on her face.

"You told me not to call you. Remember? You said, 'Don't call me. Don't get in touch.' That you couldn't be around me right now."

Maggie's face burns. Had she said that? Those exact words? They don't sound like something she would say. But she remembers anger coursing through her in the driveway that day. How it burst out of her.

As though a lifetime of keeping it hidden away had allowed it to grow and grow until it became too enormous to contain.

"I'm sorry," she says now. "I was angry. And not just at you. That's no excuse——"

"I have to go," Agnes announces, turning and opening the door.

"Wait——" Maggie calls, but the door shuts. And Agnes is gone, leaving Maggie alone in the quiet room.

She stands for a minute, trying to swallow the lump that's formed in her throat. On the side table, there's a newspaper, the front-page picture catching her eye.

She's avoided looking online or reading anything other than her book ever since the picture of Pete had appeared in the paper. Now there's another one of him in his uniform. "Ichabod Police Chief Cleared of Allegations" headlined above the picture.

She scans the article. Reads how a third-party was hired to investigate claims that are not being publicly disclosed. The complaints were found to be *trivial* and *exaggerated*.

She drops the paper on the table, thinking she should feel relieved. Elated. Instead, she's numb. As if the article she just read isn't about her husband. But a stranger.

Someone she doesn't even know anymore.

By the time the school day ends, she's in a full-blown panic. Worried sick about Agnes. Had her cancer come back, and she hadn't said anything?

She barely got through the day without abandoning her students, running down to the nurse's office and making Agnes tell her exactly what the hell was going on.

But she didn't. Agnes was just about the most private person she'd ever known. Not about other people's business—only her own. She hadn't even told anyone in school that she was sick until her hair disappeared.

Even then, she was close-mouthed about it.

Still here, aren't I? she'd say when someone asked her how she was feeling. Or Maggie's favorite: *Shitty.* That was it. Not *Shitty, thanks for asking.* Or *Shitty, how about you?* Just one word. The air between the person asking the question and Agnes suddenly thick with an uncomfortable silence.

But Agnes didn't seem to mind. She'd just walk away.

As though, in her mind, the person got what they deserved for asking someone with cancer how she was feeling in a light, chirpy voice.

She waits until she's home to walk over to Agnes's house. She knocks on the door and waits. She turns to leave after several minutes when no one answers.

She's on the sidewalk when she decides to walk over to Agnes's other house. The front door is open, so she knows Lillian is home. The smell of gingerbread drifts out from the house when she reaches the door.

"Lillian?" she calls through the screen. "It's Maggie."

She hears a chair scrape against tile, and Lillian appears in the hallway, a surprised look on her face, the newspaper in her hand.

"Maggie. How nice. I was just going to have some cookies and tea and catch up on life on Ichabod. Come in!"

She opens the screen door and steps in. "Thank you, but I can't stay. I really just wanted to ask you something. About Agnes, actually." She can't keep the worry out of her voice.

Lillian tilts her head and walks forward tentatively, a concerned look on her face. "Of course."

"I mentioned that Agnes and I aren't really speaking. And I just have this awful feeling that maybe she's sick again. Did she happen to say anything to you? I knocked on her door, but she's not home."

Lillian shakes her head. "I haven't really seen much of Agnes. She's been avoiding me, I think, since I told her I was moving out at the end of the month. I'm looking for a different place on Ichabod."

She notices Lillian glance around the house after she says this. "Are you not comfortable here?"

"Actually, no. Not really." She lowers her voice. "I'm grateful that Agnes invited me to stay. But I just can't do this house. The vibe is just . . ." She grimaces.

"You're not into an early-nineteenth-century-Quaker vibe? I can't believe it."

Lillian laughs. "Nothing against it. But it's time for me to look for something else." She holds up the paper. "There are a few long-term rentals in here that I'm going to look at. I wanted to ask if you could keep your ears open and let me know if you hear of anything. Word of mouth has always worked for me in the past."

Maggie glances at the paper and winces when she sees Pete's picture.

"Or not," Lillian says, reacting to Maggie's expression. "I don't want to put you in a position."

"That face was completely unrelated to you." Maggie sighs. "I'm actually happy to look at places with you. If you want. I can give you the inside scoop on the neighborhoods."

A part of her feels as though she's betraying Leo. But she has to admit—she likes Lillian. She enjoyed Lillian's company at the cookout at his house.

Sky had sat with them through dinner. She wondered if Lillian would ask Sky about school or sports or her favorite color. All normal questions when you're trying to get to know someone, but exactly the type of questions that would force Sky to be the focus of everyone's attention at the table.

Something Sky did not enjoy.

But Lillian blended easily into the conversation. And when Sky asked to be excused and Leo said of course, Lillian merely looked up from her plate and smiled.

"See you soon, sweetie," she said. "Thanks for your help with George."

"That would be great." Lillian pauses. "I didn't know how you'd feel about me staying. I know you weren't happy when I moved here."

Maggie doesn't answer for a moment. What had changed? She couldn't say. Maybe it was just that she had a good feeling about Lillian. It was as simple as that.

And from what she knew, Lillian had respected Leo's wishes. She didn't seem to be someone who came to the island with bad intentions. Or to meddle in Sky's care. If anything, she had gone out of her way to be part of the community—a job at the island's dog-care service and frequent trips to the local shops. Maggie had seen her walk by her house with a yoga mat slung over her shoulder several mornings this past week. Most likely joining the class on the town green by the harbor.

She lifts her shoulders, lowers them. "I guess I changed my mind. No—wait. That sounds shallow. It's sort of . . . have you ever heard about a person you've never met? But you hear enough that you form an idea in your mind of what this person is like. Then when you do get to know this person, you find that she was nothing like you thought she would be."

Lillian looks sideways at her. "Am I this person?"

Maggie smiles. "You are this person." She pauses. "I am curious though. Why are you staying? I mean, is it just for Sky?"

Lillian twists her mouth as though she's considering this. "I'm not really sure. I always wanted to move back here. It just wasn't a possibility with Ann in school and my work. Then Ann grew up and sort of claimed this space. She made it clear that I was only welcome when asked. And she didn't ask often." She shrugs. "Honestly, I didn't know what to expect when I came here. But there's something so freeing about being on an island in the middle of the ocean. It sounds silly to say that I'm looking to start over—I'm aware I'm past middle age. I guess I'm still just looking—" She shakes her head. "It's hard to explain."

They don't speak for a moment. Maggie's eyes drift back to the picture of Pete on the front page of the paper in Lillian's hand. When she pulls her eyes away, Lillian is gazing off in the distance.

Looking for something she can't explain.

"It doesn't sound silly," Maggie says. "I know exactly what you're talking about."

And she does. She really does.

40

When Leo opens his eyes on Saturday, for the first time in as long as he can remember, he simply stands up. There's no weight on his chest. No pain in his back.

Only a list of things he needs to do today. And a house that's becoming an actual thing—straight out of his dreams.

He drew the plans faster than anything he's ever drawn in his life. Years and years of ideas spilling onto the page. In the end, it's a simple design. Clean lines. A good-sized house, but not more than what they need. The scale appropriate for the neighborhood.

He's always had a thing for Craftsman-style bungalows. Exposed beams in every room. Open concept in the main living area. Four bedrooms upstairs. Each one with a view of the water.

The master and Sky's room are positioned so they have the best light. Almost the entire back of the house is glass. Sliders or windows that look out at the sloping grass lawn with the ocean in the distance.

"Oh, thank God," Joe had said when he looked at the plans for the first time.

"I was afraid you were going to ask me to build a McMansion. What do you think, boss?" he asked Sky, who was standing next to them.

"It's perfect. Except there's no tree house."

"Let's build one house at a time here," Leo said distractedly, looking at his watch. "Speaking of—I've got a call with the Realtor for this place in ten minutes. She said she has someone who's been dying to move into this neighborhood. We might not even need to put it on the market."

"Hope they don't mind living next door to an old guy who waters the garden in his boxers," Joe said.

"It's not you I'm worried about. When I was trying to find a tenant for the house after my parents died, the property manager kept complaining about my neighbor. Turns out Agnes was telling everyone he brought over that the street was monitored. No noise after a certain hour. No street parking. The whole bit."

Joe shook his head. "Did she chase everyone away until the right person came along?"

"Enter Mrs. Pearse. The whitest, richest, oldest person on the island. Right up Agnes's alley."

"I hope the new family who moves in doesn't speak a lick of English. Goddamn place could use a little diversity." Joe smiled. "Not telling you anything though."

Leo smiled back. "Joe Armstrong—man of the people. You surprise me every day." He slapped him on the back, left him staring at the house plans.

Leo's future spread out on the table, waiting to take shape.

Now the house is gone. Demolished in a day. Joe insisted he'd have the frame up by the end of next week, and Leo hadn't believed him. But now that he's seen the speed at which Joe works—the crew he pulled together seemingly out of thin air—he doesn't doubt it.

He's noticed a change in Joe and wonders if he has a crush on Maggie. He'd heard about Pete moving out from Joe, who told Leo to keep it to himself in a way that made Leo wonder why Joe had mentioned it at all. He's not sure he would have noticed that Pete wasn't around with the odd hours the police chief kept, his truck rarely in the driveway.

He doesn't really know Pete at all, even though he grew up down the street from him.

He was always just the cop who lived a couple of houses away. When Leo moved back months ago, they'd met on the street once, both of them getting the mail. Leo had said it was good to see him—it had been a while. And Pete smiled and waved, a look on his face that made Leo wonder if the man even remembered who he was. He'd just assumed, after all, with Maggie's involvement in Sky's life. But it made more sense when he'd lived on the street for several weeks.

He could count on one hand the number of times Pete was home.

Then Maggie and Joe showed up at Agnes's Fourth of July party together.

He thought about asking Joe about it, but he wasn't one to pry right now. He flinched when anyone asked him about Xavier. Made up some excuse about how Xavier was traveling for work. Even though he was just a ferry ride away on the mainland.

Apparently never coming back to Ichabod.

Now though, he's walking past Maggie's house, and the thought briefly passes through his mind again.

Joe and Maggie.

For some reason, he feels a heaviness imagining this, even though he likes both of them. Loves them, really.

But Maggie's marriage breaking up only reminds him of his own.

How he never imagined a future without Xavier. And here he is, building a house all on his own. On an island his husband despises. How long had Maggie and Pete been married? A quarter of a century, maybe?

And just like that, it was over.

But was it just like that? Or was it a series of blows. Or nicks. Or cuts. Injuries that damaged the foundation of the marriage.

His future is taking shape before his eyes. Soon there will be walls. Rooms. A house, waiting for a family to move in.

As the days pass, reality sets in. His family might not include Xavier.

It's almost dark when Sky and Frankie walk through the back door. They freeze when they see him, as though he's surprised them.

He's equally surprised.

"What are you doing here?" he asks. "I thought Frankie's mother was picking you up?" He looks at his watch. "Three hours ago."

He glances at Frankie, then Sky, who look at each other, then him.

"She was picking us up. Is, I mean. She *is* picking us up!" Frankie corrects, then laughs nervously.

Leo tilts his head. Wonders briefly why they both seem jumpy. But he's in a rush.

Joe's waiting at the other house for Leo to bring back a spare set of plans. He rifles through the papers on the table, half listening to Frankie, who's talking again.

". . . then my brother missed the bus to his game, so my mother had to drive him. Then we were going to walk, but Sky wanted to show me something in the tree house, so we went there. And now we're back——"

"Is she getting you or not?" he interrupts, digging the plans out from under a stack, his eyes on the clock on the wall. "The plumber's waiting, so I have to run."

"Yes." Frankie nods. "She'll be here any second. We're actually going to start walking and meet her. Like around the corner. Right?" she asks Sky, who nods dumbly, then clears her throat.

"Sorry we didn't tell you we were still here. I didn't want to bother you. I know you're busy working——" Sky begins, and he holds up his hand.

"It's fine——look. Just walk down to the other house if you end up needing a ride. I have to get back. Okay?"

The girls nod, and he turns and rushes out the door. He's halfway down the street before he realizes that his entire car is loaded with cedar shingles. The back seat unavailable.

But it's another hour before he remembers the girls, and by then, he knows they've been picked up. He thinks about calling Frankie's house to confirm they arrived, but just as he pulls his phone out, Joe calls his name.

And the night gets away from him. Just like that.

41

They hold their breath until the door closes behind Leo. Then Frankie turns and glares at her.

"I told you we shouldn't have come back!" Frankie hisses.

"And do what? Sit in the dark all night?"

They were settled in the tree house when Sky turned the knob on the lantern, and nothing happened. They spent the next hour arguing about it.

Frankie insisted they didn't need light. Sky insisted they did.

Frankie said it was stupid to go back and risk getting caught. Sky said there was no way she was staying without a light. The lantern was always on at night in the tree house. Otherwise with the door shut and no windows, it was pitch-black.

Leo was working at the other house anyway, she argued.

Finally Frankie gave in. And they left the tree house, walked straight through the back door of Sky's house, and nearly bumped into Leo.

Luckily Frankie came up with a story, and Leo was distracted enough to fall for it.

Now Sky digs in the junk drawer, looking for two C batteries, but all she sees is a handful of stray AAs.

"What about this?" Frankie says, reaching in. She holds up

a small lighter, igniting the flame. Then throws it back in the drawer as though she knows it's a ridiculous suggestion.

"Wait." Sky digs it out, an idea forming in her mind. "Follow me."

They go out the back door and she leads them to Joe's garage. His truck is gone, and she knows he's at the other house with Leo.

Still, she's quick.

Frankie keeps watch by the garage door while she hurries inside and grabs the glass lantern off the shelf and tucks the bottle of fuel under her arm.

She'd asked Joe about it the day she was working on the easel, and he said he'd show her how it worked sometime. He explained how the fuel went in the bottom of it, and she just had to light the wick and the flame would burn for hours.

She's out the door in less than a minute, handing Frankie the bottle and cradling the lantern against her body while they both run through the backyard.

Sky glances behind her once to make sure they haven't been seen. And then they're on the path, dusk threatening to turn to darkness just as they climb the ladder and collapse on the bed in the tree house, breathing hard.

"Okay—you were right. It does get dark fast when the sun goes down," Frankie says, giving Sky a *sorry* look.

She removes the glass from the lantern and unscrews the top while Sky takes the cap off of the lamp fuel.

"You do it. Your hands are steadier," Sky says, eyeing the small opening. "We should have brought a funnel."

Frankie nods. "Here goes nothing," she says, putting the bottle close to the lip, tipping it until the clear liquid rolls toward the opening. But she tips it just a little too far, and the fuel spills over the edge onto the wood floor.

"Crap!" Frankie mutters while Sky searches for something to clean it up. There's nothing in the tree house besides their bedding and a handful of paintings taped to the wall. She digs a T-shirt out of her backpack and presses it against the liquid, the smell of the fuel making her eyes water.

She wipes up as much as she can while Frankie screws the top on, then presses the flame from the lighter to the wick.

"That was a disaster," Frankie says. "But it's working." She puts the lantern on the floor near the wall, and they both look up as a soft light spreads through the room.

She feels Frankie's eyes on her, and when she glances over, Frankie lifts an eyebrow.

"You don't look any better," she tells Sky.

An hour ago, they'd left another painting on the easel. Another half-done picture of Sky, an action shot of her from last summer at camp, riding a speckled pony in a ring.

"Let's see if our mystery artist can draw animals as well as humans," Frankie had said, clipping the actual photograph to the easel.

Then she looked at Sky and pointed at her face. "You're kind of green. Are you feeling okay?"

"I don't know," she replied, pressing her hand to her forehead. "It's probably just the leftover tacos we had for lunch. Come on, let's go."

Now, between running into Leo and spilling the fuel on the floor, both Frankie and Sky have been too busy to think about her green face. But she can't deny that her head is pounding, and it's suddenly hard to breathe, and she wants nothing more than to lie down on the feather bed on the floor and close her eyes.

"You should lie down," Frankie says, as though reading her mind. "I can take the first watch. I'll wake you up if I see anything. Or in a couple of hours. Whichever comes first."

"I feel bad," she says, toppling over onto the bed. Her body melting into the covers. "This was supposed to be fun!"

Frankie stands, grabs a bag of chips from their snack bag and hangs the binoculars around her neck. "Who says it isn't? Your company isn't *that* great. Close your eyes. Sleep away the green, please. You're making my stomach turn."

Sky reaches for a pillow to throw at Frankie, but when she puts her head down, she's drifting off to sleep before the door shuts.

She dreams she's in a burning car, trapped in the back seat. She's curled in a ball, pressed against the hard cushion, the heat searing.

She tries to scream, but nothing comes out of her mouth. Then something slams into her leg and she opens her eyes, swimming out of the nightmare until she blinks herself fully awake, screaming when she sees the fire.

Her nightmare isn't a nightmare.

The tree house is on fire. A roaring wall of yellow and orange flames across from her, so hot she can barely look at it.

She doesn't know how long she's been asleep. The last thing she remembers, Frankie was outside on the landing, waiting for the mystery artist.

She blinks through the smoke and sees Frankie standing above her. Frankie turns and steps on Sky's leg, in the same spot that woke her out of her nightmare, and Sky gets a look at Frankie's face, slack and expressionless, and she knows immediately that Frankie is sleepwalking.

"Frankie!" she screams, reaching for her, but her hand grazes Frankie's fingers, the fire pushing her back against the wall.

The lantern is shattered at Frankie's feet. She must have kicked it over, the glass broken, fire climbing up the far wall.

She lunges forward, grabs Frankie's arm and tugs, pulling her down to the bed next to her, where she watches Frankie snap out of sleep, blinking until terror flashes in her eyes and she looks at Sky and lets out a scream.

"Get up!" Sky shouts and they start to stand, backs pressed to the wall, when there's an explosion in the corner by the door, knocking them both down.

An orange light blinds her, smoke filling the room.

She pictures her T-shirt. The one she'd used to clean the spilled lamp fuel. The one that was soaked and balled up in the corner, now a bonfire, loud and crackling.

She can't see Frankie anymore, the smoke from the fuel black and dense, her eyes burning. Her throat closing. She tries to move, grabs for Frankie, but the fire is big, too big—the wall across from her too hot to even look at.

The fire is headed for the door, trapping them in the tree house.

She's paralyzed. A hot glow blazing in front of them. The heat suddenly unbearable. Black, thick smoke all around them.

She hears Frankie call her name, and they fumble in the dark until they grab hands. Sky tries to stand but Frankie yanks her down.

"Stay on the ground!" she hears Frankie shout.

But her throat is closing. She gulps for air. Fire fills her lungs. She gasps again, but there's nothing left in the room but heat and fire and darkness.

And then nothing. Just a black hole tugging at her, swallowing her until she curls in a ball, closes her eyes.

*   *   *

Her body is being dragged. She feels the wood under her heels and hands underneath her armpits. She wants to scream for it to stop—the heat on her face is too hot. But she can't speak.

Can't do anything besides die in this fire.

Then she's outside. A surge of air fills her lungs and she gulps, coughs, clawing at her throat. She presses her hand into her eyes, forcing them to open so she can see. She's lying on the tree house deck, the black night in the distance, flames touching the treetops above her.

Someone is shoving her to the edge of the landing to the ladder. But there's no way she can climb. She can't even feel her arms or legs.

Her body is pushed forward, her legs fall over the edge, and suddenly there are hands in her own, a foot pressing against her lower back until she slips over the edge into the air where she hangs, the hands holding her tightly, then loosening slowly when her body is fully stretched out, closer to the ground.

She holds her breath when she knows she's going to be dropped.

How far is it to the ground? she wonders briefly, and then she's falling through the air. She doesn't even have time to scream before she lands on her side, her body bouncing off the hard earth. She can't feel anything, just a buzzing in her head.

"Crawl!" someone shouts from above, and she listens, gathering all her strength, willing her body to move. She turns over and claws at the dirt, drags her body away from the tree house.

She doesn't know how far she's gone when she turns, squints up at the fire, now a blazing ball of orange in the trees.

She screams Frankie's name. Over and over.

Then two figures appear. Straight out of the fire. She watches as they stumble through the door and onto the narrow landing in front of the stairs, the fire blazing behind them.

She stares at the figure behind Frankie. Tall and thin. Long hair. A woman, though she can't see her face.

Suddenly a noise rips through the forest. A *SNAP* so loud, Sky screams, reaches her hand out just as the tree house buckles, folding in on itself.

A body is launched in the air. Pushed, it seems, with such force that arms and legs flail, and hang suspended in the air for a moment, before dropping.

Frankie.

Darkness dots her vision, but she rises to her knees, starts crawling, inch by inch, toward her best friend, who's motionless.

A body crumpled on the ground.

42

She hears the screams before she sees the fire.

This was going to be her last night. She'd packed up all of her belongings into her duffel bag. Not one thing left behind in the studio. Then she'd walked to the cliff, threw it over the edge into the ocean, and watched as it splashed into the sea. Next, she went to the easel, left all the paintings in the box. She wrapped them in a clean sheet of paper and tied them with a piece of string she'd found in a drawer.

She saw the unfinished painting they'd left on the easel. The photograph next to it. She smiled, traced her finger over the girl on the pony, then unclipped both from the easel and placed them on top of the other paintings in the box.

It's time. She can't finish this one for the girl. What she's left in the box will have to be enough.

She stands on the edge of the cliff. The portrait she'd painted of her daughter in her hand. She's ready. Counts backward from three.

A scream breaks the silence. And she turns, watches as fire shoots from the treetops.

By the time she sprints into the forest, it's impossible that the ball of orange before her is the tree house, but she hears the screams.

She's watched the girl climb up there so many times from her hiding spot, she has the number of rungs on the ladder memorized.

Good thing too, because the smoke is so thick—the fire so hot—she can barely open her eyes, barely breathe. She finds them in the corner, huddled together, both of them unconscious.

She doesn't think—just moves. Lifting and pulling. She's weak. Too weak. All she can do is drag and pull and tug. Finally, she's holding the girl over the edge, the weight of her almost pulling her off the landing. It's a drop, but not too far with the way she's lowered her. She shoves her as hard as she can with her foot, and when she lands, she screams for her to get away from the flames.

When she looks behind her at the tree house, she almost gives up.

But there's another girl trapped. Someone's daughter. She runs through the door, the heat searing, burning her legs and arms and face. The girl is screaming—awake now, trapped in the corner. She grabs her and pulls her out of the door just as the roof splits and the floor beneath them tilts, threatening to give way.

They're going to crumble with the house.

The girl screams, and their eyes lock. She takes a step forward, and with all her might pushes the girl off the landing, watches her fly through the air toward the ground.

Before the flames engulf her body, she looks down at the girl who's crawling, trying to reach her friend.

When the floor beneath her gives out, she falls into it.

Willingly. Finally.

How glorious it is to die in this way. How her last moments on this earth have proven to be her best.

How, for once, she's the mother her daughter always deserved.

43

They're sitting on Leo's patio sipping cocktails and waiting for the burgers on the grill to cook.

Maggie accepted Joe's invitation to join him for dinner at Leo's even though what she really wanted to do was put on her pajamas and disappear in front of the television.

But that's what she's been doing most nights lately. So she made herself walk across the street, a bowl of homemade potato salad in her arms.

It was Saturday night, after all.

Leo's sitting next to her at the table, and he sniffs at the air and looks at them, stands abruptly and walks to the grill.

"I think I'm burning our dinner," he calls out.

"That's a fire somewhere. Must be some idiot burning leaves when he shouldn't be." Joe looks at her. "Speaking of idiots. Has your husband come to his senses? Begged you to forgive him?"

She feels herself bristle. "I thought you liked Pete?"

"I do like Pete," Joe says. "I can like him and think he's an idiot for letting you go."

"He's not letting me go," Maggie corrects. "Nobody has to be in the wrong here. We're just two people who want different things."

She feels her face redden, aware that it wasn't long ago that she asked Joe to pick sides. Hers or Pete's. Now listen to her.

"I'm sorry," she says to Joe. "I'm all over the map lately."

But he's not listening to her. He's on his feet, stepping away from the table, looking at the woods behind them.

"What?" she and Leo ask at the same time, turning to see what he's looking at.

There's a moment when nobody speaks. All three of them staring at the ball of fire spurting out of the forest.

In the exact spot where the tree house sits.

"Thank God Sky's at Frankie's house," Leo says. "I'm calling it in." He turns to leave when Maggie says his name.

"Frankie's parents are taking their sons to college," she blurts. "Frankie's brothers. The twins."

"I thought Frankie's mother picked them up—" He stops, looks at the woods, as though something has just occurred to him.

The same thing that occurs to all of them at the same time. They take off running for the woods without another word.

"Someone should stay and call it in!" Joe shouts, but the sound of a siren wails in the distance, growing louder.

Maggie hasn't sprinted like this in years, and her side is throbbing when they see the flames in front of them.

The tree house is no longer a tree house. Just a burning ball in the trees.

"Jesus," she hears Joe say.

But when she turns, Joe's not looking at the fire. He's running in the other direction. To two girls on the ground.

She reaches for Leo, but he's gone, following Joe. She can't move. Her feet are lead weights attached to her legs.

"Maggie? Is that you?" someone calls. She turns to see Lillian rushing toward her. "I saw the fire from the house."

"Me too," says Agnes, joining them, a fire extinguisher in her hand. "It's probably silly but I thought I'd see if I can help. Oh, Sky's going to be heartbroken," she says, looking at the tree house, then at Maggie. "What's wrong? You're as white as a ghost—"

Maggie pushes past Agnes and stumbles over to the girls. Frankie is sprawled on the ground, her eyes closed, her arm bent at an angle. Maggie drops to her knees, next to Joe, who's crouching over Frankie.

"She's breathing," he shouts.

Agnes appears, kneeling on the ground across from Maggie, her eyes searching Frankie's body. "Go help Sky. I have her."

Someone is screaming. A howl so raw, Maggie's heart feels as though it might burst out of her chest.

She crawls the few feet to where Sky is lying on the ground. Leo has Sky's head in his lap, and he's yelling at her to stay still. He doesn't know what's broken.

But Sky's not listening. She's screaming, pointing at the tree house that's exploding in front of their eyes.

"What is she saying?" he shouts at Maggie. "Sky—I can't understand—"

But Maggie is right next to Sky's head. So close they're almost touching. And she hears her. Hears exactly what she's saying.

She grabs Leo's arm, holds on to it so she doesn't collapse.

"She's saying there's a woman in there," Maggie says. "There's a woman in the fire," she says softly at first. Then loud.

As loud as she can.

Maggie stands, shouts it at the top of her lungs. Over and over until the firefighters who rush by hear her too.

Then she's on the ground, shielding Sky from what's happening right in front of them.

The tree house dissolving. The ladder brought in by the firefighters dropped to the ground.

There's nothing left to climb. Just a ball of fire that's burning. Waiting to become a pile of ash.

44

It's his fault the girls were in the tree house. All his fault.

He didn't have a second to think in the ambulance on the quick ride to the hospital, and then doctors and nurses were in the room and then they'd kicked him out to examine Sky and sent him to sign forms. By the time the nurse brought him to the waiting room, he hadn't even processed what happened.

Maggie and Agnes and Lillian are sitting in the windowless room with him. Joe stayed behind with the firefighters, and Leo wonders if they've put out the fire by now.

But mostly, he can't stop thinking about how it's all his fault.

"Stop saying that," Maggie says softly.

Leo looks up, surprised. He hadn't realized he'd actually *said* it out loud.

"Well, it is," he argues. "I'm the one who didn't call Frankie's mother to make sure they were staying there."

"Who the hell were they with anyway?" Maggie asks. "There's a woman more than likely dead back there, and we have no idea who it is!"

"Are we sure it's a woman?" Agnes asks. "Don't let it be a child. One of their friends!"

"No." Maggie shakes her head. "Sky said woman. Over and over. You heard her screaming it—"

"I heard her," Lillian says, nodding. "She kept shouting: *There's a woman in the fire*—"

"Lillian, please," Maggie interrupts, covering her ears at the sound. The way Lillian says it sends a shiver through her.

"I'm sorry—I think I'm still in shock!" Lillian drops her head back, stares at the ceiling.

"What did Frankie's parents say?" Leo asks Maggie. He had wanted to call them, but Maggie insisted. Told him to stay in the ambulance with Sky and she'd take care of it.

"They had no idea who it could have been. Absolutely none. Granted, they thought Frankie was in bed at her grandmother's house, so I think all of it was a bit overwhelming. Frankie's mother is on a flight home now. But I don't think she's going to be able to tell us anything."

The door opens, and Joe appears, his hair wild, the smell of smoke following him in the room.

"How are they? What did the doctor say?" he asks.

"They're both okay," Leo says. "But I don't have details. They kicked me out of the room so they could examine her."

"Can I get you a water?" Agnes asks Joe. "A wet towel?" She studies him, concern on her face.

He shrugs, and Agnes disappears out the door, happy, it seems, to have something to do.

"Is the fire out?" Leo asks, and Joe sighs, nods.

"It didn't spread. Just the tree house and some of the surrounding brush. Police are on the scene."

Agnes returns with a towel draped over each arm and a cup of water in her hand. She stands in front of Joe and extends her left arm.

"This one first. Head and face. Hands and arms."

Joe takes the towel, a suspicious look on his face. He lowers his head and rubs the wet towel over it, dragging it down over his face. Then up and down each arm. When he's done, Agnes gestures for him to drop it on the floor.

"Now the same with the dry one," she says, and he takes the towel and repeats the process.

"Now, drink," she says, handing him the cup.

Agnes leans down and gathers the towels and disappears out the door without another word.

Joe chugs the water. When he's done, he looks like a new man.

"She's good," he says, looking at the door.

"Yup," Maggie agrees. "Bedside manner not included, she's one of the best nurses on the island."

"So?" Leo asks impatiently, waiting for Joe to tell him what he knows. "What happened? Who is the woman? What was Sky talking about?"

Joe slumps in the chair. "No clue to all of the above. They found a body. Not exactly identifiable. A woman though. Just like Sky said. Cops will be here soon. I told them where to find us."

Joe stands suddenly, peering out the glass door.

"I wish they'd send someone in to give us an update," he says just as the door swings open and a man in scrubs steps in. It's a different doctor than the one he met earlier in Sky's room, and the man's eyes roam over them.

"Sky's family?" he asks.

Leo stands. "That's me. I'm Leo. Her, um . . ." He can't seem to find the word. "How is she?"

"She'll be fine. We'll keep her overnight. Give her some oxygen for the smoke and pain meds for the bruise on her back. It'll be sore, but nothing serious. You can see her in a bit. We're moving her to a room with her friend."

"Frankie—she's okay? Did you talk to her parents? They're probably worried sick."

The doctor holds up his hands. "I spoke with them. Frankie did as well. She's a tough kid." He smiles. "Broken arm, a good bump on her head, and some minor burns, but I almost had to strap her down on the bed. She kept trying to go see Sky. I'll send a nurse to get you when they're in the room."

He waves and disappears out the door.

Leo stares at the wall. *Guardian.* That's the word he was looking for when the doctor came in.

He wants to say *parent*. He's her parent. But he's not. Not really. A parent would have called to check with Frankie's mother. That's what a parent would have done.

Instead, they're here in the hospital. Two young girls with burns and bumps and bruises.

A woman dead.

All his fault.

45

Frankie sleeps straight through the night.

She was asleep when they first got to the room, and Sky thought Frankie might wake up when Leo came in. But he barely spoke. He just came over and kissed Sky on the forehead, told her to close her eyes and get some rest.

Then he sat down in the chair next to her bed. She could tell he wanted to ask her a million questions, because every time she opened her eyes, he was looking at her. He'd lean forward, tilt his head in a way that made her feel as though he wanted her to say something.

Finally, she told him what she'd been wanting to tell him all along.

"I'm sorry I lied," she said. "About staying at Frankie's."

He nodded, as if he already knew this, and then the nurse walked in and said Sky should try to get some sleep, and Leo stood up.

"Do you want me to stay the night? I can sleep in the chair," he said.

"You can't with your back," she said quickly, relieved when he came over and kissed her forehead again and said he'd be back in the morning, because she couldn't think of anything worse than having him stare at her all night, waiting to ask what happened.

When she had absolutely no idea what happened.

She almost went over at one point and shook Frankie awake so they could talk about it. But then she closed her eyes and fell asleep.

Now it's morning and she's been waiting for Frankie to wake up when a nurse comes in again, and by the time she leaves, Sky looks over to see Frankie sitting up, her eyes open.

Sky turns over, leans as far as the bed allows toward Frankie.

"I can't come over with this thing in my arm!" She points to the IV.

"Me either." Frankie holds up her arm. "Can you believe I broke it again?" she says, gesturing to her other arm.

She pictures Frankie in the burning tree house. Then falling through the air.

"If you start crying, then I'm going to. So don't!" Frankie warns as Sky's eyes fill with tears.

"You could have died—"

"And I didn't. And you didn't. Besides, I should be crying over you—I'm the reason we're in this stupid hospital."

"What *did* happen? I went to sleep, and you were outside. Then I woke up and there was fire everywhere."

"I watched the easel for a couple of hours and then I got tired. I went inside to wake you up, but you were all curled up, and I didn't know if you still didn't feel good. So I just lay down for a second, thinking I'd listen for footsteps. Go back out in a couple of minutes. Then I woke up to you screaming. Then—" She looks over at Sky, who doesn't speak.

Both of them are silent, staring at each other. The woman, Sky wants to say. But she can't make it pass through her lips. She knows she's dead. She saw her drop straight into the flames.

There's a knock on the door, and Leo walks into the room, followed by a policeman.

"Hi girls. This is Officer Mike," Leo says in an upbeat voice, as though he's just brought a clown into the room instead of a cop. "He just wants to talk to you guys about last night. Nothing to be afraid of—you're not in any trouble. Okay?"

He nods to Officer Mike, who Sky and Frankie already know from surfing at the beach. He's not that much older than Frankie's brothers, and she's glad it's him standing in front of them and not Maggie's husband, her neighbor, who seems much scarier.

"Sky and Frankie, right?" He points to Sky first and then Frankie. They both nod, and he slaps his hands together. "We're off to a good start. That's about as hard as the questions are going to get, okay?" He flashes a smile, trying to make them comfortable.

But Sky can't breathe, and when she glances at Frankie, she's as white as the sheets on her bed.

"First—I have some hard news." He pauses, glances at Leo, who nods, as though giving him permission to say what he's about to say. "There was a woman in the tree house with you. She, um, didn't make it. I'm sorry." He waits, folds his hands in front of him, and puts his head down.

Sky slides her eyes over to Frankie, who widens her eyes briefly and looks back at Officer Mike.

"We didn't know her," Frankie offers. "I mean she saved us. But we were sleeping when the fire started. And then she just showed up."

"You had no prior dealings with or knowledge of this person?" Officer Mike asks, looking at Leo, as if he should add something to the conversation.

"Girls," Leo cuts in. "Anything you can tell us is helpful. Even if you think it's not important. They're having trouble identifying the bod——" He clears his throat. "We want to find out who she is. You know, for her family."

Sky looks over at Frankie, who nods, as though she knows what Sky is about to say.

"We don't know who she is. But we have an easel by the cliff. We paint there sometimes. And someone started finishing our paintings. We wanted to see who it was. We left a picture and were hoping whoever it was would come back. That's why we slept there. Except we both fell asleep, and Frankie started sleepwalking and kicked over the lantern. And then the tree house lit on fire. Then she just was there. To save us."

"Did she say anything? Did she know your names?"

They both shake their heads.

"Okay," Officer Mike sighs. "How about looks——can you describe her? Color of her skin? Hair? Any physical description would help."

"I couldn't see anything," Sky says. "I just felt someone dragging me, and then when I looked up after I was on the ground, I saw just a woman and Frankie."

"How do you know it was a woman?"

Sky pauses, closes her eyes and pictures the moment when she looked up from the ground at the tree house. "Her hair, I guess. It was long. And she was skinny. Like tall, taller than Frankie, but like a skeleton. You saw her," she says to Frankie. "You had your back to me, so you must have looked right at her."

Frankie holds Sky's eyes, then looks away. "It was dark. Smoky. I don't remember anything." She looks down, picks at the blanket on her legs.

"Nothing?" Officer Mike presses. "Think. Maybe close your eyes and try——"

"I don't remember," Frankie says, her voice suddenly hard.

"I think that's enough for now," Leo says. "We'll call you if we can think of anything else, okay?" He extends his hand to Officer Mike, who shakes it.

"Thanks, girls. Feel better, okay?" He waves, walks to the door.

"Wait," Frankie calls and he turns. "There's an artist studio. On Crow Farm. I don't know if it has anything to do with it. Or this woman. But whoever kept finishing our paintings was good. Really good." She shrugs. "Maybe check if anyone was staying there."

Officer Mike nods and gestures for Leo to follow him out to the hallway.

"Be right back," Leo says, and closes the door behind him.

Sky looks over at Frankie, who takes a deep breath and blows it out.

"You okay?" she asks.

Frankie shakes her head, a tear slipping down her cheek.

Sky holds her breath. Frankie never cries.

"What?" she whispers, leaning over the side of the bed.

Frankie leans over too.

"I wanted to tell you first. Not him," Frankie says. "I did see her. She was right in front of me. Like as close as you are to me. And I looked right at her."

Sky waits. "And?" she asks finally.

Frankie swallows. "It was you," she whispers, her voice catching. "I was looking at someone who looks just like you."

46

She was the one who suggested sending the rookie cop to talk to the girls.

Pete had called her on the phone. He was heading to the hospital to interview Sky and Frankie, but he wanted to stop by first to see what she knew.

It was the first time they'd seen each other in weeks, and Maggie had been nervous about it. Maybe things would be different between them.

But Pete had walked in the door without knocking, as though he'd never left. And they'd argued almost immediately.

"Tell me what you know about all this. I heard pretty much the whole street was at the scene of the fire," he said.

"I know very little. We were having dinner, and Joe turned around and saw the fire—"

"Joe Armstrong? From across the street?"

"Yes—and then we heard the fire trucks and ran into the woods. The tree house was on fire. Sky and Frankie were lying on the ground—"

"Why were you and Joe having dinner?" he interrupted, folding his arms across his chest. He spread his legs and leaned back.

The cop stance, she called it.

It infuriated her. Always had. Made her feel as though she were being interrogated.

In her own kitchen.

"I didn't know you guys were friends."

"Yes, you did," she said tightly. "We've been friends with Joe for a long time."

"We have. Yes. Me, you. Joe. That's three people. Not two people having dinner together."

She could've told him that Leo was there. Instead, she walked over to the door, opened it.

"If these are the questions you want to ask me, you can leave."

"I don't know why you're so angry all the time." He threw up his hands.

"I know you don't," she said calmly. "Who are you sending to talk to the girls?"

He shrugged, walked past her. "Probably me. Why?"

"They're two ten-year-olds who are hurt and scared. Send one of the young guys. And tell him not to cross his arms and stand like you do."

He rolled his eyes, pushed the screen door open. "Any other suggestions?" he mumbled over his shoulder.

"Yes. Next time, knock," she said, slamming the door behind him. Not giving a damn that the whole house shook.

She found herself humming as she poured herself a cup of coffee. She went out on the deck, sat in the sunshine, and thought about how light she felt.

How free.

She makes a pan of lasagna in the afternoon and thinks about walking it over to Leo's house an hour after she sees his car pull in the driveway. But she wants to give him some time alone. Some space to deal with what's happened.

She'd come home from the hospital last night equal parts relieved and gutted. Relieved the girls were going to be okay.

But her body numb, her mind reeling.

Someone has died tonight, she kept thinking. Over and over and over.

She took a shower, curled up in bed, and just stayed there for hours, the scene at the tree house replaying in her head. Finally, she went into the bathroom and opened the bottle of sleeping pills she rarely used. They'd make her groggy in the morning, but she needed the relief.

Now she leans against the window frame when she sees another car pull into Leo's driveway. Lillian emerges from the driver's seat, carrying a bouquet of flowers. She walks tentatively to Leo's door, as though she's not sure she really wants to be there.

Maggie grabs the lasagna off the counter and walks out of the house.

"Lillian," she calls as she crosses the street. "We had the same idea. I've been waiting for a good time to drop this off. We can visit together."

"Oh, I don't want to visit. I'm just dropping these—" She pauses, glancing over Maggie's shoulder.

They both turn as a police car parks in front of the house. A man Maggie doesn't recognize gets out of the car. Although calling him a man is a stretch. He looks like a boy dressed up in a Halloween policeman costume.

"Afternoon," he says, tipping his head. "Is this Leo Irving's house?"

The door opens, as though Leo's heard his name. He squints

at the crowd on his doorstep. "Officer Mike," he greets. "Hi, Maggie. Lillian. Come in."

"Oh, no. I'm just dropping these off." Lillian thrusts the flowers at him. "I don't want to intrude."

"Me neither," Maggie says, holding out the lasagna. "It just needs to be warmed. Or it can go in the freezer until you're ready."

"Just come in," Leo says, stepping back and opening the door. "Everyone."

"Good idea, actually," Officer Mike says. "We have a picture of the potential woman. The more eyes on it, the better. Maybe someone will recognize her."

They file into the house and follow Leo to the kitchen. Maggie opens the refrigerator and puts the lasagna on a shelf while the officer recounts how they went to the artist studio at Crow Farm.

"I spoke to the owner," he says, looking at the notebook in his hand. "Greer McCallister. She said a woman has been staying at the studio most of the summer. We took a look, but it was empty. Owner hasn't seen her for days. Not uncommon, apparently. She likes to give the artists their privacy. Owner said the woman's name is Henley. Didn't have a last name. Paid in cash."

He looks up, raises his eyebrows. "Anything ringing a bell?"

Leo shakes his head. "I didn't even know there was a studio there. I'm not exactly in touch with the artist community here."

Officer Mike looks at Maggie then Lillian. "Either of you? Woman is midthirties, maybe. Tall, thin. Brunette." He pulls a picture from the back of the notebook. "Owner had this picture. She called me back to the farm after she stumbled across it. I guess she was taking a picture of one of her horses and the woman happened to be in the background. Take a look."

He hands the picture to Leo. Maggie and Lillian look over his shoulder.

It's a close-up of a black horse. Far off in the distance, there's a woman, looking the other way, only her profile in the picture.

"I wish it was closer," Maggie says.

Leo nods. "I don't think I know her, but there's something about her that's so familiar. I just can't place it."

Lillian doesn't say anything.

"Do you know her?" Officer Mike asks.

There's a long pause. Lillian's eyes don't leave the picture. She doesn't blink or breathe, it seems.

"No," she says simply. In a voice that doesn't leave room for discussion.

"Can I hold on to this?" Leo asks, putting the picture on the table. "Maybe it'll come to me. And the girls will be home tomorrow. I'll show it to them."

Officer Mike nods, turns to leave. "You have my card. I'll call you if any new information comes in."

They're silent, listening to his footsteps through the house, the sound of the door closing the only sound in the room.

Lillian stands, crosses the room, and studies a picture that's framed on the wall. It's an eight-by-ten family photograph of Brian, Ann, and Sky.

"I think you should sit down," she says, picking up the picture of the woman that's sitting on the table, and looking up at Leo.

47

Sit down?" Leo pulls out a chair.

He's tired. And irritable.

He hasn't even called Xavier to tell him what's happened. He's afraid to—this is exactly what Xavier was talking about when he said they weren't cut out for this parenting gig.

One woman dead. Two girls in a hospital.

All his fault.

Lillian glances at Maggie. "I have to tell you something. I don't know if you want anyone else here—"

"Oh, I can leave!" Maggie stands.

"No—" Leo puts a hand on her arm. "There's nothing you can't be here for." He is surprised by how forcefully he believes this. "Something to do with this woman?"

He takes the picture from Lillian, the light hitting it at a different angle. The tilt of the woman's face catching his eye.

So familiar.

"Her name is Charlotte Waters," Lillian says. "She was my daughter's best friend. They went to high school together, back when we lived in New York."

Leo brings the picture closer, studies it. "I met her best friend. Once. Years ago. She had light hair. And her name was different—" He stops, embarrassed.

He should remember the name of the only woman he ever slept with.

Lillian takes out her phone, searches for a moment, and shows Leo a picture. It's of Ann, young and smiling. An arm around the shoulders of another girl. Blond and young and smiling as well. He recognizes her immediately.

He can't speak.

"She went by Charlie," Lillian says softly.

And Leo can only nod.

Maggie leans over, looks at Lillian's phone. "Oh my God, she's the spitting image of Sky." She covers her mouth with her hand. "Is that her . . ." She looks at Lillian.

"Birth mother." Lillian nods, takes a deep breath. "I'm going to just start at the beginning." She looks at Leo, clears her throat.

"Ann was a difficult teenager. Mood swings. Manic behavior. We finally got a diagnosis. Various disorders, but she took her medication, and she seemed better. Then she met Brian and moved here. Our relationship was already strained. I was sober then, but she was angry. She blamed me for pretty much everything that was hard in her life." She gave them a sad smile. "My side has a history. Alcoholism. Depression. Schizophrenia. Bipolar—you name it. Ann didn't want me to be a part of her life here. She said she was a different person with Brian. She even changed her name when she moved here. From Mackenzie Ann—Mac to all of her high school friends—to just Ann. She told me she felt different here. With Brian. She said she no longer felt crazy. Her word. Not mine."

"She wasn't crazy," Leo says. "Ann was great. Happy, it seemed."

Lillian nods. "I'm sure she was happy." She pauses. "She wanted a big family. But she was convinced she would pass on these diseases. That's what she called them—*our family diseases*. She told Brian she couldn't have children. They started looking into adoption."

She pauses. "Can I have a glass of water?"

He pushes his chair back, but Maggie puts a hand on his arm and stands. They're quiet while Maggie fills a glass and places it in front of Lillian, who brings it to her mouth.

Leo notices her hand shaking when she puts the glass on the table.

"Ann called me one day. We hadn't spoken in almost a year. She wouldn't return my calls." She takes a breath. "She told me she was a new mother. I was excited, of course. Thinking they had adopted. Then she was quiet on the other end. I asked her what was wrong. And she told me she had a secret that she needed me to keep. That I had failed her as a mother, but now she needed me to be there for her. And she wanted me to be part of the baby's life."

Lillian takes a sip of the water, pauses again, then looks at Leo.

"She told me Charlie had contacted her. She was modeling at the time. Had no idea she was pregnant until the photographer told her to skip dinner because she looked bloated. It was too late for an abortion."

Lillian traces her finger on the rim of the glass, her eyes filling.

"Apparently the two hatched a plan. Charlie stayed in the artist studio on that farm. I guess you can walk there from here and not be seen. Brian never knew anything about it. Ann took classes, became a midwife. The hurricane hit the night Charlie went into labor. The plan had always been to leave the baby at the fire station, where Ann would say she found it. The storm made it easier with the station empty. Charlie left when the ferry started running again. The owner of the studio thought she was going back to the mainland to have the baby."

Lillian stops, quietly sips the water. "I was stunned. I had no idea what to say." She brings the water to her mouth again. Then stares at the glass after it's back on the table.

"What did you do?" Maggie asks finally.

"What could I do?" Lillian shrugs. "Ann was elated. Didn't see anything wrong with any of it. Charlie had a modeling career. She was always a screwed-up kid. Hated her family—there was a reason the two of them got along." She sighed. "They agreed to keep it a secret. Ann said she was only telling one other person in this world and it was me. And she was only doing that because I knew Charlie so well. She thought I might see a resemblance. She didn't have to worry about that with Brian. He'd only met Charlie once when she came to the island. I guess everyone was pretty drunk."

Leo leans over and puts his face in his hands. He looks up after a minute. Lillian is watching him.

"I thought it was wrong. All of it. I begged Ann to tell the truth. Told her I wasn't sure I could be part of their life—Sky's life—unless she did that. And she wouldn't. She refused. She said it wasn't possible. That two lives would be ruined—Charlie's and the father's, if she did that."

"And the father? Did she tell you who he was?" he asks.

He already knows it's him. He can do the math. Count back nine months from when Sky was born. It never occurred to him to do such a thing because he never heard from the woman again. He never even told Brian about it. He was too embarrassed.

Lillian looks down. "No. She said Charlie wouldn't tell her. And I believed her. But I don't anymore."

Maggie raises her eyebrows. "Why? Do you know who it is?"

Lillian doesn't answer. She just looks at Leo.

"There's something you asked me a few months ago. About Ann. If she was taking any medication. I told you I didn't know. And that was true. The last time I was here, I noticed that Ann was acting strange. I confronted her, and she admitted that she was on and off with taking her medication—she said it made her feel like a zombie. We argued. I told Brian not taking it wasn't an option for Ann. That if she didn't, Sky wasn't safe. They asked me to leave, and I did. They both ended any communication with me. That was two years ago." She pauses. "Then out of the blue, Ann called me. I missed the call. Only got the voice mail. She was angry. Ranting about how I'd cursed her for life. And now Brian was leaving her. I called back. Tried Brian. Called again and again. I was going to call the police, but they called me first. It was the night of the accident."

Leo shakes his head. "She said he was leaving her? They were on a date. For their anniversary."

"I think he may have given her the same ultimatum that I did. That she needed to get help. Or lose him. It doesn't matter really. But she was driving that night. I can't help but wonder if she wasn't in the middle of an episode."

Leo stands now, almost knocking the chair over. Anger surging through him.

"Why didn't you tell me any of this? Now you just dump all this on me?"

Lillian doesn't react. "I didn't know you were involved as anything other than her guardian. It didn't seem worthwhile to—Ann was so ashamed of her disease. So angry at me for insisting that she take her medication. And then I came here, and everyone loved her. And Brian. I wasn't going to tarnish her memory. The reputation of their *family*."

Lillian glances at the family picture on the wall. "I think something wonderful was created from a difficult situation. I wish it had started with the truth. I think it would have been an easier life for my daughter. For Brian. And Sky. You have a chance to fix that. To start over. I hope you do."

His mind is racing. Lillian stands to leave, and he puts his hand up.

"Wait a second. And what about you? Does this change things? Do you still want custody?"

Lillian blinks. "Custody? Why in the world would you think I want custody?"

"You moved here. I just assumed that was the ultimate goal—"

"Goal? Oh, heavens no." Lillian lets out a long sigh. "I already raised a child, Leo. As a single mother, no less. These past years I've been so consumed with work and worrying about Ann and trying to be a good partner to someone incapable of being in a relationship—no. I have no interest in custody. Don't get me wrong. I'm here for Sky in whatever way I can be—whatever *you* need, as well. But this time in my life is really going to be about me. It's actually a bit overdue."

"Amen to that," Maggie mutters.

Lillian crosses the kitchen and puts a hand on his shoulder. "Call if you need anything," she says and walks through the house and out the door.

Leo sits in the chair, stares blankly at the table.

Maggie clears her throat. "I feel like I'm missing something here."

Leo looks at her. "She's mine," he says softly. So soft Maggie blinks and he wonders if she's heard him.

"Yours?" she asks finally. "But how—I mean—I always thought you were— I just didn't know you were into—"

"Women? I'm not. Unless I've had a bottle of tequila the same night I bury my father." He runs his hands over his face, stunned. He stands quickly, pushing the chair back abruptly.

"I need to tell Xavier," he blurts, turning and looking for his keys.

"Now?" Maggie asks.

"Yes, now! Look—I have to talk to him. I have no idea what I'm going to say to Sky. She's in the hospital until tomorrow. I'll be back first thing in the morning to get her—"

"Don't rush. I had already decided to take the day off. Sky can come back here with me. She'll be just fine. Just call over and make sure they'll release her to me."

He doesn't even bother packing a bag. Just leans over and gives Maggie a quick hug and he's out the door. Running, it seems.

Though he's not sure if he's running toward something.

Or away.

48

Before Sky leaves the hospital, Frankie makes her promise that she'll go to the easel. Her back is sore, and she has some scrapes on her from crawling in the woods, but the doctor said she's ready to go home.

"I wish you were going home too," Sky says. "I hate leaving you alone here."

Frankie looks so small in the large room with her own bed empty next to where Frankie is propped up, a pillow wedged under her arm.

"My mother will be here any minute. Go before you're trapped." Frankie smirks. "They're only keeping me an extra night anyway. Seriously—you need to call me the minute you're back from the easel. I'm dying to know if she left anything." She winces after she says it. "Bad choice of words. You know what I mean though."

"I'll try," she says, giving Frankie a quick hug when she hears Maggie's voice in the hallway.

"Try hard!" Frankie whispers, squeezing her hand. She knows Sky is afraid to go back to the woods.

She'll have to pass the tree house. Or what was the tree house. Now it's probably just a black patch of ground. Smoky and ruined.

Maggie meets her in the hallway, waves the sheets of paper in her hand. "Got your walking papers," she says, slinging an arm around Sky's shoulders. "Let's get you home, shall we?"

Maggie is cheery today. More cheery than usual. A smile on her face that wobbles now and then, as though it's tired and needs a rest. Her voice chirpy and bright. All of it makes Sky's heart race because she knows it's because Leo isn't here to pick her up.

He called her on the hospital phone yesterday and said he had to go to the mainland for an emergency. He sounded far away, the call dropping every other word until she told him she could barely hear him, and then he said something else and all she could make out was the word *back*.

All night she thought about that word. Ran through the list of things he could have said.

I'll be back.

See you when I get back.

I'm not coming back.

It's the last one that sticks in her mind now. She wouldn't come back either if she were Leo. Not after she lied and then almost burned down the forest. And the woman—her throat closes every time she thinks about that.

"Here we are," Maggie says, and points to a car waiting by the curb. She's relieved to see Joe in the driver's seat.

She can always count on Joe to be Joe. He's never extra cheery. Not even when her parents died.

"Hi, Sport," he says when she gets in the back seat. "They finally got sick of you here, huh?" He winks when she smiles and pulls away from the curb.

She closes her eyes, rests her head against the seat. She doesn't know if Maggie takes the hint that she doesn't want to talk, because Joe starts rambling about the house, rattling off the stuff the crew has been doing.

She doesn't open her eyes. Doesn't speak.

Is he coming back?

That's what she wants to ask. But she can't make the words come out of her mouth.

It's almost lunchtime when she wakes up after taking a nap in the den. In the kitchen, Maggie is at the table, flipping through a magazine. The box Joe made for her paintings is on the counter.

Maggie smiles when she sees her in the doorway, gestures for her to come in.

"Joe brought this back from the cliff while you were sleeping. He's had it in his garage since the night of the fire. He still has your easel, but he said there are some things that belong to you in here." Maggie stands, puts her hand on the lid of the box. "I'm going to be outside on the patio. Call me if you need me." She walks over and kisses the top of Sky's head, squeezes her arm.

After the door shuts, Sky walks over, lifts the lid.

Inside is the unfinished painting Frankie had left on the easel. The one of Sky on the speckled pony. The original photograph resting on top of it.

She takes them out, squinting at what she sees underneath them.

The box should be empty. Instead, there is a package, wrapped in plain white paper and tied with string.

She carefully lifts it out, the smell of dried paint drifting up to her. She unties the knot, pulls the string until it slides off, the two sides of the white paper opening to reveal a painting. Several more sit underneath.

She holds the top one in front of her.

It's a painting of two women at a table. Leaning into each other. Both blond. One of them is her mother. The one who adopted her. The one who raised her.

The other woman is pregnant, a hand resting on her middle. She's crying, her profile wet with tears on her cheek.

She studies the pregnant woman. She could be looking at a picture of herself if the woman's hair was brown, and her skin a darker shade. She remembers Frankie's words about the woman.

She puts the painting aside, looks at the next one.

A woodstove sits in the center, a fire burning inside. Behind the stove is a window, a storm raging outside from the way the trees bend and the leaves scatter in the wind.

The next painting is of a baby in a basket on a table. She knows she's the one in the basket. And in the belly of the woman in the painting.

The mother she never met until the other night.

Just minutes before she died.

She puts all the paintings on the table. There are three of them. Lined up together, they tell the story of how she was born.

The screen door opens. Maggie's face appears.

"Are you okay—" Maggie stops when she sees the pictures, steps inside, and walks over to the table.

"It was her," she says, and Maggie nods, studying the paintings. She picks up the one of the two women at the table and glances from Sky to the painting.

"You look so much alike," she says.

"I didn't always. I need to show you something," Sky says, and walks out of the kitchen to her bedroom while Maggie follows behind her.

In her room, she walks over to her desk, opens the drawer, and takes a picture out. She sits back down on the bed and hands it to Maggie.

It's a photograph of a newborn, wrapped in a striped blanket.

"You gave me this at the other house. When we slept there."

Maggie smiles. "I found it in the basement. You were the cutest baby. Look at those cheeks." She touches the picture.

Sky walks over to a bookshelf, grabs a photo album, and flips the pages. She pulls out a picture and walks back to the bed, holds it up for Maggie to see.

It's a picture of a newborn, wrapped in a blanket, identical to the first picture, except the blanket has darker stripes.

"That's me," Sky says. "The day after they found me in the fire station."

"You had a copy already," Maggie says. "I thought you might."

She points to the one in Maggie's hand. "Look at the back," she says.

Maggie turns the picture over. In small handwriting on the lower corner of the picture there is a name and age of the baby.

Leo. 2 days old.

Maggie flips the picture over again and holds it up to Sky's. Side-by-side pictures of two babies.

Almost identical.

Maggie puts her arm around Sky's shoulders and doesn't speak.

She should put the pictures away. Ask Leo about it when he comes back. But she can't stop looking at the same thick black hair sticking straight up.

Eyes that look so much alike. Hers are blue now. Leo's are dark brown. But in the pictures, they're the same dark gray.

She's pressed against Maggie, and she sits up straighter, but Maggie pulls her tighter.

"I'm not going to take the easy way out here." Maggie looks at her and takes a breath. "A lot has happened since the fire. We learned about your birth mother. And Leo just found out he's your father. He went to talk to Xavier." She stops, doesn't loosen her grip.

"How come I don't look anything like him now?"

Maggie tilts her head, her eyes on the pictures. "That happens sometimes. PJ looked just like my baby picture. By the time he was your age, he was just a miniature version of Pete."

"Do you think Leo's coming back?" she asks.

"Of course," Maggie says quickly.

In that chirpy, bright voice.

49

Turns out all his rushing to get to the mainland is for nothing—the condo is empty when he arrives.

No Xavier. No furniture. Not even a television.

Just moving boxes upon moving boxes lining the walls. Nearly every single item in the house packed away, meticulously labeled in Xavier's handwriting.

He calls Xavier's phone, but it goes straight to voice mail. He sends him three texts over the course of two hours.

I'm at the condo.
Where are you?
Call me ASAP!

Finally, after midnight, when he can't keep his eyes open anymore, he lies down in bed, the only remaining piece of furniture in the entire condo.

He doesn't know how long he's been asleep when he opens his eyes to the front door clicking shut, then footsteps walking toward him. The light flicks on, and he blinks, and Xavier is standing over him, a backpack over his shoulder.

"What's wrong?" Xavier asks. "I've been trying to call you since I landed!"

Leo glances at his phone, dead on the table. He'd rushed out the door without a charger and couldn't find one in the condo.

"Landed from where?" Leo says, standing and walking into the kitchen. His head is pounding, his mouth dry. Xavier follows, watches him open the cabinet for a glass, only to find it empty.

"Here," Xavier says, grabbing a bottle of water out of the refrigerator. "From LA. I didn't bother to tell you I was going. It was a quick trip."

"I thought you weren't going until October." He glances at the boxes, then at Xavier. "But obviously I don't know anything anymore. When were you going to tell me we were moving? *You* were moving, I should say."

"I'm not going at all," Xavier says. "To LA. The scope of it kept growing and growing. It was obvious I'd be out there more than I originally thought. I told them I didn't want the project."

"What? Why? You've been trying to sell that pitch forever."

Xavier shrugs. "I have other things I can work on. Local things."

"Local to where?" Leo asks.

Xavier digs in his pocket, hands him a piece of paper. "The movers come at the end of the week. Hope I got the address right."

Leo looks down. It's an address with both their names. Winding Way as the location.

He stares at it. Speechless. When he looks up, Xavier is studying him.

"I thought you hated the island," he says finally.

Xavier shrugs. "I hate being without you more."

He wants to step into his husband, take him in his arms. Instead, he leans back against the wall, away from him.

He's not sure if he's giving Xavier space to hear what he's

about to say. Or distancing himself from his husband before he tells him something that might break his heart.

"There's something you need to know," Leo says. And then begins with the story of his father's funeral. A bottle of tequila. A woman named Charlie.

And a baby named Sky.

When he's finished, exhaustion spreads through his body, and he wishes his favorite couch was still in the living room so he might curl up on it and go to sleep.

But, it's empty. Just a bare room.

"What did you do with our furniture?" he asks suddenly.

Xavier doesn't answer. Just looks at him with the same blank expression he's had since Leo began his story.

Suddenly Xavier blinks, his eyes filling. A crease forms on his forehead.

"Are you crying?" Leo asks, tilting his head. Xavier rarely cries. As in never.

"Maybe. Yes." Xavier presses the heel of his hand to one eye.

"Are they good tears or bad?"

Xavier pauses. "Good, I think. Maybe a little bit of shock mixed in. But good."

"I'm surprised. You haven't really wanted to be part of any of this. Me and Sky. Our life—"

"Your life." Xavier nods, as if that's exactly the point. "Brian and Ann didn't name me as a guardian. They named you. Only you. I always felt like the third wheel. I didn't know your friends very well—we met once at our wedding! And then to suddenly live in their house. Raise their daughter—it was . . ." His voice trails off.

"A lot," Leo finishes.

"Yeah," Xavier agrees.

"And now?"

Xavier blinks at him. "She's your daughter. Our daughter! Look—the past few months have been awful. In my worst nightmare, I never imagined my life without you. And then all this happened, and I was suddenly alone in this house. I hated it. But I had to stay here and feel what that was really going to be like. It was never going to be fair to you or Sky if I wasn't fully in. Fully willing to be your partner and Sky's parent. So that choice was already made. I was coming to the island to be with you both before you showed up tonight. This just feels . . . I don't know." He shrugs. "We can learn to be dads at the same time."

"What if we screw it up?" Leo asks.

Xavier raises an eyebrow. "Well then it's your fault. You're the real dad," he jokes, nodding to the bedroom. "Let's get some sleep before we become parents for the rest of our lives."

They wake up to the sun blazing through the window, the curtains packed away. Leo glances at the alarm clock and moans.

"It's almost nine o'clock. We need to get moving—"

Xavier throws an arm over him. "Stay," he says. "I don't even remember what it's like to be in bed with you."

Leo laughs. "I forgot how dramatic you are."

Xavier sits up and looks down at him. "I'm serious. Let's stay here one last night. Just us. We'll take the ferry over in the morning."

"I don't know if Maggie can stay—"

"I'll call her right now," Xavier says, standing up. "You stay right there. And our neighbor. Jim? Give me his number. I woke up with an idea, and I'm hoping he can help."

"It's Joe. Joe Armstrong." Leo sighs. "You have to start getting his name right—"

"Joe—I got it. I promise." He picks up Leo's phone, his finger scrolling until he finds what he's looking for. Then he puts the phone to his ear. "Don't get up." He points at Leo. "Hey, Joe," he says into the phone in a friendly voice. "This is Xavier, Leo's husband—"

His voice fades as Leo cranes his neck, watches him walk out the bedroom. He should follow him. Take a shower. Get dressed and go back to the island.

There's a house to finish. And a child to raise. A list of things to do that seems to grow each day.

"We're all set," Xavier says, walking in and getting in bed next to Leo. "Maggie has everything under control, and Joe's on top of it."

"On top of what?" he asks, but Xavier shakes his head, presses his lips against Leo's.

And Leo closes his eyes, leans into his husband. His marriage had almost slipped through his fingers. He lets the house that needs finishing and the child who needs raising and the list that's growing fade into the background of his mind. There for the rest of his life.

Just not right now.

50

When Maggie tells Sky that Leo isn't coming home for another day, there's a long silence between them.

"Why not?" Sky asks finally.

Maggie doesn't have the answer, given that she only briefly spoke to Xavier, not Leo, and the only explanation Xavier gave was that they had a lot of *things* to figure out. She hadn't wanted to pry—*things* seemed a reasonable enough explanation given the circumstances—so she told him not to worry.

Everything was just fine on their end.

From the look of panic on Sky's face, Maggie is wondering if she may have spoken too soon.

"Something to do with work, I believe," she says breezily. "How about a sandwich for lunch?"

"Leo doesn't work. He lost his job a month ago."

Maggie swallows. "I meant Xavier's," she says quickly. "Soup?"

"I'm not that hungry. I'll just have cereal. Did you talk to Xavier? Is he coming back with Leo?"

Worry is etched in the girl's features. Maggie sighs, walks over, and wraps her arms around her, feels Sky stiffen and finally relax in her grip.

"I have an idea," Maggie says, turning to the table, the paintings spread out. "How about we get these framed? You can put them in your new room."

Sky is quiet, studying the paintings.

"Your mother was talented," she says softly.

"Birth mother," Sky corrects, and opens the cabinet, searching for the box of cereal.

As though it's just another typical day.

They spend the afternoon picking out frames.

Then Maggie takes Sky for an early dinner on the harbor at a fancy restaurant with a rooftop deck overlooking the water. She called Joe to see if he wanted to have dinner with them, but he rushed her off the phone. Something about a project he was working on.

When they get home, Sky tells her that she's going to bed. It's not even dark out, and she wonders if Sky is upset about Leo not coming home, but Maggie can't find it in herself to argue because she's exhausted and the only thing she really wants is a glass of wine and to put her feet up and relax.

Tomorrow is an in-service day for teachers, so she tells Sky to sleep in and take advantage of the day off. She's already decided she'll get to school when she gets there.

After Sky disappears into her bedroom, Maggie finally sits at the table, but her mind is racing and she stands, paces the small room.

Something has been bothering her since dinner, and she hasn't been able to put her finger on it until now.

It's Agnes.

She'd been sitting on the roof deck with Sky watching the ferry unload when she thought about the lunch she never got to have with Agnes.

The lunch they had every year when Agnes would snicker and make fun of the tourists on the dock and Maggie would shush her and they'd laugh until Maggie thought her side was going to split wide open.

Before she can change her mind, she picks up her phone.

Agnes answers on the second ring.

Within the hour, they're sitting at the kitchen table, the paintings on the table between them.

"So Leo is the father?" Agnes repeats for the third time.

"Yes!" Maggie says.

Agnes puts her hands up. "Okay, okay! Sue me for having a question or two. So where is he then?"

"He went to talk to Xavier. Look—I didn't call you so we could talk about Leo or Sky or any of it." She looks at Agnes. "Are you sick again? Tell me the truth."

"No. I'm healthy. Scout's honor." She holds up two fingers.

Maggie narrows her eyes. "Then what's with the circles." She draws in the air under her own eyes. "And the weight loss."

"Let's see. My best friend of thirty years—really my only real friend if you want the truth—told me she doesn't want to talk to me. And for some reason, I haven't had much of an appetite and I can't seem to sleep at all." She tilts her head at Maggie, who lets out a long, ragged sigh.

"I've missed you too. I was just so . . ." She can't find the word.

"Angry," Agnes says quietly. "You were angry, Maggie."

"Yes! I really was! But it wasn't just at you. I was angry at myself, for acting like everything was fine all my life when it wasn't. I was angry at Pete, mostly."

"About time," Agnes says, then sighs. "I'm sorry. I promised myself I was going to be less judgmental. About everything."

"Everything?" Maggie's eyes go wide.

"Grace called the other day." Agnes plays with the cross around her neck. "She had some news. Apparently, there's going to be a wedding. In Vermont."

"Well then give my congratulations to Grace and Julie. Are you going to stop referring to her as the roommate?" Maggie smirks.

"I don't have the first clue what I'm supposed to call her!" Agnes drains her glass and slams it on the table. "Fill it, will you? This conversation requires alcohol." She shakes her head, but a smile forms on her lips.

"You're going to the wedding, right?"

"Of course I'm going. Somebody once screamed in my face that it wasn't about me. This person is suddenly very bossy and outspoken." Agnes looks at her. "But she also happens to be right."

Maggie tops off Agnes's glass, watches her friend take a long sip. "We'll have to shop for a dress for you—"

"Wait." Agnes holds up a hand. "I'm not done. I'm sorry I sent that picture to the newspaper. It was a rotten thing to do. I was mad at you too. For something that wasn't your fault. You know my marriage isn't perfect. I married a good man, but he eats, breathes, and sleeps his work. After the MRI came back clean, I was looking forward to a summer with you. Just us. Day trips and beaches and lunches. And then you got so involved with Leo and Sky." Agnes shrugs. "I was hurt."

"I'm sorry," Maggie says. "I wished you had told me."

"I hope that picture didn't ruin things with Pete. I heard he moved out."

Maggie snorts. "The only thing that ruined my relationship with Pete was Pete."

She knows it's true when it passes her lips. She also knows they were in love for a lot of years. Then something between them changed. And Pete kept telling her she was wrong. That everything was fine. And everything did *look* fine. On the surface. But leaving him feels right. She's less lonely living alone than living with Pete.

"And Joe?" Agnes smirks. "You two seem to be spending a lot of time together. I think he has a crush on you."

Maggie grabs the bottle of wine, tops off their glasses.

"Cheers," she says, holding up her glass.

Agnes raises hers. "What are we cheering?"

"Beets," Maggie says, remembering how Joe had grown them in his garden. Just for her. "And to men willing to try new things."

51

The house is freezing when Sky wakes up. She left her window open when she went to bed, only a sheet covering her, and she opens her eyes to goose bumps covering her arms and legs. She wraps the blanket at the end of her bed around her and shuffles out of her bedroom.

In the living room, Maggie is standing by the far wall, tapping the round thermostat.

Sky pulls the blanket tighter around her body. "It's only the middle of September," she complains. "Why is it so cold?"

"New England is why." Maggie smiles. "The weatherman said it'll warm up by midmorning."

The door opens, and they both turn to see Leo step into the house, Xavier pushing in behind him.

"Don't bother," Leo tells Maggie. "It's one of the reasons we're selling this place. Needs a whole new heating system."

Xavier is in shorts and a tight T-shirt, rubbing his hands over his arms. "I'm getting one of your sweatshirts. Don't go without me," he calls over his shoulder, disappearing down the hall.

"You're here early," Maggie says. "It's not even eight o'clock. Go where?" She looks at Leo.

Sky realizes she's been holding her breath when Leo walks over and gives her a hug, pressing his lips to her cheek.

"You two need to get dressed," he says.

Maggie shakes her head. "I haven't even had coffee—"

"Come on! Go!" Leo slaps his hands together. Xavier emerges from the hallway dressed in a heavy sweatshirt and long pants.

"You're going to be dying in an hour," Leo tells him, but Xavier waves him off and walks over to Sky.

"I'm glad you're okay," he says, and gives her an awkward hug.

She lets him because Leo is smiling in a way that she hasn't seen him smile in a long time. And she doesn't know if it's because he's glad she's his daughter or he's glad that Xavier is on the island.

But she doesn't care.

She skips to her room, changes into a shirt and shorts and pulls on a long-sleeve T-shirt she can tie around her waist when it warms up.

She doesn't know where they're going, and Leo and Xavier won't tell her while they wait for Maggie to come out of the bathroom.

"It's a surprise," Leo repeats.

"I don't like surprises," Sky says honestly.

Xavier nods. "Me either. I *hate* them," he whispers.

He makes a face, and she laughs, not because it's funny, but because it's the first time they've all been together—her, Leo, and Xavier—when Xavier has actually spoken to her without being prompted by Leo.

It's a small thing.

Still.

"Ready?" Leo asks when Maggie steps into the room, finally dressed.

"I was ready to stay in my bathrobe and have a cup of coffee," she says grumpily. But she rolls her eyes and grins when Leo puts an arm around her shoulders and leads her out the front door with Xavier and Sky trailing behind.

"Where are we going?" she asks when they're all on the street.

"Home," Leo says with a wink, tilting his head in the direction of the new house.

She looks at it while they walk toward it. But there's nothing there. Just Joe standing next to his truck in the driveway, sipping from a mug.

She says this out loud, and Leo glances at her.

"Just trust me," he says.

She studies the empty spot where the house used to be while she walks. Thinks about what it will look like when it's done. When it's really her new home.

They walk to where Joe's standing, and he holds his hand out to Leo, who shakes it.

"All set?" Leo asks and Joe nods.

"Hi, Jim," Xavier says, and laughs when Joe's cheeks color. "Just kidding! How are you, Joe?" He extends a hand, and Joe brings his fist back as though he might punch Xavier, but he smiles and shakes his hand.

"He'll grow on you," Leo promises.

"So?" He looks at Sky. "Think you'll like it here?"

She nods, doesn't know what to say.

Mostly because it's just an empty space with a basement she can look straight into and she's not very good at imagining these things all on her own. Frankie can. Which is probably why Frankie is such a good artist and Sky is still a beginner.

"Come this way," Leo says. "There's something out back for you."

She walks next to him around the hole in the ground to the backyard and onto the lawn.

"Look," he says, his eyes on something in the corner of the yard.

She follows his gaze, looks to where the yard slopes off into a line of trees.

There's a tree house perched between two pines. Not as high up as her old tree house, but high enough to see the water. A window faces the ocean.

It takes her breath away. She swallows. Waits until the lump in her throat disappears before she turns and looks at Leo.

"Thank you," she says.

Leo holds up his hands. "Don't thank me. This was all Xavier's idea."

She turns to Xavier, who shakes his head and points at Joe.

"This is the guy who made it happen."

"Good thing you have deep pockets," Joe tells Xavier, slapping him on the back before he walks over to Sky. "Your easel is up there already, Sport," Joe says, putting an arm around her shoulders and giving her a squeeze. "Go check it out. I'm off to get some sleep. Oh—and no lanterns! I installed a battery-powered light in there. Leo can show you how it works."

He raises his hand, and Maggie joins him. "I'm off to have that cup of coffee," she calls over her shoulder.

Then it's just the three of them. Out of the corner of her eye, she sees Leo glance at Xavier and tilt his head to the street, as though he wants to be alone with Sky.

"I'm going to make a latte run. Hot chocolate for you?" Xavier asks Sky, and she nods, steps forward, and puts an arm around him.

"Thank you," she says, and it's a minute before she feels his hand on her back, patting her in a way that makes her choke back a laugh.

"I'm so awkward," he announces, and she straightens and shrugs.

"You're not that bad," she says.

"Go," Leo tells him, and they watch him walk across the lawn, ripping off the sweatshirt that Leo warned him not to wear because he was going to be hot when the fog wore off.

"Told you——" Leo shouts.

"Don't say it," Xavier calls over his shoulder.

When they're alone in the backyard, she turns back to the tree house. Thinks of all the pictures Maggie helped her frame. She can put them on the walls. She and Frankie won't have to go to the cliff anymore. They have their own studio now.

She looks at Leo, and he shifts, clears his throat.

"We need to talk," he begins. "I don't even know where to start but——"

"We already did," Sky interrupts. "You were here when my parents died, and you're here now. Can we go see the tree house?"

She doesn't wait for him to answer. They have the rest of their lives to talk about it.

Right now, there's a tree house waiting.

And a view she can't wait to paint.

Acknowledgments

I am indebted to the following people for their contributions to this book:

My brilliant editor, Kaitlin Olson, for her vision, insight, and ever-vigilant eye that helped shape this book into what it is.

The entire team at Atria for their enthusiasm and support. Special thanks to Megan Rudloff, Maude Genao, and Erica Ferguson.

Danielle Burby, who is simply a perfect agent.

My deepest gratitude to these book lovers who bring authors and readers together. My spam the shit outta Insta gals: Stacey Armand (Prose and Palate), Kate Olson (kate.olson.reads), Chandra Claypool (wherethereadergrows), Kourtney Dyson (kourtneysbookshelf), and Jessica Robins (jessicamap). As well as Laurie Baron (booksandchinooks), Kristy Barrett of A Novel Bee, and Cindy Burnett and Krista Hensel from Conversations from a Page.

Peg Hamilton, who has read early drafts of each of my books within twenty-four hours, this one no exception. She's not only my best reader and greatest advocate, she's my mother and one hell of a remarkable woman. Her belief in me is a gift for which I'm eternally grateful.

A special thanks to my family and friends for their continued enthusiasm and support. In particular, Jen Tuzik, Nancy Scho-field, Lisa Roe, Chris and Tina Hamilton, and the fam squad: Lauren, Mitch, Heidi, Scott, Alyssa, and Hutton.

Samantha, Matthew, and Mia, for your light and love and laughter.

For my husband, Tom Wheble. As always, for everything.

About the Author

Lisa Duffy is the author of *The Salt House*, named by *Real Simple* as a Best Book of the Month upon its June release, as well as *Bustle*'s 17 Best Debut Novels by Women in 2017, and *This Is Home*, a *Publishers Weekly* starred review novel and 2019 favorite book club pick.

Lisa received her MFA in fiction from UMass Boston. Her writing can be found in numerous publications, including *Writer's Digest*. She lives in the Boston area with her husband and three children.

My Kind of People is her third novel.

My Kind
of People

Lisa Duffy

This reading group guide for My Kind of People includes an intro-
duction, discussion questions, ideas for enhancing your book club, and
a Q&A with author Lisa Duffy. The suggested questions are intended to
help your reading group find new and interesting angles and topics for
your discussion. We hope that these ideas will enrich your conversation
and increase your enjoyment of the book.

Introduction

On Ichabod Island, a jagged strip of land thirteen miles off the coast of Massachusetts, ten-year-old Sky becomes an orphan for the second time after a tragic accident claims the lives of her adoptive parents.

While grieving the death of his best friends, Leo's life is turned upside down when he finds himself the guardian of young Sky. Back on the island and struggling to balance his new responsibilities and his marriage to his husband, Leo is supported by a powerful community of neighbors, many of them harboring secrets of their own.

Maggie, who helps with Sky's childcare, has hit a breaking point with her police chief husband, who becomes embroiled in a local scandal. Her best friend, Agnes, the island busybody, invites Sky's estranged grandmother to stay for the summer, straining already precarious relationships. Their neighbor Joe struggles with whether to tell that all was not well in Sky's house in the months leading up to the accident. And among them all is a mysterious woman, drawn to Ichabod to fulfill a dying wish.

Topics & Questions
for Discussion

1. The novel alternates between points of view in every chapter. Do you think this was an effective storytelling technique? What overall effect did this have on your reading experience?

2. Ichabod Island is home to a wide variety of family archetypes, both traditional and nontraditional. Compare the defining outward traits of each of the families in *My Kind of People* to what is really going on behind closed doors.

3. Joe and Maggie find Xavier to be abrasive; however, Maggie would like to be on good terms with Xavier simply because he is Leo's husband. Have you ever felt you should keep the peace for the sake of a loved one?

4. Agnes is described as bossy, rude, and the town busybody. Maggie is a kind-hearted schoolteacher. The pair are best friends, but Maggie thinks they've lasted so long because "they don't talk about religion or politics." Do you think it is realistic that a friendship spanning decades can survive current events having opposing points of view on these topics?

5. Xavier is adamant not to change the life he and Leo had before the accident, but, despite previously not wanting to have children, Leo feels he owes it to Ann and Brian to take care of Sky. Do you think either of the men is right or wrong in his reasoning? Why or why not?

6. "Sky has two favorite places in the world: One is next to Frankie and the other is roaming Ichabod" (p. 48). Think of your favorite places. Do they connect with a specific person or defining moment in your past?

7. It is frequently touched upon that Leo is the only gay *and* black person on Ichabod Island. How do you think the topics of race and sexuality were handled?

8. Discuss the accusations against Maggie's husband, Pete (p. 183), and their swift dismissal. Compare this situation to the national discussion around sexual assault and the #MeToo movement. Do you agree with Agnes's decision to send a compromising photo of Pete with another woman to the newspaper?

9. At what point in the novel did you realize who Sky's birth parents really are? Were you surprised? Did you notice any similarities between the three that tipped you off?

10. When Frankie and Sky walk around in the dark, Sky often feels that someone is watching them. After finding out the mystery painter's true identity, do you think there is a biological connection that causes Sky to have these senses?

11. Consider the number of characters on the serene Ichabod Island who are in turmoil but constantly put on a happy face. Why do you think that is? Do you think the community would be better off if more members spoke their truths?

12. Discuss the title and what you think "my kind of people" means in relation to the people on and off Ichabod Island. What does this mean to you personally?

Enhance Your Book Club

1. Consider reading Lisa Duffy's previous novels, *The Salt House* and *This Is Home*, with your book club. Discuss any themes that are similar to those in *My Kind of People*.

2. Sky becomes an orphan for the second time when her adoptive parents die in a car accident. Review this article from KidsHealth about helping children to cope with the death of a parent: https://www.kidshealth.org.nz/helping-child -cope-death-parent. Discuss the ways in which the adults (and Frankie) adequately help Sky grieve her parents.

3. The characters on Ichabod Island are interrelated in many ways: Maggie was Leo's schoolteacher. Joe did work on Brian and Ann's house. Leo is Sky's biological father. Make a *My Kind of People* chart about the connections in your own communities and share with the group.

A Conversation with Lisa Duffy

Q: Congratulations on publishing your third novel, *My Kind of People*! What was the inspiration behind the story? Did you find it easier, having written two novels before this?

A: I wrote a short story years ago about a middle-aged married couple who come home after a session with a marriage counselor and find themselves spontaneously in bed together, but unfortunately instead of a passionate tryst, they have this awkward, cringeworthy moment that goes horribly wrong. I knew I wanted to explore these two characters in a novel, but I wanted that scene to be the jumping off point. When I started writing more about this couple—what they did for work, where they lived, and who they interacted with—the story began to evolve, and I found myself writing about people on one street who become intimately involved in each other's lives when their young neighbor is suddenly orphaned.

As far as it getting easier, I'd say no, but there is a sense of confidence that grows with each finished project. I learn something new about my process with each book, and I sort of know the ups and downs that I'll experience with wrestling with a first draft. Once the first draft is done, the real fun begins for me. I love revising and shaping the book into its final form.

Q: Throughout *My Kind of People*, we quickly become acquainted with the labels in this community that deem its members either insiders or outsiders. Was this something you wanted to write about?

A: I'm fascinated by the idea of belonging—what it means to some people and how we construct that in our lives. It was something I wanted to explore through these characters with the current conversation about immigration and who belongs where and why and how a piece of land can be at the center of it all.

Q: Relationships between the islanders (in all forms) are central to the novel. Was there one relationship in particular that you felt most compelled by?

A: I'd say I'm compelled by every relationship that doesn't get cut from the novel in the draft process. There is such satisfaction in digging as deep as I can into every relationship, so by the end, I don't have any favorites. Each character, and how they relate to other people in the novel, holds an equal space in my mind and in my heart.

Q: Was there a particular place you had in mind while setting the scene? What inspired you to name the Island Ichabod?

A: Ichabod was loosely inspired by the New England islands—Nantucket, Martha's Vineyard, Block Island to some degree. Places rich in history with a year-round population and a robust summer crowd.

There wasn't one specific inspiration for the name of the island. I was looking for something that would ring true as a man's first name when the island was first discovered, but also something that just felt right. Naming locations and characters is almost something innate—the name needs to feel as if it's essential to the story. My husband actually came up with Ichabod when we were out on our boat one day, just relaxing in the sun and talking about the book. The minute he said it, I knew it was perfect. And as I soon as I typed it in the manuscript, I had a clearer sense of the island.

Q: Ichabod is an idyllic setting full of characters experiencing emotional hardship. Was this contrast intentional? Did you begin writing the story with a specific outcome in mind?

A: I knew when I first started the draft that Ichabod would play a certain role in the novel. It's certainly idyllic for some characters. For others, it's a refuge. And for one character, it's a place he'd rather leave behind. It was intentional that all of these characters would have very strong feelings about Ichabod because I think to live year-round on an island requires a certain dedication to that way of life. It requires adjusting to taking a ferry to get off the island and dealing with crowds in the summer and shops and restaurants closing in the winter. So, for some, the hardships they are facing are in direct contrast to how they feel about Ichabod—that it's a place of peace and beauty and belonging. For others, the hardship is the island itself—the emotions it stirs inside of them and the desire to be part of something that's really just out of reach.

Q: Several characters are artistically inclined. What artistic mediums (aside from writing) do you think play a role in healing emotional wounds?

A: I think any medium or activity that pushes you to a deeper level of self-awareness has the ability to heal. To find joy and purpose in an activity that requires you to tune-in rather than tune out. It's one of the reasons I thought the epigraph in the novel was fitting: "I shut my eyes in order to see." A quote from Paul Gauguin. Everything he needs to create as an artist is inside of him. In a lot of ways, this translates to the characters in the novel, who each have to find their own way by looking inward as opposed to looking outward.

Q: Can you tell us what the title means to you in relation to the story?
A: In relation to the story, the title highlights how little we can actually know about someone by only an outward appearance. It's a statement made about a couple who seem to have it all, yet behind closed doors, they are struggling with things like addiction and mental health. On a larger scale, the title challenges some of the individual belief systems in the novel—hopefully reinforcing the idea that we can always find a point of connection with each other even if we don't look the same or think a certain way or adhere to a particular way of life

Q: What do you hope readers take away from the novel?
A: My hope is always the same. That my readers will enjoy the time they spend with these characters and this story.